TRIGGER WORDS

A Cape Trouble Novel

By Janice Kay Johnson

ISBN-10: 0-9976638-3-9
ISBN-13: 978-0-9976638-3-9

Trigger Words
Copyright 2017 Janice Kay Johnson

Cover Design by Carrie Divine/Seductive Designs
Image: prometeus (Kiselev Andrey)/Depositphotos
Image: gemenacom (Lisa Quarfoth)/Depositphotos
Image: logoboom (Konstantin Sutyagin)/Depositphotos

This book is a work of fiction. All names, characters, locations and incidents are products of the author's imagination, or have been used fictitiously. Any resemblance to actual persons living or dead, locales, or events is entirely coincidental.

License Notes

CHAPTER ONE

Staying behind the protection of her department-issue Tahoe, Rebecca Walker squirmed to adjust the fit of the Kevlar vest she wore under her black POLICE windbreaker. Day One of her new detective gig, she gets called away from it. A crisis situation always came first.

And this crisis…they should have seen it coming. Two irascible old men living next to each other, one sour, the other a genuine asshole. Sour now held asshole at gunpoint. As much as she usually liked people, honest to God, she'd have been tempted to leave them to go at it if only Kurt Gordon's wife Mimi wasn't also in the house.

Telling herself to do her job, she dialed the Gordons' phone number.

It was snatched up on the first ring. "Nobody here has time to talk."

"Mr. Brodsky—"

Slam. A real landline that let you do that.

Rebecca hated negotiations when she knew the people involved. It was a bad idea on a whole lot of levels.

She dialed again. This time, he said, "You can just clear out that circus in front of the house. I may start tossing bodies on the porch if you don't. And you know what son-of-a-bitch I'll start with!"

Circus was about right. Half a dozen police cars, the armored SWAT truck and an ambulance blocked the street. A television truck had already showed.

And…*bodies*? Somehow, that sounded like more than two.

"Mr. Brodsky, I'm Detective Rebecca Walker. Will you tell me what's going on?"

"All I ever asked is a little consideration!" he snarled. "And *some* kind of response from the police. How many times did I call you folks? Twenty? A hundred? Did any of you ever do a damn thing but politely knock on Gordon's door and say, 'Why don't you let your dog in so he'll quit barking?'"

He was right. That was about all they'd ever done. Noise complaints fell in the nuisance category. There were always speeders, traffic accidents, burglars, rapists, embezzlers and pimps to pull them away.

But the non-stop barking today, regular as a metronome, already had her on edge. Given years of listening to that…well, Ed Brodsky ran on anger *and* possessed an alarming collection of guns. Nothing they could do about that. License for an AR-15? Here you go, sir. Enjoy.

"You sound really frustrated," she forced herself to say, hoping her sympathy sounded close to genuine.

"Don't think you're going to talk me out of here," he snapped. "With Cecelia gone, I don't have a damn thing to live for. I'll be doing the world a favor to take Gordon and a bunch of lazy-ass cops with me!"

Oh, boy. He had just upgraded himself to the most dangerous type of hostage taker: a man who intended to die no matter how this scene played out. She didn't like his verb tense, either. His intentions sounded written in stone. A gravestone was what he had in mind.

"I was sorry to hear about Cecelia," she said gently. "I remember your little dog, too. Last time I saw the two of you out walking, he was getting up there."

The moment of silence gave her hope. She'd startled him.

"Didn't care enough to ever stop by and say you were sorry, though, did you?"

She shut down the pang of guilt and regret. She couldn't afford to let him dwell on the fact that *she* was one of the deputies who had failed him. She had to be his lifeline, not his enemy.

"How long had you been married, Mr. Brodsky?" she asked, and settled in for the long haul. In fact, she prayed it *would* be a long haul. She needed plenty of time to wear him down, remind him of his humanity.

Rebecca just hoped her critical new boss didn't hurry to show up. Her own annoying physical reaction to him was hard to shut down. While she was juggling nitroglycerin in fragile glass balls, the last thing she needed was his angry presence to ignite them.

*****

Lieutenant BJ Wilcynski parked in front of the ambulance, giving it room to get out if the shit hit the fan, then strolled toward the black Tahoe assigned to Detective Walker.

Sure enough, there she was, leaning against the fender. Her ponytail bobbed as she waggled her head at something said by the hostage-taker. Will had been told she had direct communication with him.

If she heard Will approaching, she didn't give any sign, her gaze never leaving the house across the street. Her posture stayed relaxed, her voice smooth as warm maple syrup. "Really gets on your nerves, doesn't it?" She listened for a minute. "Yeah, that's a lot of years to live next to the same people."

Textbook crisis negotiation responses, Will thought, except Rebecca had the gift of sounding as if she was chatting with a good friend. As sympathetic as her tone was, the guy she was talking to probably thought they were getting to be best buds. Of course, that was the idea.

In one way, he was reassured that she knew what she was doing. In another way…damn, he wished she wasn't the department's primary negotiator. And he wasn't real thrilled to now be her commander in these situations.

Or her lieutenant on a day-to-date basis. That warm maple syrup voice didn't make *him* feel like a buddy. Instead, he imagined that voice sliding over his bare skin, whispered against his mouth. He could get aroused just hearing her talking to someone down the hall.

Damn it.

Then she did glance his way, waving him over. When he stepped to her side, she handed him a note he assumed was in her handwriting.

Husband, wife, daughter and three grandkids 10, 7 and 5 inside!!

Shit. A different kind of tension ratcheted right up. Not two hostages. Six. And three of those were kids.

She scribbled again on a notepad. *Plans to commit suicide. Wants to take cops with.*

Better yet. He nodded acknowledgement before his gaze raked the surroundings, changed from pleasant residential neighborhood to surreal crime scene. The other houses on the block had been evacuated by the SWAT team as they arrived. Easy to see that people had been required to drop whatever they'd been doing and run. Two lawn mowers sat abandoned in the middle of half-mowed yards. It being late October, people probably hoped this was the last mow of the season. Kid-sized bikes lay on their sides up and down the block. His eye fell on a soccer ball that had come to a stop against the curb a few feet away.

On the way, he'd checked 911 calls to addresses on this street, and had winced at the number. Loud dog. Rusting heap of junk on cinder blocks in the driveway. Knocked down fence. Barking dog. Dog shit in flower beds. On and on.

Given the theme, he wasn't surprised that a dog was barking non-stop in that backyard. Every now and again, the poor animal would reach a crescendo that brought wolves to mind. There might be a whine in there. Why hadn't they gotten him out?

Scanning the scene, he picked out the SWAT members crouched behind vehicles or positioned to go in, weapons at the ready. A sniper lay flat on a rooftop, and another had somehow found a perch in an aging apple tree. More disturbing was the sight of TV news vans parked at the barricade, huge cameras aimed at the scene. He didn't want any of their faces to appear on television or the internet, but it was probably inevitable.

All of this because two sixty-something men had been squabbling for years, and one had finally snapped. The sad thing was, Will could identify. He'd been here five minutes and, in other circumstances, he'd have been hammering on the door.

"Let me give you another phone number," Rebecca said, apparently oblivious to any stresses as well as nearby activity. "I'm on my cell, and I'd hate to have the battery give out on us." Pause. "Yeah, if you can find a pen and something to write on."

Smart not to use the word 'die'.

Of course she was smart, he thought irritably. Despite some serious reluctance, he'd about had to promote her to the opening in the detective unit he headed. What excuse could he give? She's hot, and I don't trust myself if I have to work closely with her? Sheriff Mackay would have loved that one.

Her record on the job was rock solid. No real screw-ups, and a fair number of triumphs. Rebecca was well-liked even among the men in the department who hated the idea of women cops, and that was saying something. She'd been persuaded to train to be the negotiator because she'd proven herself so good at talking people off ledges. She'd been wounded once while saving the witness she was protecting, in doing so displaying courage and tactical thinking.

So here she was, standing on the sidewalk to negotiate on a cell phone.

In Los Angeles County, where Will had served for almost eighteen years, an entire team of experienced crisis negotiators would have turned out with SWAT. They'd have a command center bus. While the primary negotiator was talking to the HT – hostage-taker, in police jargon – the others would have been analyzing his intonation, his trigger words, keeping sophisticated communications equipment up and running, and serving as liaison with the SWAT commander and with Will in overall command. Someone would have been researching the HT, trying to determine any criminal background or mental health history, info about his finances, his family, close relationships.

From what Will knew, nobody had to do the last. Every deputy in the county had met these two. The liaison part was covered when he and she passed notes. Almost like being in third grade.

Will had known she was a trained negotiator. Until he had promoted her into his unit, he hadn't realized that she was pretty much it, not only for the sheriff's department, but also for the two cities in the county that had their own police departments. The second deputy trained to take turns with her in lengthy negotiations had little experience.

Will had also been surprised to learn he'd just inherited the job of commander at these scenes. It made sense, given that they would be working together day-to-day, and even more when the sheriff knew Will had done a stint in SWAT earlier in his career. Didn't mean he had to like it.

Taking his time – abrupt or hasty movements might scare the HT into hasty action – Will made his way behind the police vehicles to the SWAT commander's post.

Headed by Lieutenant Donald Nobach, the team had members from all three law enforcement agencies within the county: Cape Trouble P.D., North Fork P.D. and the sheriff's department. They did a lot of training, but this wasn't a dedicated unit. When needed, members dropped whatever they were doing, whether it was patrol or interviewing a suspect, grabbed their gear and got wherever they were needed as fast as they could.

Nobach, probably in his early forties, kept his graying hair buzz cut and looked at home in body armor. The first words out of his mouth? "We can go in anytime." That was the trouble with SWAT people – they always wanted to go in. Understandably, given how useless they felt standing around. Nobach added hopefully, "Rambler, lots of windows, slider in back, no problem."

Will handed over the note he'd stuffed in his pocket.

"Kids?" Nobach said in dismay.

"Kids."

"Can we shoot the dog?" he asked, downright plaintive.

"That might cool our HT's jets," Will conceded. "But it might also set him off if he's a dog lover, or just because he hears a gun fire. Let me go see where Detective Walker is at with him."

Despite the chill autumn afternoon, Rebecca still appeared relaxed and comfortable. Her long, lean body was as tantalizing as ever despite the bulk of the vest. Encased in form-fitting jeans, her slim legs, taut with muscle, could set off fantasies for him. Locked around his waist—

Get a grip, or get a new job, he thought grimly.

When he approached, she handed him another note. *Call Shelley. Say I can't make it tonight.* A phone number was at the end.

What? He was her social secretary now?

Nonetheless, he backed away. No, it wasn't looking good for her making it for any kind of appointment this evening.

He dialed and a brisk, woman's voice answered, "Shelley here."

"Rebecca Walker asked me to call to let you know she can't make it tonight. She's on the job."

"Tell her thanks. I appreciate the notice to find someone else to cover her shift."

Shift? Will didn't know why he was surprised. Cops did moonlight. Did she know she'd have to quit whatever it was now? Detectives worked erratic and sometimes long hours.

Did that damn dog never take a *rest*?

Stalking back to her, he scribbled in his own notebook and stuck it in front of her. She glanced down at the single word. *Dog?*

Without looking at him, she said, "Uh huh," a couple more times. Then, "Mr. Brodsky, how about if we let the dog out of the backyard? The barking is getting on all of our nerves, too. Would you mind if someone went up to the gate?" After a minute, she said, "Crying, huh? Did you and Cecelia have children? No? Me, either, but I do know it's hard to reason with a five-year-old, Mr. Brodsky. Why don't you let us take her off your hands, too."

Not a question. A casual offer – why should you have to be bothered with the kid? The implication was that she didn't really care about those kids one way or the other, but if her taking responsibility for the child would be a help to the old guy, she was willing.

Will held his breath, waiting for the answer.

"Well, I don't know. If you explain to one of the older kids and let him bring her out..." As if she'd had a lightbulb moment, she said, "In fact, if you let all the kids leave, it would cut the stress level out here a whole lot, and probably in there, too. I know you better than to think you'd ever hurt children."

More talking. Rebecca never met Will's gaze, but she grabbed his notebook and wrote 'Who to gate?'

He tapped his chest.

She frowned, but finally nodded.

"My boss offered. He's a big guy, but good with kids." She chuckled, a ripple of sound that felt like fingertips lightly exploring his bare skin.

Goosebumps.

"Okay, let me clear that." She held the phone away and met his eyes, hers a clear gray. "Lieutenant, Mr. Brodsky asks you to go unarmed. Hold your hands in the air as you approach the house. Gate's on the south side. Kids'll meet you there. One of them has a leash for the dog. Bring them straight back across the street. No slipping away across the neighbor's yard. He wants to see you coming and going. Nobody else moves."

"Got it, Detective," he said, pitching his voice to be heard through her phone.

He unsnapped his holster and laid it on the hood of the Tahoe, then walked around the front bumper, his hands in the air. He'd done things like this before, but always felt the tension. This could be a setup. The guy had already said he wanted to kill cops. Here was his chance. If Brodsky really was suicidal, he wouldn't care that SWAT officers would storm the house the minute they saw Will go down. Choosing suicide by cop wasn't uncommon. This was a throw of the dice on the hope Brodsky might be serious about letting the kids go.

Will's flesh flinched in anticipation of the bullet that could strike before he heard the sound of it being fired. He appreciated the Kevlar vest, but felt naked anyway. He was a big man, making an oversized target.

He knew the blinds were closed, but now the house windows all glinted a reflection of the sun dropping low in the sky. More time had passed since he arrived than he'd realized. Also textbook; Rebecca hadn't been in any hurry. She'd listened, empathized, established rapport, and now moved into influencing the HT into behaving like a decent human being.

The closer Will got to the house, the more his skin prickled. A shaft of reflected sunlight blinded him momentarily and he had to avert his face. Blinds separated, Mr. Brodsky probably stood behind that very window with the cross-hairs of a semi-automatic rifle on Will's head. No, maybe not. Gordon was the one he really hated. He might still have the barrel of one of his four licensed handguns aimed at his nemesis. All depended on how much he hated the cops who in his eyes hadn't done their jobs versus Kurt Gordon, the guy who had made baiting his neighbor a hobby.

Will continued up the driveway, no hesitation, but felt bunched muscles ease when he passed the corner of the garage. Garbage and recycling containers parked against the wall served as a reminder of everyday life. He rolled his shoulders in relief at having cover and strode to the gate.

The dog was still barking, but excitedly, as if he was leaping around the kids. Will heard a voice.

"Kids?" he called. "I'm Lieutenant Wilcynski, here to escort you across the street. Do you have a leash on the dog?"

"Yes, sir," said a young voice.

With a click, the gate swung open. Tail swinging, a black lab lunged at Will but came up short, although the oldest kid, a boy, was having to lean back to restrain him.

"Here, I'll take him," Will said, reaching for the leash. The dog whirled around him and he had to step free. "Are any of you hurt?"

Both boys shook their heads. Their eyes were puffy, faces splotched with red. The little girl breathed in hitched, half-sobs. "I want Mommy!"

"I know, honey." What he knew about children fit in a shot glass, but he could try. "Son, would you close the gate behind you?"

The taller boy did it.

He gave them simple instructions. Once they passed the garage, they were to bunch together and walk in front of him. Let his bulk shield them. "We'll be heading toward the ambulance." He pointed toward it. Their dad was behind it, but he wasn't telling them that in case one or all of them bolted.

Walking back across the street was even less pleasant than going the other way. He truly did hate having his back turned to a threat, and now he had to think about these terrorized children. His shoulders hunched and the back of his neck crawled as he escorted them at an even pace, always conscious of where they were in relation to those blank windows behind them.

When they reached the ambulance, he herded the kids around it. Despite the chill of a fall day, he'd sweated big, wet patches under his arms.

"Daddy!" screamed the girl.

The waiting man fell to his knees and pulled all three children into an embrace. The face he lifted to Will was both exultant and bare-to-the-bones terrified. "My wife."

Will squeezed his shoulder. "We're working on it, I promise. I'll keep you updated." He handed the leash to a nearby deputy. The dog bumped against these familiar people, tail whapping.

There to meet him, a scowling Lieutenant Nobach drew him aside. "What the fuck? We should have sent one of my men."

Will shook his head. "With all that armor? Brodsky wouldn't have let him close, and I don't blame him." He shrugged. "I'm wearing a vest."

Nobach snorted his opinion of how much protection that offered. "Now what?"

"Let me talk to the kids."

Will squatted down to their level and asked what they'd seen and heard. They talked over each other, but he got the essentials. In the background, the Lieutenant listened as attentively. In his notebook, Will wrote in big letters, *Everyone still alive. All in living*

*room. Not sure how many guns – saw at least one big black rifle –
AR-15? – and handgun. Grandpa goading him.*

The guy was really that stupid. Did he not *want* to walk out of
there? Or was his ego too shaky to let him back down in front of his
wife and daughter?

This time, Rebecca watched him approach. Even so, she kept
talking, with those long pauses for listening. "They're real glad to
see their father, Mr. Brodsky. That's a good thing you did. And no
more barking. Now that we can all relax a little, let's talk about how
we can resolve this situation. What do you hope will happen?"

Her face tightened. She made some *uh huh* and *yeah* noises.
Will held out his notebook. She took a look, then momentarily
closed her eyes. When she opened them, Will saw an expression so
bleak, he flinched. In response, she gave a small nod. No, she
didn't think she could pull this fat out of the fire.

He wrote, *Go in?* Hey, *someone* might survive if they did.

Rebecca shook her head vehemently.

He went to his Suburban and poured a cup of coffee from a
thermos he'd brought along. When he handed it to Rebecca, she
looked so grateful, he was afraid she might cry.

Crap. He wanted to say, "This isn't on you. Don't take
responsibility for what happens," but he knew the words would be
wasted. Any good cop was haunted by ghosts, a crowd that grew in
size as the years passed.

The sun set, purple dusk deepening. Huge white lights snapped
on, illuminating the Gordon home as if it were the infield at Yankee
Stadium. Will stuck by Rebecca's side, not interfering, hoping she
read silent support in his presence even though he knew he wasn't a
comfortable man to be around.

After another hour of expressing her understanding, she finally
said bluntly, "Mr. Brodsky, has Mrs. Gordon ever done anything to
you? And her daughter. Even if you remember her as a snotty
teenager, she's now the mother of three children who need her
desperately."

Rebecca listened for a minute, then said, in a voice that held the
faintest tremor, "I'm asking you to let the two of them go."

Oh, hell. Will straightened away from the side of her SUV. A
negotiator focused on the taker, not the hostages. Always. Solving
his problem, that was her ostensible goal. The taker needed to forget

that the hostages were really who mattered to everyone but him. Throwing that away after all these hours meant Rebecca knew she'd failed. Brodsky didn't want anything she could give him. He didn't want a solution. This was her desperate bid to save the real innocents trapped in that house.

When she let out an exhalation of relief, he did, too. Even as she said a husky, "Thank you," Will signaled the SWAT lieutenant.

Within minutes, two women emerged through the front door, the younger one supporting the older with an arm around her shoulders. The door stayed cracked open. Another dangerous moment. Hostage-takers often changed their mind – or enjoyed setting people up to think they'd survived, only to take them out. If Brodsky really wanted to hurt Kurt Gordon, what would be better than killing his wife and daughter where he could see it happen?.

The tension was huge, felt by everyone watching.

A fast walk turned into a trot by mid-street. SWAT members swarmed the women and hustled them behind their armored truck. Front door on the house closed.

More relieved than he'd have admitted, Will went to get them, escorting them in a big semi-circle to the lawn behind the ambulance, where they caught sight of the kids. With glad cries, the two groups merged, the man yanking his wife into an embrace so tight it looked painful. She held on just as hard, before pulling away to hug their children.

The older woman turned a tear-streaked face to Will. "My husband…"

His throat closed. He squeezed her arm. "We'll do our best." The despair on her face told him she heard the underlying truth: their best was unlikely to save her husband.

He returned to Rebecca to hear stress creeping into her voice.

"Mr. Brodsky, despite all the hoopla out here, nothing all that bad has happened. You still have the chance to take some classes at the senior center, see those gladiolas in bloom again, adopt a dog that needs a home." She swallowed. "Please."

A gun barked once. Twice.

SWAT members closed in on the house, slammed through the front door.

It was all over.

Hearing an odd sound, Will spun to see that Rebecca had slid down the side of the SUV and now sat with her back to it, her head tipped toward the sky, her eyes closed – and tears slipping down her cheeks.

Seeing her like that, he wanted to go to his knees and take her in his arms. The stabbing pain in his chest told him he was in deep trouble.

CHAPTER TWO

Lieutenant Wilcynski was the absolute last man Rebecca would have chosen to see her break down. Or would have expected to insist on taking her to a diner instead of letting her drive away on her own.

He had also ordered for her. Still dazed, she gazed at her plate. She couldn't remember the last time she'd had a cheeseburger. But with her mouth watering and her stomach growling, she snatched it up and took a big bite. Best to eat before he started critiquing her performance.

Rebecca gobbled, while he ate more slowly, watching her with the darkest eyes she'd ever seen. Now and again, he scanned the mostly empty restaurant and what he could see of the parking lot outside. Typical cop behavior. When she was done, he paused in his own meal.

"Feel better?" he asked, in a voice deep enough to set off some kind of vibrations inside her.

"Yes. Thank you."

"Good." He took the last bite of his own burger.

Rebecca braced herself. If he wanted to debrief, why not do it at the scene? Because she, the fragile little woman, had cried? Remembering made her cringe. Had he fed her only to salve his conscience before he fired her, or at least lobbed some grenades?

She'd never had any trouble dealing with Lieutenant Driscoll, her boss on the patrol side. With Wilcynski, she instantly became tongue-tied.

Shouldn't have applied to become a detective. Except a familiar stir of anxiety told her she couldn't have continued in her old job. Sure, he caught her eye every time their paths crossed, but she noticed other men, too. She'd get over finding this new boss so…disturbing. Or so she thought until he closeted them in his small office for the interview and she found out how overwhelming he was in close quarters. At which point it seemed too late to say, Whoa, maybe this isn't such a good idea.

Broad, blunt cheekbones made his face arresting, along with deep-set eyes and midnight-dark hair. Probably six foot two or three, he had a powerful build that could be useful for intimidation, although the effect might be unconscious. Most people shifted into idle some of the time. Wilcynski had an aggressive energy she felt even when he sat outwardly relaxed behind his desk skimming a file. The simmer went to a boil with lightning speed, although she had yet to hear about him actually losing control. Whoever he was chewing out just felt his fury, as if he projected his energy in a way that should be impossible.

The only real fact known about him was that he'd left a job as head of a homicide unit in Los Angeles County to move to a relatively minuscule sheriff's department on the fog-bound Oregon coast. The *why* was an endless source of speculation within the department. An ugly divorce. He'd been fired. A wife and children had died. He got sick of southern California traffic.

She blurted, "The suspense is killing me. Are you planning to critique my performance, or what?"

If he fired her, she'd be forced into another line of work. Would that be so bad?

"Critique? I've never heard a negotiation handled better." Wilcynski tipped his glass at her before taking a swallow.

She automatically shook her head. "I don't deserve that. I failed tonight."

"You saved every single hostage," he said. "You told me yourself that Brodsky intended from the get-go to commit suicide."

"He's the first one I've ever lost. At the end..." She still felt the hammer-blow of finality. Only, when SWAT officers got inside the house, they found that Brodsky had shot his neighbor in the leg before swallowing his gun. He had chosen not to kill even the man he had hated enough to take hostage.

That somehow made his death harder for her to accept.

"I'm sorry." The lieutenant sounded gentle. Who knew he could? "I suppose, after all those hours on the phone with him, you really do connect."

"Yes." Blast it, her eyes stung again. She looked away. "Not always, but... I kept thinking of him walking that scraggly little dog after his wife died. And I thought, why *didn't* I ever stop and say,

'Mr. Brodsky, I'm sorry to hear about your wife. How are you?'"
She hoped he couldn't tell she'd become choked up.

"On patrol, you encounter a lot of people. You can't keep up with all their lives."

She tried with some. She followed up with a few she'd spoken to when answering the crisis line, too, the ones she'd sensed were fragile. Why not Mr. Brodsky? Because his constant complaints were annoying, even if they were justified? Because he was a grouch? The answer was *probably*, even if she wasn't proud of herself. Why hadn't she guessed he'd be sinking into depression?

She shrugged.

"Rebecca. Look at me."

The order was too compelling for her to disobey.

"I asked around about you before I interviewed you for the detective position. Do you have any idea how well-liked you are?"

Heat blossomed in her cheeks. "I, well, I like people." Yep, there she went, stumbling over her words.

"I can tell. So can everyone else."

Wait. Her eyes widened. Had he just called her by her first name? She'd heard him address the guys in the unit. 'Detective', with a sarcastic inflection, was the usual. Or she'd expect a snapped, "Walker".

"That's why he didn't shoot the dog," he said suddenly,

Rebecca blinked. Where had that come from? Oh – scraggly dog. "No. I mean, yes. He wouldn't have blamed the dog." She let out a huff. "I hate that Kurt Gordon comes out of this smelling like roses," she exclaimed. "If he keeps letting that damn dog bark…"

"I heard his son-in-law saying they'd take the dog, whether Kurt liked it or not."

"Really? You think he'll have the grace not to get another one?"

"If he does, what do you say we become dognappers?" her lieutenant suggested.

Rebecca giggled. Completely inappropriate, it had to be part of the crash. To her shock, Wilcynski grinned at her, the expression both friendly and wicked. He was not known for smiling.

"Feeling better?"

Had he fed her just to be nice? No - more likely, he considered her a responsibility. Driscoll and Mackay and even Chief Colburn of

CTPD had never bothered, but nobody had died at those previous scenes.

"I guess I am," she admitted. "The tranquilizing effect of carbs." Wilcynski's effect sure wasn't tranquilizing, but he'd settled her in a different way.

"You done?" he asked.

"Sure." It embarrassed her that she'd eaten every morsel. And what a stupidly girly thing that was to think. Who cared how much she ate?

Her heart spasmed as Mr. Brodsky's face rose in her mind's eye. He'd gone out in a blaze of anger, but mostly because he was sad. She brooded as Wilcynski handed a credit card to the waitress.

When he pocketed his wallet a minute later, resignation appeared on his face. "Any good I've done is wasted, isn't it?"

"What?" She focused on him.

He only shook his head and slid out of the booth, waiting until she did the same.

They were almost to the door when he stopped. "Shit!"

Going on alert, she turned her head until she saw what he did. A television hanging on the wall. Evening news, volume turned low. She recognized the street, the vehicles. The camera panned the two women hurrying across the street and the SWAT officers meeting and protecting them.

Rebecca's heart drummed as she stared. The reporter's words were only a jumble. The muted sound of two gunshots...that she heard. Her body jerked in response, and then started when a strong arm came around her.

"Damn them," he said fiercely. The segment still running, a pretty blonde talked to the camera, but he hustled Rebecca out the door into the sodium-lit parking lot. He didn't stop until they'd reached her vehicle, where he spun her to face him, still gripping her upper arm. "How the *hell* did they pick you out?"

She gaped at him. "What do you mean?"

"They showed you talking on the phone. It was obvious you were wearing a vest, and you turned so viewers could see the 'police' on the back. Then they zoomed in on your face."

"Oh, my God." She'd missed that part.

Over the years, she'd had to participate in post-crisis press conferences twice, but they'd been handled by Sheriff Mackay or

Chief Colburn, and she'd been kept in the background as much as possible. She'd hated having to say even a few words.

"I've been doing this long enough, the press all know I'm likely to be the negotiator at a scene like that," she said. "They must have looked for me."

He released her, his scowl making him formidable. "I don't like you being in the public eye."

"I don't like it either, but what's your solution?"

"The Tahoe has tinted windows for a reason. You should have sat inside."

Rebecca shook her head in immediate repudiation. "I can't spend hours sitting down. Besides, I'd feel disconnected. I want to come as close to looking into the eyes of a person in crisis as I can."

"Even if it puts you at risk?"

Chilled, she hugged herself before realizing what she was doing and dropping her arms to her sides. "Why would I be…?"

"You're a woman, you're beautiful, you represent something powerful. You're lucky someone hasn't fixated on you already."

"Are you *trying* to scare me?"

"Yes."

What if he knew how scared she was already?

Then he seemed to shake himself. "Nothing we can do about it now." He nodded at the Tahoe. "Do you still live in the same place?"

Momentarily startled, she remembered that he'd probably been there after the shooting, when it was a crime scene and she was in the hospital.

"Yes." Completely casual. She finally realized she had the remote in her hand, unlocked and opened the door of her SUV.

She'd just as soon avoid the subject of where she lived, given that he'd just talked about someone fixating on her, about putting herself at risk. She'd finally gone home to her log cabin a few months ago, having stayed with her father while she rehabbed from the wound that had torn up her shoulder. What she hadn't told a soul was the panic she'd struggled with ever since. How poorly she slept, starting awake at every tiny noise. Before the shooting, she had loved the peace she found at her home in the forest, the wildlife wandering through her yard, the brilliance of stars at night because there were no nearby lights to dim them.

She kept thinking she'd regain her pleasure in the solitude, but it wasn't happening. Now, she'd gone so far as to start thinking about putting her dream home up for sale. Her disappointment in herself was one more thing to deal with.

"Is it smart to live so isolated?" His big, broad-shouldered body imposing, Wilcynski gripped the top of her open door and looked down at her. "Cops like to think we're invulnerable, but we acquire enemies in a way other people don't."

Oh, there was the pep talk she needed.

She couldn't tell her lieutenant how vulnerable she did feel these days. His understanding would only go so far. She definitely wouldn't admit that she had applied to become a detective because she'd become afraid every time she walked up to a car she had pulled over, the front door of a house when the call was a domestic. Her shoulder ached all the time, but the pain spiked to match her tension.

Rebecca had no doubt a counselor would slap her with the PTSD label, but she wouldn't be allowed to do her job if that ever happened. They wouldn't want her as negotiator, either. She knew for sure she'd lose the respect of the macho men who were her co-workers. Being shot had raised her status in the department, dumb as that sounded. Unless she planned to quit, she couldn't jeopardize her reputation. This was where she belonged. What she'd wanted to do since she was a girl. Her purpose.

Anyway, being a detective was supposed to be way safer than riding patrol. She just had to make sure Lieutenant Wilcynski didn't see right through her. If he hadn't already, with those piercing dark eyes.

Diversion, that was the ticket.

"So," she said, "you could help me win the jackpot."

One dark eyebrow rose.

She blurted it right out. "What's BJ stand for?"

The second eyebrow joined the first, although she thought his mouth twitched in what might be a near-smile.

"You can call me BJ, you can call me Will—"

Rebecca rolled her eyes and climbed in behind the wheel. "Or you can call me lieutenant. I know." She frowned, stopping in the act of pulling out her seatbelt. "How do you think of yourself?"

He cocked his head. "You know, people don't ask me that."

"Really?"

"They might ask what I prefer to be called, but that's different."

"Yes, it is." In welcoming her, other detectives had hinted that whatever he had said after hiring her, what he *preferred* to be called on the job was lieutenant.

"Will," he said abruptly. "In my head, I'm Will."

"Oh." Her heart beat faster. Telling her that felt like a gift. As if he was letting her in. And he did say she was beautiful.

No, no. She was imagining things. Becoming delusional. Lieutenant Wilcynski couldn't possibly be suggesting... No.

But, oh God, she was afraid her nipples had tightened and heat had definitely settled between her legs.

No.

"Well, um, thanks for dinner."

Expression suddenly guarded, he nodded and said, "Goodnight." He slammed the door and walked away toward the even bigger SUV she knew was his personal vehicle.

He was driving it because he had been taking today off. Weird, when she'd dreaded his arrival, but Rebecca was very glad he'd quit whatever he was doing, jumped in that Suburban and raced to the scene to support her.

Backing out, she made a face. He'd probably been sure she would screw it up if left on her own. Uh huh, and hadn't she? Hearing a man kill himself because she hadn't been able to help, that was hard.

Deciding whether there was anything she could have done differently would be a process, excellent material to keep her awake tonight and every night for a while. Right now, she couldn't help hugging to herself what Wilcynski said, though, about never having seen a negotiation handled better.

And she couldn't forget that he said she was beautiful.

She groaned. Working under him would be more challenging yet if she seriously started wishing the man was more than her boss.

*****

"The parents swear the girl would never do anything like this. She's not really a girl," the deputy said over the phone, "she's twenty-three, so usually I'd just tell mom and dad to hold off before panicking, but… Part of it is, she has a kid. A two-year-old who's with them."

Despite not being able to see his face, Will heard Desoto's discomfort. Even so, it was ridiculous to suggest they launch an investigation into why a twenty-three-year-old woman hadn't come home after a party. To her parents' house, no less. She'd know they would take care of their grandkid. She was probably still sleeping off the booze or recovering from a night of wild sex.

Something he hadn't had in too long, Will thought irritably. Phone to his ear, he walked out into the squad room to find half the desks unoccupied. Their occupants were either out on interviews or off today. Worley seemed to be having an intense phone conversation. He was working that mess at the Castaneda's organic farm. Likely teenagers high on something had thought it would be fun to commit some vandalism, but they'd done extensive and expensive damage.

Will's gaze stopped at Rebecca, who was also on the phone, probably making calls Sean Holbeck had assigned to her yesterday morning before she got yanked away in her role as negotiator. Will intended to pair her with Holbeck for a few weeks, since he was the best detective in the unit – skilled, intuitive, methodical. But Sean had taken an unusual full weekend off.

His gaze latched hungrily onto her delicate nape, the skin creamy beneath a bundle of shiny dark hair. Bending over, touching his lips to that pale, vulnerable spot was way more appealing than it should have been.

He swore under his breath. Maybe not quite under his breath, since Detective Britton lifted his head to stare at him, and Desoto stopped talking.

"Sorry," Will muttered into the phone, realizing he'd missed part of what the deputy had said.

Desoto cleared his throat. "Well, uh, the mother called a couple of the friends who were with her daughter last night. They all swear she said she was going home."

Stopping at Rebecca's desk, Will said abruptly, "I can't promise anything. You know it's too soon to mount any kind of search."

"I just have a bad feeling about this."

Will grunted. "Give me the info." He grabbed a blank pad from her desk and made hasty notes. She'd finished her own call somewhere in there and was gazing warily at him. Probably braced to find out what he wanted.

He ended the call, thinking this could be an excuse to get Rebecca out learning her job. A training exercise, yeah. The benefit to him was that he wouldn't have to see her again today. Her very presence was a distraction and an annoyance.

"Do you know Deputy Desoto?" he asked.

She nodded. "He's steady, careful. I think he just passed twenty years on the job."

That was a lot of experience, which didn't sway Will's thinking.

"Why?" she asked.

"He got called to take a report on a missing young woman." Saying it out loud clarified his thinking. He couldn't in good conscience waste any of their time on this, even hers. As an investigator, she'd learn this reality soon enough, but it wouldn't hurt to let her in on his reasoning. "You know the odds," he said brusquely. "She hooked up with some guy, went home with him and was inconsiderate enough not to let anybody know. But her parents are scared and the friends she was with last night swear she was heading home."

"You want me to take it."

Trying to decipher her expression, he shook his head. "We need to wait a day, minimum. Give her a chance to come home."

"Why did Desoto call you?"

"He has a bad feeling."

Rebecca bristled. "You don't think instincts count?"

Aware other detectives were eavesdropping, he scowled at her. "Of course I do. But there's a reason we don't act on this kind of report. Or, usually, even take it."

"So why are we talking about it?" she demanded.

"Into my office," he snapped. Once there, he half sat on his desk, one foot braced on the floor. "I'm trying to give you some insight into one of the decisions we make here."

Temper slashed color across her cheeks, and she crossed her arms. "The twenty-four hours after a murder is critical. If this woman has been abducted, not even looking for her until twenty-four hours has passed could be fatal."

His exasperation was turning into something more cutting. "You're the expert now?"

"It's common sense!" she snapped.

"I've been doing homicide *and* missing persons for years, Detective Walker. Or should I call you that yet?"

He could see her biting back fury. Smart enough not to push him too hard?

"Let me look into it," she said at last. Was she pleading with him? "I don't have anything important to do yet." Adding a tinge of sarcasm, she said, "It would let Desoto think you respect him. Pacify the parents. Earn us some brownie points."

She made a good argument. He wouldn't be able to send her out as primary even if something important came in this afternoon. Uh huh, and if she'd been any other detective in this unit except maybe Holbeck, Will would have already slapped him down. His hesitation wasn't just because this was Rebecca, already a problem for him. No, what bothered him was the look in her eyes. It was close to the anguish he'd seen after they all heard those two gunshots yesterday.

Did she feel a desperate need to atone for what she saw as yesterday's failure? See this as her chance? Or did the idea of a missing woman shake her on a fundamental level?

Suddenly, Will wished he knew more about her background. He could ask whether her reaction was personal, but...what was the harm in letting her go ahead? Training exercise, he reminded himself. And when the idiot young woman showed up, Rebecca would get her first solid lesson. This is why we don't launch an investigation every time an adult goes 'missing' for a whole day.

"All right," he said curtly. "Having you sit around here with your feet on the desk doesn't gain us anything."

Her jaw worked and her eyes spit fire at his unfair jab, but she had the self-control to keep her mouth shut.

"Here's what I know," he said, handing over what information he'd jotted down.

She glanced down. "She has a young child?"

"Safe at Grandma and Grandpa's." Maintaining the relaxed pose was becoming an effort. "Have at it."

Without a word, she turned her back on him and strode to her desk to grab her jacket.

He pushed himself up and went to the doorway. "Oh, Walker?"

Her glare seared him.

"Stay in touch." Will hardened his voice. "You do anything but chat with the girl's family and friends, I want to know about it. You hear me?"

"Yes, Lieutenant, I hear you."

*****

All residual warm feelings from yesterday erased, Rebecca stalked out to her vehicle, parked in the gravel lot right behind this wing of the sheriff's department headquarters on the outskirts of North Fork, the county seat.

"What a jerk," she muttered.

Humiliation and anger hot in her chest, she sent some gravel spurting behind her when she pulled out into the alley. Then she made herself brake before turning onto the street. It would be good to know where she was going. And…she had to acknowledge her deeper fear. Say, *This isn't the same thing. This is just me doing my job.*

Except that was a lie. It never had been. And if Wilcynski knew her past, he wouldn't have let her take on an investigation involving a young mother who didn't return home to her child. Rebecca shuddered, but made herself scan his notes.

Amanda Shaw. Oh, crap. Rebecca took in the address. More people she knew. She'd babysat for Mandy and her little brother Jerry. Jeremiah.

Rebecca and her dad had moved to the wooded neighborhood surrounding tiny Bow Lake on the east side of Highway 101, after Mom died. He hadn't wanted her to have to go to school with people who knew what happened. Not until Rebecca left for college did he sell this house and move back to Newport. As a cop, she'd had reason to visit the neighborhood, but never happened on anyone she remembered from growing up.

Wilcynski might not have let her go if he'd been aware she had a history with the family, too. Except, she couldn't do her job at all if she had to pull back every time she encountered someone she knew. Burris County didn't have that many citizens. It was fine for Sean Holbeck, who hadn't grown up here, but Worley had, and he must have the same problem she did.

In this case…Mandy Shaw would have been about ten when Rebecca left for college. Long time ago.

She drove straight to the address, her head turning as it always did when she passed the two-story that had become home when Rebecca herself was ten. The paint color wasn't the same, but otherwise it hadn't changed. She had no idea who owned it now. Didn't want to know. There was something creepy in thinking about strangers living in a house so filled with her memories.

The Shaws' split-level home was gray now instead of the brown she remembered. The spruce and Douglas firs surrounding it had grown. Parking in the driveway, she got out, inhaling the woodsy scent mixed with the faint, salty smell of the ocean not that far away. This house was about a block from the lake, which had a couple of community access points for swimming or launching canoes or rowboats. It wasn't big enough for speedboats, but offered neighborhood kids a lot of fun.

For the first time, she really looked around with a cop's eye. Half acre lots, if memory served her, all wooded. Lake. A lot of places to hide a body.

No, Wilcynski was undoubtedly right. *Please let him be right.* Mandy would walk in the door rolling her eyes because her parents had called the *police*? Really?

Nope, Rebecca was here to practice her interview skills. Because she hadn't learned a thing in nine years on patrol and handling negotiations. As cover for the fact she was flat-out scared, she let irritation rise again.

She hadn't reached the porch when the door opened. Seeing the barely contained fear on the woman's plump face, Rebecca knew.

A repentant Mandy had not come home.

CHAPTER THREE

"Mrs. Shaw," she said gently. "I'm Detective Walker. You might remember me. I babysat your daughter, a long time ago."

The woman peered at her. "Rebecca?"

"That's right." Rebecca would have known Vicky Shaw if they'd come face to face in the grocery store, but not her husband, she realized, who waited in the living room. Stuart, he said, when he shook hands. He'd lost most of his hair, but she had a feeling it was fear that made him look so gaunt.

"Mandy is always considerate," he insisted. "She wouldn't do this to us." His voice shook.

"I understand she has a child?"

"Samantha. She's napping."

"How old?"

"Two and a half."

Fortunately, too young to understand much.

Rebecca sat down and took out her notebook. "Tell me about Mandy."

Vicky talked while her husband struggled to hold onto composure.

Their daughter had left home to get her associate degree in nursing from Clatsop Community College in Astoria. She liked the idea of a small town but easy access to Portland. She managed to finish the degree despite her pregnancy, but after moving to Portland for a year because of the baby's father, she came home, saying she wasn't a city girl.

"Brian – Sammie's father – is worthless. He didn't want to have a kid. His words. He left them for some girl who worked at a bar. He sends a support check every three or four months." Anger infused Stuart's voice now, momentarily overriding the fear.

Vicky said, "Fortunately, the small hospital in Cape Trouble hired her right away. We suggested she live at home for now, so we can help take care of Samantha. We're glad to have both of them." Vicky's hands twisted in her lap. "Jerry – do you remember him? –

is a sophomore at Harvey Mudd in southern California. He's big into computers, and I can't see him ever coming home for more than visits."

Rebecca kept them both talking until an image of a vivacious, warm-hearted, stay-at-home young mother emerged. Mandy had apparently melded right back into the same group of friends she'd had in high school, but she didn't go out evenings more than once or twice a week, and rarely stayed out much past midnight.

Oh, yes, Mandy had had boyfriends before Brian and had dated since coming home, but hadn't been serious about anyone, Vicky assured her. Rebecca smiled and nodded, although from experience she reserved judgment. There was a lot teenagers and young twenties didn't tell their parents.

She recognized names of a couple of the friends and one former boyfriend. She'd babysat him and his younger brother, too. The idea made her feel old.

Mrs. Shaw leaped up to hand several framed photos of Mandy to Rebecca. Amanda Shaw was an exceptionally pretty young woman, blonde and blue-eyed. In one, she held her daughter, maybe eighteen months or so then. Useless daddy or not, Samantha had a sunny smile and looked a lot like her mother had at the same age.

The party last night had been thrown to celebrate one of the friends getting a coveted job. With a brand new degree, she'd been hired to put on educational programs at the aquarium in Newport.

Vicky drew a deep breath and gazed beseechingly at Rebecca. "Mandy's crowd isn't into drugs or anything like that. I'm sure they drink, but…"

Withholding her opinion on that, too, Rebecca asked, "Where was this party held?"

"One of the boys rents a cottage at Jasper Beach. Mandy and two friends from the neighborhood walked. She was sure she could get a ride home."

"All right," Rebecca said. "I need names, phone numbers and addresses of as many of her friends as you can come up with."

Eventually, if Mandy didn't turn up, Rebecca would need access to her laptop, get phone records. But she'd start with the obvious, and keep hoping the perfect daughter showed up.

Rebecca would really like to kick her ass for scaring her parents like this. Nobody should have to go through what they were, not if she wasn't in trouble.

And if she was… Alone in the SUV she hadn't yet started, Rebecca closed her eyes and dealt with emotions she *could not* let influence how she did her job, or get in the way of doing it. Several minutes passed before she released a breath that seemed to empty her. Finally, she reached for her phone.

*****

Rebecca hadn't been gone an hour when Will took a call on the internal line from Sheriff Mackay.

"I'm spreading the word that a Tillamook County deputy was just ambushed and shot," he said tensely. "Report was about a break-in. When he got out of his vehicle, multiple shots were fired and a car on the other side of the road took off."

"Was he killed?"

"Alive but in critical condition. This may have been personal, they don't know yet. But just in case it was motivated by a grudge against law enforcement in general, we need to have our people be extra cautious. I'll let Colburn and Lundy know about this, too."

Daniel Colburn was the police chief in Cape Trouble, Howard Lundy chief in North Fork. Smaller communities all contracted with the sheriff's department for law enforcement.

"I'll pass the word to my detectives," Will said. "Where did this happen?"

"Near Garibaldi."

Picturesque, but not a very big town, if memory served. Also an easy drive along the coast highway from Cape Trouble. In other words, too close.

"Any leads?"

"Nobody in the vicinity agrees what color the car was, forget make. They were too shaken to think about looking at the license plate."

Off the phone, Will went out into the bullpen. Four detectives were there, one having plopped himself at his desk since Rebecca left.

"Listen up." He repeated what Mackay had told him. "Use a little extra care. Take a look around before you exit your vehicle. Be especially cautious if you're going to see someone who called out of the blue to volunteer information."

"Shit," Worley said, "it's been happening in other parts of the country, but here?"

There was grumbled agreement to cover the anxiety every cop felt. They spent their lives approaching strangers. Trusting that they'd been called because they were needed.

"There are plenty of reasons why someone can feel wronged by authority, and police in particular," Will reminded them. "You know that."

As he went back into his office, some of them were already going online in search of more answers. He didn't blame them. Things like this hit home.

Frowning, he called Rebecca first.

"Checking up on me?" she said testily.

He'd be amused by her attitude if it didn't also turn him on.

"You learn anything?" he asked.

"She has not yet appeared." Now her voice held unfamiliar tension. "The party was in Jasper Beach, a mile and a half from home. She walked there with a couple of friends, who both found alternate ways to get home. She promised to be home by midnight. According to her parents, she keeps her promises. Haven't pinned down anyone yet who actually saw her get in a car or walk away down the street." She paused. "Crossing the highway on foot in the middle of the night, not a good idea for a woman alone."

That gave him pause. A girl who'd had a little too much to drink, maybe smoked some weed, might think nothing of setting out by herself late at night. It probably never occurred to her there was any real danger. She'd undoubtedly done it plenty of times over the years and gotten away with what was actually high-risk behavior. Like Rebecca, Will knew how many dangers that young woman could have met. A car pulls over, the driver asks for directions... The parents would never recover.

"Stick with it," he said. "But that's not why I'm calling."

Rebecca listened in silence before saying, "The uniformed deputies are most at risk."

"Probably, but don't count on being immune."

"I won't." And she was gone.

He made other calls, but he felt most uneasy about her. He tried to convince himself she wasn't any more vulnerable to this kind of attack than a male officer, but knowing she'd already been shot once in her career disturbed him. Shot, as it turned out, by a fellow cop, who used a jacketed hollow point bullet designed to achieve maximum damage. Most cops reached retirement without being shot or ever discharging their own weapons. Having that happen had to impact her reactions now.

Will had worked with female cops without gender being an issue on his part. With Rebecca...he wasn't sure he could get past thinking about her as a woman.

So what was he supposed to do about it?

*****

All Mandy's friends were scared for her. None were especially helpful, although not for lack of trying. Three agreed that she had said goodnight to them and they didn't see her again, so she must have left, right?

If Mandy was still missing by tomorrow, Rebecca knew she'd need to go back to them, learn the intricacies of relationships, whether there might be jealousy or obsession everybody pretended wasn't there. These were the friends who she would have told if a guy was making her uneasy, or if there was new tension with Samantha's father. For now, Rebecca was determined to find out who had last seen the girl.

Jen, a weepy brunette, had been, well, with her boyfriend. "You know." She blushed as she pleaded for understanding. "Mandy knocked on the bedroom door and said she was going home, she'd call tomorrow. Well, today." Yes, Jen agreed, she'd walked over with Mandy, but Damon drove her home.

Nicole, the other girl from their neighborhood, left around eleven because she had to be at work at seven. She made a face to express her opinion of that. "Now I wish..."

Too little, too late. Persisting, Rebecca asked, "Did you walk home?"

"Uh uh. Scott Cardenas said I shouldn't, so he drove me."

"Did he go back to the party?"

"Um...I think so? He said he might."

And so it went. They all sounded absurdly young, even though she had only six or seven years on some of them. Rebecca had never felt those years so acutely. And truthfully, she'd never been so careless. Even if she'd lost her mother in a different way, she still would have tried to fill some of her role. Between the additional responsibility and her awareness that tragedy could strike at any moment, that danger could have a familiar face, she'd always been older than her real age.

She kept thinking, *This is how it was after Mom disappeared. Cops doing what I am.* A part of her had stayed angry they hadn't found her mother in time. Now she understood, and felt increasingly futile as the afternoon went on and the interviews proved fruitless. What if nobody *had* seen Mandy leave? And if someone had...did that really mean anything? If Mandy had been snatched by a passing predator on the highway, they'd never know what happened until her body was found. If it was found.

At least I am *trying,* Rebecca told herself. Nobody would be if she hadn't argued with Wilcynski.

Her knock on Scott Cardenas's door prompted his mother to drag him out of bed. Like so many of the group of friends, he still lived with his parents, in his case, only a couple blocks from the beach in Cape Trouble.

Light brown hair streaked with blue standing on end, he seemed bewildered by her visit. Turned out he hadn't heard yet about Mandy's disappearance.

"Shit. Wow. Really?"

Yeah, he'd gone back to the party, but he didn't remember especially noticing Mandy after that. "A bunch more friends showed up. It got kind of out of control." He sounded like that was a good thing. In the background, Mom looked less enthusiastic. Like Mandy, Scott was twenty-three. Why was he still living at home? "I didn't leave until, like, three?" he said.

Rebecca thanked him for his time and asked him to call if he recalled anything that might be helpful. "You did a good thing, driving Nicole home instead of letting her walk."

"Yeah. Wow. I can't believe..." Still dazed, he closed the door behind her.

Rebecca stopped on the sidewalk and breathed deeply. She had to clear her head, and she did love the ocean air. If she hadn't been working today, she could have gone for a walk on the beach. They might not have many more days this warm. She could have rolled up her pants, gone barefoot and joined the tiny brown sandpipers in dodging the foam of incoming waves.

Unfortunately, it would have been more fun with a companion. Too bad the only someone who interested her was taboo, even assuming he had any interest. She tried to picture her dark, brooding lieutenant rolling up his pants and digging bare toes into the wet sand but failed. On a sharp pang, she realized the last time she'd held hands with a man was Sean Holbeck, who'd gripped her hand as she was wheeled into surgery after the shooting. Didn't count, given that he had been in love then with the woman he'd since married.

Okay. Back to the moment. Taking out her phone, she hit re-dial.

So far, Carson Crandall had eluded her. A relative newcomer to Cape Trouble, he was reputed to be Mandy's current boyfriend. Apparently from the west side of the mountains, he was an EMT she had met at the hospital.

No answer again. Rebecca didn't leave another message.

Okay, if she couldn't find the current boyfriend, she'd talk to the high school boyfriend who had broken up with Mandy before she left for college. Timothy Spiva, whom Rebecca had babysat so long ago. She had dreaded calls from his mother and been relieved when they quit coming. He and his brother were both butts, certain *they* didn't need a babysitter. Tim had been a couple years older than Mandy, Rebecca seemed to remember, which would make him twenty-five now.

Another of Mandy's friends had told her Tim worked at a fencing and decking business in North Fork, the county seat twenty miles inland. When Rebecca arrived and asked for him, his boss called him to the front. Several other employees and a couple customers gaped, a familiar reaction even when she wasn't in uniform.

Spiva jogged out from the back. "This about Mandy?"

"It is," Rebecca said.

His eyes widened. "Hey! I know you. You used to come to the house."

"Long time no see," she agreed.

"You were on TV last night! Plus, you got shot last year. That was awesome. They said on TV you got a slug in him, too. I mean, none of us ever saw a woman cop."

The times were theoretically changing, but not very fast in little Burris County. To date, there were only three female cops, all employed by the sheriff's department. Her promotion to detective was a first.

"Awesome?" It took an effort to keep from sounding sharp. "Not how I'd describe it. It hurt, and I didn't get back on the job for three months."

To his credit, Spiva flushed. "Well, sure, I didn't mean..."

She suggested they go outside to allow them to talk privately. He led the way into the side yard, a chain-link surrounded space where decking, fence and railing styles were displayed. They currently had it to themselves. Probably not all that many people got inspired to build a new deck in the fall.

Rebecca asked the first of the questions that were starting to come by rote.

"I saw her come out of the house," he said, forehead wrinkling. "I offered to drive her home. But I think she expected us to hook up again now that she's around, so she was kind of mad that I've been seeing someone else. She said no way." Timothy Spiva swallowed. "Man, I should have pushed her in the car anyway."

Tim Spiva wasn't a kid in the same way as Scott, Rebecca became uneasily conscious. Maybe the extra two or three years made the difference. At five foot ten or so, he was stocky and strong in build, with beefy hands that he clenched in frustration or distress. Brown hair was buzz-cut, and he either hadn't shaved for a couple days or sported the stubble because he liked the look.

He never took his eyes off Rebecca. Mostly her face, but every so often his gaze slid lower, pausing on her breasts or her legs. She hadn't gotten this kind of male assessment much in the past, possibly because she'd been in uniform. Police uniforms came across as masculine no matter how they fit, and they never really fit any woman right. She hadn't expected to miss wearing it. She might have to rethink what she *did* wear. The slim-cut black pants she had on with knee-high boots were apparently a bad idea.

No way she could let him know he was making her uncomfortable.

"Tim, do you think you were the last person at the party to see Mandy?" she asked.

Spiva twitched, his eyes returning to her face. "I…maybe?"

"Did she appear drunk?"

"Not really."

"Had she started to walk away when you went back into the house?"

"No. I just shrugged and said something like, 'Have a nice walk', and left her there."

"Was anyone else outside?"

He frowned. "I don't think so, but I'm not sure. I mean, I know people were spilling out of the house into the back yard. Someone else might have been leaving. And once I got in the house, it was kind of loud. I wouldn't have heard a car leaving or anything like that."

"This guy she's currently dating. Carson Crandall. Why wasn't he driving her home?"

A flash of something intense crossed Spiva's face. His feelings for his successor weren't warm, but might have nothing to do with Mandy. "I don't know. I didn't see him, although I heard he was coming late because he had something he had to do first. So maybe he wasn't there, or… Hey! Maybe he picked her up."

That was still a distinct possibility. Two people seemed to be unreachable: Carson and Mandy. If that was the case, if it turned out she'd been with a guy all this time, Rebecca wasn't sure she could hold onto her temper.

"Did you drive your own girlfriend home?"

"Who said I have a girlfriend?"

That almost sounded aggressive. Rebecca said calmly, "You mentioned that Mandy was annoyed you were already seeing someone else."

"Oh." He grimaced. "Yeah. Sorry. I just don't like people talking about me."

Rebecca waited.

"No. She left way before Mandy. She had her own car."

Had Tim really been chivalrous in offering Mandy a ride? His girl had blown him off. Did he imagine getting some from Mandy for old time's sake? Good reason for her to prefer walking.

"Her name?"

He looked puzzled. "Why do you want to know, when she was already gone?"

"She might have heard Mandy talking about meeting someone later, or a guy who came onto her in a way she didn't like."

"Oh. Yeah." His expression became earnest again. "Jordan Torgerson. But she's not really my girlfriend. We've just been hanging out some. You know."

Rebecca smiled. "I do know. And with luck Jordan can steer us to some more people who might know something. Thanks for your help, Tim. It was good to see you. I just wish the circumstances were different."

"Yeah, about that. Will there be a search? Because I'd really like to be in on it if there is. Mandy..." His shoulders jerked and his tortured expression seemed genuine. "I mean, I've known her, like, my whole life."

"I know." Rebecca laid a hand on his muscled forearm. "If there is, we'll put out the word. There's a lot of ground to cover."

"This just sucks!" he exclaimed.

She left him standing there, grappling with his emotions, and cut through the storefront to go out.

Her phone rang just as she got in her Tahoe and tried to decide what to do next. Lieutenant Wilcynski, of course.

She wanted to snap, but this *was* her first day in a new job, and he *was* her supervisor.

"Lieutenant."

"Any word?"

"From Mandy? No." What if there was something she should be doing but wasn't out of ignorance? Pride had no place here. She took a deep breath. "I'm really starting to share Deputy Desoto's bad feeling." Foreboding.

"Tell me what you've done." He listened, then said, "You really need to find that boyfriend."

At the realization that he was taking her seriously, she let her fingers loosen on the steering wheel. Gazing blindly at the cinder-block wall of the decking business, she said, "He's an EMT. I'm headed to the fire station to see if they can reach him."

"Good plan."

Her heart skipped a beat or two. "What if she's not with him?"

"What's your gut say?"

He hadn't ridiculed her yet. Didn't mean he wouldn't. Mandy still hadn't been missing even twenty-four hours. But nothing Rebecca had learned about her suggested she would do this kind of thing.

"Mount a search," she said finally. "I know you think it's premature, but everything I've heard says the parents are right." She was talking too fast, afraid of what he'd say. "This isn't like her."

She waited through a pause.

"Okay," he said finally. "I let you start. Now we have to follow through. Let's hope we locate the boyfriend. I'll have her phone pinged, which may give us an answer. Searches are costly and scare the public. Not something you want to do unnecessarily."

He wasn't saying they'd mount one, but he hadn't categorically refused, either.

"I've taken part in them before, but I've never called for one. I'm not quite sure what to do."

"If it becomes necessary, I'll walk you through it. But with it heading toward sunset now, we won't be able to start until daybreak." Now he sounded grim. "Tell you what, I'll meet you at the fire station. Which one?"

"You don't think I can find him on my own?"

"I think it's time you have some backup," he said. "With Holbeck off, that would be me. We'll check there, then go by this guy's apartment again."

Embarrassed by the flood of relief, she said, "Okay. Thanks. It's the station in Cape Trouble a couple of blocks from the hospital. Um. I could come by and get you. I'm in North Fork right now." In fact, not a half mile from the sheriff's department headquarters.

"You do that." And he was gone.

Rebecca rolled her eyes as she set her phone on the passenger seat. Having Wilcynski join her might be a mixed blessing – except she remembered how glad she'd been of his presence yesterday.

*****

However much he disliked being a passenger, Will didn't suggest switching to his vehicle. How people drove said a lot about them. After her years on patrol, he'd expect Rebecca to be capable. If she was a little hesitant, though, he wanted to know. Or too aggressive, although that seemed unlikely.

Since he'd bought a house in Cape Trouble, wanting to be close to the ocean, the highway between it and North Fork had become all too familiar to him. What he used to consider a scenic trip along the forest-shrouded Mist river had become just a drive, exasperating when he got stuck behind gawking tourists, flat-out irritating when he felt compelled to pull over a speeder. Today, he was conscious only of Rebecca – intonations, fleeting expressions seen in profile – as she told him who she'd talked to and what she'd learned.

He wasn't surprised that she'd done everything he would have except for initiating a search for the phone. She'd probably never had a reason to do that on patrol.

Something he'd meant to ask her, though.

"The shift you had to cancel yesterday. You know you won't be able to keep a second job now."

She flicked a quick look at him. "It's not a job. It's something I do as a volunteer."

"Something."

Her fingers flexed on the steering wheel. "I man a crisis line one or two nights a week."

Of course she did. "That'll be hard to keep up with the irregular hours you can expect from now on."

"I know that!" she snapped. "But I talked to Sean and a couple of the other guys, and they said the really long days are the exception, not the rule."

"That's true," he said mildly. "Just need you to know your priorities."

"I do."

"Do you identify yourself as a cop?" he asked.

"No. I'm aware it's against regulations." She hesitated. "Some people would refuse to talk to me if I did."

"Does the phone ring off the hook?" he asked, curious.

Rebecca slowed as they approached the outskirts of Cape Trouble, an historic seaside town built originally to support the early logging industry. It had continued to thrive first because the deep river channel made it a port as well, supporting a small fleet of fishing boats, now thanks to tourism.

"Some shifts are busier than others," she answered. "Around the holidays, for example. A lot of volunteers become convinced the moon and tides influence people's stress level." A movement of her shoulders indicated a maybe, maybe-not opinion. "I can go a full shift without the phone ringing once, or I'll get several calls. We have regulars, too, who just need to talk."

"Can you do it remotely?"

"No, it's something the family counseling center started fifteen years ago. I'm happy to sit there and read. I'd probably be alone at home, too."

Her tone did not invite him to ask why she didn't have anyone waiting at home for her. And if he asked – he'd open himself to the same question.

So he only nodded, staying silent when she braked for the red light at the highway. A couple of turns, and the firehouse appeared ahead. Apparently, Rebecca's tension was contagious. The odds still said Mandy would come home with a lame excuse for her absence, but Will felt a twitchy sense of wrongness he'd learned to pay attention to. He, too, was beginning to believe that someone had kept Mandy Shaw from making it home by midnight – and very possibly from making it home at all.

CHAPTER FOUR

"We have no justification for asking volunteers to search in the dark." Arms crossed, feet planted apart, Wilcynski had the flexibility of a mountain.

Rebecca strove for a reasonable tone, knowing it was the only way to deal with this man. "We have another hour and a half before sunset." The sun sank behind the curve of the earth at almost exactly six-thirty right now, in the latter part of October. Now that they knew Mandy's phone had been disabled, she didn't want to waste a minute.

Ignoring the uniformed firefighters washing and polishing an already shiny red rig across the parking lot from them, he shook his head. "It takes at least that to turn out the volunteers. I'll make calls tonight, arrange for search and rescue people to begin first thing in the morning."

Rebecca knew he was right, that her need to search *now* was irrational. Snatched before midnight, Mandy had been gone for seventeen hours. What were the odds she was alive? Yes, predators did often hold a woman for hours to days, but it wouldn't be in any of the places a search would cover. No, they'd be looking for a body.

Breathe. That's right. And again.

"Okay," she said, the word about choking her. "Seven-thirty?"

"Plan to be here half an hour before that. If you're organizing this one, you need to be ready to give direction to early arrivals."

"Some of Mandy's friends want to search. Her father does, too."

"That's fine, as long as they work with trained personnel."

Because one of those friends might already know where Mandy was, and either make sure *he* was the one who looked there, or steer other searchers away.

"I wish we'd been able to talk to Carson face to face," she muttered.

"That's always better."

Crandall had returned her call just as they walked into the fire station. He had climbed Mount Hood yesterday, one of his days off. Yeah, he admitted he'd told everyone he would do a one-day climb and drive back late last night, but at the last minute he changed his mind and packed what he needed to sleep partway up the mountain, completing the climb this morning. Since he hadn't promised Mandy he'd be at the party, he hadn't seen any need to let her know his plans had changed.

He had no idea if he'd had cell coverage or not on the mountain; his phone was buried in his pack and he hadn't thought to check messages. Why would anybody call? The station knew where he'd gone and that he wouldn't be available to cover for anyone or come in even if they had a major emergency call-out.

Did Mandy know where he'd gone?

"Yeah, sure. I invited her to come along, but switching days off would have been a hassle for her, and I kind of got the vibe that she was glad to have an excuse." There had been a pause before he exclaimed with sudden violence, "If she'd come with me, this wouldn't have happened!"

Until that moment, Rebecca hadn't been sure he was all that upset.

With the phone on speaker, Will had asked whether Carson had climbed with a partner.

No, his buddy Shawn was supposed to go, but he twisted his ankle Wednesday, running on the beach, and had to cancel. Carson claimed to have hooked up with a small party that didn't mind an extra. Well, no, he didn't know their last names. It had been really informal. They must have registered to climb, though.

He'd stopped in Portland, but said he would come straight home. "I've got to help look for her." To his credit, he sounded as desperate as Mandy's parents, but the suspicion inculcated by her years in law enforcement suggested that would be easy to fake.

Now, Will said, "I'll make the calls tomorrow to try to identify the group from the names he gave us."

Ryan, Kayla and John. There'd been another guy, but he couldn't remember the name.

Practically, verifying Carson Crandall's alibi wasn't urgent. If he'd been where he said he was, that meant he hadn't had anything to do with Mandy's disappearance. If he'd lied, it wasn't as if he'd tell them where he'd stashed her in time to call off the search.

Rebecca nodded and swung herself into her Tahoe. "I'll take you back to headquarters."

"Let's do some canvassing instead." He circled to the passenger side.

Rebecca waited only until he got in. "Really?"

Pulling out the seatbelt, he shook his head. "This is why I said you can't knock off at five because you have something else planned.

"Yes, but...I just thought you—" She had to be turning beet red.

He tipped his head, his eyebrows raised. "Intended to go home and have a good dinner?"

"Weren't convinced."

"I'm not," he said bluntly. "You can't be that naïve. She's twenty-three. Burdened with a toddler when her friends are still free to stay out as late as they want, to blow off work if they're hungover or just have something better to do. People break, you know that. She could have run away from too much responsibility, or just met a guy and desperately wanted to be young and wild, if only for a couple days. Her kid would be safe, she knew that."

"You're telling me I'm going to feel like an idiot when her mother calls and says, 'Oh, thank goodness, Mandy is home! It was just a misunderstanding.'"

"No." The lines on his forehead deepened. Rebecca couldn't look away from brown eyes that, in sunlight, did warm with a hint of caramel. "If that happens, *she* should be ashamed of herself. Not you. Caring is never wrong."

"But early on, you said—"

Without moving, he withdrew. "My job is to balance what we all want to do with what we can afford to do." His voice was virtually expressionless. "Statistically, this was one of the times we shouldn't have launched an investigation. As it's looking now, you were right to dig in your heels."

"I... Thank you," she said huskily.

He only scowled. "Why are we just sitting here?"

The brusque complaint reassured her, in a way. The moment hadn't been as…intimate as it felt. Will hadn't softened, let her see that he knew he sometimes made the wrong call.

Will. She couldn't even start *thinking* about him that way, or she'd slip up. Wilcynski. Lieutenant. She refrained from wrinkling her nose. Probably not BJ.

Benjamin Joseph? Byron Josiah?

She had to say something as she started the engine, released the emergency brake and swung in a circle to take them back out to the street. "The timing is good with people coming home after work."

"It is, although the likelihood of someone having happened to see a woman leaving the party at approximately the right time and be able to identify her as Mandy is close to zero."

Was he *ever* optimistic? "It's possible," Rebecca argued. "Scott Cardenas said the party livened up right about the time she likely left. If 'lively' means louder, neighbors might have woken up, looked out the window."

"Nobody called in a complaint."

"I know." She turned onto the highway to bypass the headland crowned by a now-decommissioned lighthouse. The small cove that formed Jasper Beach lay just on the other side. "Someone might have seen a scuffle, thought it was just roughhousing. Heard a scream."

"You're right." Still watching her, he said, "You intended to drop me off and do this anyway, didn't you?"

She didn't have to turn her head to feel his scrutiny. "Yes."

The sound he made might have been a rough chuckle he covered by saying, "I need to call Colburn."

Since he didn't seem to care that it was now five-thirty, Rebecca assumed that meant he had the Cape Trouble police chief's cell number.

She couldn't tell much from his side of the conversation, but when Will – Wilcynski – ended the call, he said, "He'll join us, bring maybe a dozen people to help."

"Really?"

"He says a vote is coming up to annex Jasper Beach into Cape Trouble. Apparently, the city council has their eye on Bow Lake, too, but decided to take one gulp at a time. If the Jasper Beach residents go for it in November, this will be his jurisdiction."

"The city council just wants the tax money from the fancy new resort." She shrugged. "It would actually be a good thing, though. Especially Jasper Beach. Daniel has been including it in CTPD's routine patrols for the last year or so. Our response time there isn't so good."

"No, I imagine not," Wilcynski said thoughtfully.

Rebecca had patrolled a different part of the county since her return to duty after the injury. Now, turning off the highway into the aging enclave tucked in this small cove, she couldn't help noticing how much revitalization had happened since she'd paid any real attention – and since the elegant, boutique hotel climbing the ridge between Jasper Beach and Cape Trouble had opened just this past summer. A short funicular railway allowed guests to easily reach the beach on this side. Quite a few artists had called Jasper Beach home, but sold their work in galleries elsewhere on the coast. Now, several of the old houses had been converted to galleries or gift shops, and there had been a studio tour in July. Reputedly, a high-end Italian restaurant was to open in one of the handful of mansions that had been built by long-ago lumber barons. Plenty of run-down cottages did remain available for rent by the week or to newcomers in the working world like Mandy's friends, but that might change in the near future.

She pulled up in front of a shabby clapboard cottage three blocks from the highway. It lacked a garage and there were no vehicles in the driveway.

A momentary silence fell after she turned off the engine. Out of the corner of her eye, she studied Will's hand lying on his thigh. His wrists had to be twice as thick as hers, his hands broad and powerful. A few dark hairs curled on the back of his fingers.

Not helping.

Neither did her awareness of the hard, muscled thigh beneath taut khaki.

Rebecca cleared her throat. "Shall we stick together, or divide up the houses?"

"I'll take the other side of the street," he said. "You take this one."

She nodded. They got out and slammed their doors at the same time. Rebecca didn't so much as look at him when she headed for the cottage separated only by a rotting fence and two narrow strips of weedy grass from the one where the party had been held.

*****

Nothing.

Repeating the drive to Cape Trouble after Rebecca dropped him back at the sheriff's department to recover his own vehicle, Will found he was trying to strangle the steering wheel.

No, he hadn't expected their questions to elicit much. Certainly not anything as helpful as 'Such a pretty girl, I saw her get in a blue Ford Focus with license plate XYZ 123'. But sometimes you got lucky, picked up a puzzle piece that would later slot into place. Not this evening. Nobody at all had seen a girl walk away from the cottage alone during the night. Most of the neighbors had been in bed, not happy about the voices and loud music, but philosophical. A couple had been *at* the party. Showed a photo of Mandy Shaw, both shook their heads. Nope. Didn't remember seeing her.

Will and Rebecca had door-belled all the way out to the highway, going on the assumption she'd have had no reason not to take the most direct route. They had moved faster than he expected because at least one in four of the cottages were vacant. Seasonal rentals, presumably, and October was past the high season here on the coast.

"I'll contact property management companies," he had told Rebecca before they parted. "Try to get permission to search the empty houses as well as the yards. Also find out if any that are vacant today were occupied last night."

He thought she was trying to hide her discouragement and worry. He'd opened his mouth to suggest they have dinner, but thought better of it. They'd eaten together last night. Two nights in a row? Not smart. With one of the single male detectives, it wouldn't have been an issue – except he wouldn't have wanted to have dinner with any of the men.

The steering wheel creaked and he deliberately loosened his grip. The sign welcoming him to Cape Trouble appeared ahead.

She'd be fine. She was a cop, for God's sake. Experienced and tough. An excellent driver. And she'd *chosen* to live alone in the middle of the woods.

Thinking of her that isolated…nope, not going there.

It was with deep relief that Will turned into his own driveway. He'd turn on some music, have dinner, put Rebecca Walker out of his head until morning. No problem.

*****

The sun hadn't yet peeked over the coastal range when Rebecca parked near the beach. She and Wilcynski had agreed this was the best staging area. It appeared she was the first arrival, not surprising since the dashboard clock said 6:45. Getting out, she closed the door as gently as possible out of consideration for the lucky people who were still asleep. Once volunteers started pouring into Jasper Beach, no one would be sleeping in on this Sunday morning. But why not let them have a final half hour or so of peaceful snoozing?

A dense fog cloaked the coast. As was often the case, her cabin had been above it. Dropping from clear skies into pea-soup was always a weird experience. Standing at the edge of the pebble beach, she could barely see the surf. Not that she could ever forget the ocean was there. The roar filled her ears as the salty, fishy smell did her nostrils.

She'd slept so poorly, she doubted she'd had more than three or four hours. Already on edge when she left Wilcynski, the drive had finished the job, especially once she turned onto her road, leading deeper into the wooded foothills. With the moon at barely a crescent last night, her driveway was a pitch-black tunnel, branches of fir and spruce trees joining overhead, ferns, salal and salmonberries forming the thick understory that thrived in the wet climate.

Rebecca hated how dread had begun gripping her several miles from home, squeezing tighter and tighter until she pulled into the small clearing. Last night, it had been all she could do not to turn around once she reached the clearing where her cabin stood and drive back down to civilization. She could take a hotel room for the night, feel safely anonymous behind a locked door. Sleep without listening for every sound.

She didn't, of course; surrendering to fear was not an option.

But at 4:30 she gave up on sleep. Thus her early arrival. Shivering, she decided to add a down vest over her sweatshirt before donning the POLICE windbreaker. If the fog lifted, she might not need the extra layer, but experience told her any clearing wouldn't happen until at least mid-morning.

At the sound of an engine, deep enough to be a pickup, she turned. A huge, familiar black SUV turned in right next to hers. Her boss, of course.

She'd thought entirely too much about him last night, while she wasn't sleeping. Let herself be grateful that he would prevent her from making some awful mistake that could have deadly consequences for the missing woman. Pictured his fleeting changes of expression, from a typical frown to that astonishing grin. When she became conscious that she was getting aroused thinking about him, she shut down the picture gallery. Not going there.

Instead she tried to figure out if she had missed anything in her interviews, let herself be too credulous. Then she moved on to remembering the way Tim Spiva eyed her body, and tried to figure out what she should wear today. Which made her mad. Like Sean Holbeck ever worried about what *he* was going to wear on the job. Or Wilcynski.

Okay, maybe she should copy them. Blend in. Chinos, polo shirt with long or short sleeves depending on the weather. Boots, *not* knee-high. Badge and gun at her hip.

Unfortunately, she did not currently own a single pair of khaki or olive green pants, certainly not any cargo pants like Sean usually wore, *or* a polo shirt. It wasn't a bad plan for the future, but tomorrow she'd settle for warm.

She was startled when Wilcynski got out and walked toward her to see that he'd ditched his usual and wore jeans, like she did, plus an Irish fisherman's sweater. The sweater added bulk to his muscular, broad shoulders, and the jeans had faded in interesting places.

She jerked her gaze to his face. *Not noticing.*

His eyes had narrowed a little, but all he said was "You're early."

"So are you." She cocked her head. "I hear someone else coming."

"Probably Brenda."

Rebecca had previously met the woman who headed the local search and rescue volunteers. In her fifties, she was brisk and efficient.

"We should be loaded with help," Wilcynski said. "I called Rand Bresler last night, to give him the head's up about the search."

Rebecca nodded. She should have thought of that.

"He's sending some employees and may show up himself."

"I've seen Bresler on the news," Rebecca commented, "but never met him."

"I haven't, either," Wilcynski said. "We looked at him briefly when Hannah Moss had that trouble some months back, but Colburn is the one who dealt with him."

"Bet Mr. Bresler appreciated the experience of being a person of interest."

"He took it better than a few other people I could name." Wilcynski's tone was dry.

Knowing some of the self-satisfied jerks on the city and county councils, Rebecca could imagine.

Brenda bustled up, then, clipboard in hand. She made Rebecca think of a penguin in a puffy black parka and pants, a white fleece cap and white scarf wrapped around her neck, and fingerless gloves.

"Morning." She looked around without favor. "Damn fog. Why is it *always* foggy when we have to mount a search?"

"Because this is the Oregon coast?" Rebecca suggested. She heard a smothered chuckle from Wilcynski.

The woman sighed. "That would be it."

She noted the numbers Colburn and Rand Bresler had promised, plus Mandy's friends who had insisted they would be here. Then the three of them dove into plans about how to assign volunteers, what was practical, what wasn't.

Rebecca was less ignorant than she'd been. During the drive back to North Fork after the canvassing, Will had educated her about what they could and couldn't accomplish tomorrow. A search like this was a lot more complicated than the kind Holbeck had organized last year, where a hundred or more volunteers formed a line in dense, forested land looking for a teenage girl who'd threatened suicide. That had been National Forest land; they had permission to be on it. In Jasper Beach and Bow Lake, they wouldn't ask permission to enter homes, and some residents were likely to deny permission even to walk through their yards or look into carports or sheds.

The beach and rocky points were publicly owned, so they could scour those. Around the lighthouse, and the uninhabited point to the north of Jasper Beach, too, since they were state owned. Vacant lots, they'd assume no one would object.

"As soon as I think I can reach people," Wilcynski said now, "I'll contact property management companies. Try to get permission to search as many empty cottages as possible."

Brenda tapped her pen on the clipboard. "Good. This neighborhood must be a ghost town now that the weather has turned."

"Not quite that bad," Wilcynski countered, "but I'm surprised at how many of the cottages are seasonal rentals now, which means they're vacant at this time of year except for an occasional weekend." He didn't have to say that any of them would make an ideal place to take an abducted woman. Tap out a pane of glass, let yourself in, private playground.

Brenda agreed it was worth sending volunteers on foot up and down each side of the highway for half a mile or so, poking through the long grass and scrub.

Otherwise, they'd knock on doors. She'd divide up the volunteers, start some across the highway in the Bow Lake neighborhood, where the oversized, wooded lots provided plenty of places for a body to lie unseen by a homeowner.

Cars began appearing, warmly dressed volunteers crowding around Brenda and Rebecca. Wilcynski had faded back, although he stayed in hearing distance.

Rebecca excused herself when she saw Mandy's father with another man, who introduced himself as the Shaws' next door neighbor. She squeezed Stuart's hand and said, "You haven't heard anything?"

Hollow-eyed, he shook his head. "Vicky is barely holding up. Sammie kept wanting her mommy last night." Exhaustion on his face told her he'd had even less sleep than she had. "Mandy's friends have been calling. I think a lot of them plan to be here to help this morning."

"That's good," she said gently. "I'm not surprised. She has quite a circle of close friends."

His face spasmed.

Rebecca escorted the two men to Brenda, who softened her tone for Stuart in contrast to her crisp orders to her regular volunteers.

A good-looking guy with reddish-brown hair sought her out and introduced himself as Carson Crandall. "I brought a couple of the guys from the station," he said, waving behind himself.

"EMTs?"

"Firefighters. I was supposed to work today, but the captain found someone to cover my shift." The creases in Carson's face added years to his real age, she saw.

A deep, rumbly voice came from beside her. "We spoke yesterday. I'm Lieutenant Wilcynski." His upper arm brushed hers as he shook hands with Carson. She felt warmer, just because he was next to her.

"What about the lake?" Carson asked.

Rebecca hadn't been able to argue yesterday when Wilcynski told her they wouldn't bring in divers until they had some reason to think Mandy's body might be there – or they hit dead ends otherwise.

Now, she just said, "Divers might be a next step."

Expression somber, he nodded, turning away when one of his friends called his name.

Wilcynski stuck with her as other friends of Mandy's arrived. If he was now her partner – or back-up, as he'd put it – he would want to meet the people she'd already interviewed. Several nurses from the hospital showed, along with one E.R. doctor who participated in search and rescue when her schedule allowed. Rebecca introduced Wilcynski to Tim Spiva, who came alone.

Tim acknowledged the lieutenant, but focused on Rebecca. "I walked through our neighborhood yesterday after I got home from work," he said. "Not like it would do any good, but just— That was dumb, I know. It's not like she's lost."

"Not dumb. I felt like doing the same," she admitted. She pointed at Brenda. "See the lady in the white fleece hat? She'll pair you up with someone and assign you an area to search."

"I can't stick with you?" He looked disappointed. "I just thought...you'd be the first to hear anything."

"I'm supervising today, not taking a sector. Oh – Mandy's dad is here." She looked around without spotting him.

"Yeah? I'll look for him." He headed for Brenda.

"She's good, isn't she?" Rebecca said.

"She could run Amazon with one hand tied behind her back," Wilcynski agreed. He seemed to be watching Tim, however. "That's the ex-boyfriend?"

"Long ago ex. They broke up the summer after graduating from high school. Like he said, though, he's known her since they were little kids."

"Hmm."

Something about his tone had Rebecca turning to look at him, but then Brenda waved her over and she once again became immersed in logistics. Volunteers dispersed faster than they'd arrived. Because of the fog, they simply de-materialized. The effect was eerie. Rebecca could hear muffled voices calling from the ones assigned to the beach, and see a few people knocking on the nearest cottage doors. Otherwise...everyone was on his or her own.

Fog was such a common coastal phenomenon, it had never made Rebecca feel claustrophobic before, but there was always a first time.

At least people were out there looking for Mandy. And yet, Rebecca dreaded the possibility that they *would* find her, because that would mean she was dead. Only, if the search turned up nothing, if she didn't come home... Eyes straining against the gray shroud, Rebecca swallowed, her throat tight. What next?

It's on me. And right this minute, she was all too aware of her inexperience.

CHAPTER FIVE

Will slid a key into the lock, opened the door and called, "Police! I'm coming in."

Silence. A faintly musty odor, not the acrid scent of blood or unpleasant smells associated with decomposition.

Relaxing slightly, he stepped into the small living room of one of the shabby cottages that rented by the night and were likely booked solid every summer. Most were probably furnished, like this one, although what he saw suggested garage sale or thrift store origins. Sagging springs on the sofa, formica table with metal legs, miscellaneous chairs.

He moved from room to room, scanning for blood, a weapon, a left-behind piece of clothing. Anything that shouldn't be here.

He didn't find a trap door in the ceiling, although when he crouched in an oddly-shaped closet, he discovered a partition that moved aside. There was nothing inside but dust.

Will let himself out the back door, walked through the tiny yard, unlocked a storage shed that held a lawn mower and a few yard tools, presumably owned by the property management people. Then he checked that all doors were locked behind him and walked out to the street.

Two doors up, Rebecca was just reappearing from a look-alike cottage. Both had been through several each. She was on the phone; probably had been the entire time, as any questions would get relayed to her.

They had agreed from the beginning that only law enforcement would enter houses. People at the property management companies had relaxed as soon as Will told them that. Fortunately, between the couple CTPD officers Daniel Colburn had brought and the dozen or so deputies who had volunteered, they were speedily covering the rentals in the neighborhood.

As he watched, Rebecca stuck the phone in the pocket of her vest and her head turned. Will didn't like the expression on her face. He jogged the distance separating them.

"What is it?"

"A woman out at the highway found a jacket in the weeds that matches what Mandy's mother says she was wearing when she left. It has a tear and a smear of what looks like blood."

"Verification?"

"I'm going to take it to the Shaws' so Vicky can look at it."

He nodded. "Want me to come?"

"I..." Her eyes, dark and worried, caught his. "If you don't mind."

"Of course not." This morning, he'd seen Stuart Shaw, who looked the way every parent in this situation did: as if he saw hell torn open right in front of him. Will was curious about the mother. In a situation like this, investigators always had to consider family members.

Together they jogged the three blocks to where they'd left their vehicles. He headed for his, and she didn't object. She clicked on her seatbelt then sat looking straight ahead.

A minute into the drive, she said, "This isn't good."

Had to say something. "No, but it might not be hers."

Her "No" was soft.

She needed to learn to protect herself emotionally better than she was so far, or this job would grind her down, Will reflected. Was this getting to her because she'd known the family? If so, he should yank her off the investigation. She would be mad, which wouldn't stop him if he was sure it was the right thing to do. Unfortunately, for a decisive man, he was feeling damned *in*decisive. Her composure had been absolute over the hours of negotiation Friday, until the end when everyone hearing those gunshots took a blow. No one had given her anything but rave reviews for her skill as a negotiator. So why, yesterday and today, was he seeing her buffeted by so many emotions? Uncertainty, because this was her first investigation? Maybe. But there'd been nothing timid about the woman fighting to open that investigation in the face of his refusal.

At the sight of a cluster of volunteers waiting at the highway, he shook off his thoughts. When he rolled down his window, a woman handed over a brown paper grocery sack. She pointed out where it had been found, barely twenty feet from where he'd braked. Close enough to the highway shoulder that it could have been tossed out a car window. He saw that the site had already been marked with orange cones. The search surrounding it was about to become considerably more detailed.

Rebecca bent over to thank the woman, after which Will took advantage of a break in traffic to accelerate across the highway. "You'll need to direct me," he said.

"First right."

"Rebecca…"

Holding the bag, she gave him a wary glance. Maybe because he'd called her by her first name, and not for the first time. Why was he having so much trouble with 'Detective'? Will really didn't want to think it was a sexist thing.

"We need to—"

Her phone rang.

"Walker." Pause. "Good. That was fast." She listened, but also murmured to Will, "Left at the corner." Then, into the phone, "No, the lieutenant and I are heading over to the Shaws' house." She explained why, let the man talk for a minute. "That would be great. It's marked with cones."

When she stowed the phone, she said, "Gray house on the right." As he turned into the driveway, she added, "That was Daniel. He and his officer finished their sector and will proceed out to the highway."

"Good," he agreed. He trusted Daniel Colburn, who had worked homicide for San Francisco P.D before doing a one-eighty, similar to his own, and burying himself in this scenic backwater. He, Daniel and his own boss, Sheriff Alex Mackay, had that in common. Mackay had been with the Portland Police Bureau. He'd suffered severe injuries that still hampered him physically, so his reason for moving wasn't a mystery, unlike Daniel's.

And mine, Will conceded silently. He knew there was talk in the department, and not just about what BJ stood for.

"What was it you wanted to say?" Rebecca asked, not reaching for her door handle.

He saw movement behind the front window. "It can wait."

Rebecca got out without comment. Will joined her walking up to the front door, which swung open well before they reached it. Shit. Maybe he shouldn't have come. A distraught woman waited, and having two of them approach must give off the same signal a pair of army officers in full dress uniform did when they appeared, unexpected, on the doorstep of a military wife whose husband was deployed.

"Mandy?" she whispered.

"No," Rebecca said in the voice that comforted no matter what she said. "The only thing that's been found so far is a coat that could have been hers. I hope you can identify or eliminate it."

An anguished gaze fastened on the brown paper sack. She backed in and let them step across the threshold.

"Where's Samantha?"

"In the kitchen. I shouldn't have left her."

"Then let's go in there," Rebecca said gently.

A little girl with curly blonde hair stared at them from her booster seat in front of the kitchen table. "Ga'ma?"

Rebecca smiled at her. "Hi, Sammie. My name's Rebecca. I knew your mommy when she was your age."

The idea was probably way beyond the comprehension of a kid that age, but she sounded out "Bec-ca."

"That's right."

The blue eyes switched to Will, who twitched under that solemn scrutiny.

"This is my friend, Will," Rebecca said.

He smiled, but the stare did *not* soften. He always alarmed kids, a fact of which he wasn't proud.

Rebecca moved unhurriedly to the kitchen counter. She pulled a pair of latex gloves from a pocket and put them on, then lifted the jacket from the sack.

Vicky Shaw gave a heart-rending cry. "It's hers. Oh, dear God. It's hers."

"How do you know?" Rebecca asked.

Will stayed back. She was a lot better than he was with upset people. He glanced to see that the little girl, hearing the distress, had twisted to see her grandma.

"The rip," she whispered. Tears ran down her face. "I noticed it when she was going out the door and she said she'd meant to mend it. But she decided nobody would see anyway, because she'd take her coat off as soon as she got there, and with Friday night so mild, her parka was too heavy."

Nonetheless, Rebecca showed her the tags with brand and size, and Vicky Shaw kept nodding and crying. "Where...?"

Rebecca told her, then said, "It does have a stain, but maybe that was already there, too."

Another, anguished cry told them the blood, if that's what it was, hadn't been there when Mandy walked out the door the night before last.

After asking about Mandy's blood type, Rebecca managed to calm the missing woman's mother enough to, eventually, clear the way for them to leave. Even before the front door closed behind them, Vicky was dialing her husband's number.

Will opened the rear of his Suburban for Rebecca to stow the sack holding the jacket. Their own, modest crime lab would be able to determine whether the stain *was* blood and type it. Assuming it was human blood, they'd send it on to the state crime lab for DNA testing – and be lucky to get results six months or more from now.

Rebecca gusted a sigh once they were back in their seats. "I wish I could have lied to her, promised we'd bring Mandy home."

"We probably will." One way or another.

"Alive. I meant alive."

He didn't say anything for a minute. "During negotiations, do you ever lie?"

"No. Not directly. I'd lose any chance of building trust."

"That's true with the Shaws, too."

She nodded finally, fingers twined together. "Should we go to the scene?"

"Leave it to Colburn. Let's finish what we started."

"Except the jacket suggests Mandy made it as far as the highway."

"There are ways it could have ended up there even if she was grabbed and held somewhere else. We don't yet know that the blood is hers. Maybe she left the party without her jacket. Maybe she was carrying it on the way to the party and a wind from a passing semi snapped it out of her hands. Do you know she was wearing it when she arrived?"

"No, I didn't ask."

Will made sure she was looking at him. "Somebody else could have taken it by mistake and lost it on the way home." He hesitated only a little. "It could have been planted where we found it."

She shivered. "There's a thought." Then she took what seemed to be a bolstering breath. "Okay. I know Daniel will call if he finds anything."

If Daniel hadn't been married and a new father, Will wouldn't have liked the way Rebecca said his name, with respect and something like affection. Not when *he* was stuck being 'Lieutenant'. Except she'd just said, "My friend, Will."

Irked with himself, he drove them back to Jasper Beach, parking this time on the block where they'd left off. She didn't ask what he'd wanted to say earlier, and he decided to put off that conversation. Rebecca was more emotional than felt comfortable to him, but she maintained a calm authority with searchers and even other officers, and hadn't made any common sense or procedural missteps. *So let it go*, he told himself, except he knew he wouldn't. He couldn't ignore his unease.

Being honest with himself, Will knew his need to explore her history, her personality, had a whole other cause than the job.

*****

"Nothing."

That's what Rebecca kept hearing as volunteers reported in. Nothing, and more nothing.

She joined Brenda in thanking each and every one of them, answering questions, consoling Mandy's friends who were upset upon hearing about the jacket.

She thought Carson Crandall was crying when he turned away jerkily and hurried to his car, but she had to ask herself whether he'd been hiding a different expression altogether.

Tim Spiva didn't want to leave. "There has to be something else we can do," he insisted.

"I'm afraid not at the moment," she said. "I'll be back to talk to you again tomorrow. Are you working?"

"No." Then he frowned. "Just me?"

"All of Mandy's friends. I need to learn more about her, her relationships. She might have confided in someone and not been taken seriously. Did she talk about friends in Portland?"

"Brian." Tim's face darkened. "He could have driven over here to see her."

"I'll look into that, too, I promise." Should she have verified Brian's whereabouts yesterday, first thing? Had she even heard his last name? "Now, if you'll excuse me…"

The party girl, Jennifer Starrett, checked out next with another high school friend of Mandy's, Lori Crane. Their faces were drawn. Rebecca thought they were in a state of mild shock, maybe because it had finally sunk in that something bad *really* could have happened to one of their friends. Until then, it might have all felt like high drama – Oh, my God, did you *hear*…? But having joined the searchers, each young woman almost had to have had a moment when she peeked over a fence or around the corner of a shed and realized Mandy might be there. Naked, bloody, broken.

A few more volunteers trailed in, wearily shook their heads or said, "Nothing," and departed.

At last, Brenda flipped through pages on her clipboard and said, "That's the last."

She was showing her years when she got stiffly into her car.

Daniel had left only a few minutes ago after assuring Rebecca and Wilcynski that he was available whenever they needed him.

Suddenly, Rebecca was alone with her boss, their vehicles the only two remaining. She looked around, seeing blue sky and ocean, a quiet neighborhood, the new resort blending into the rocky point. She'd hardly noticed the fog dissipating as the hours passed.

"I never met Randall Bresler," she heard herself say.

Wilcynski just stood there a few feet away from her, hands in his jeans' pockets. He'd been so quiet today, she should have been able to forget he was there for long stretches, but of course that hadn't happened. She swore she could *feel* him, as if she had an internal compass that knew where he was at all times. Every time she actually looked for him, he was watching her. His silent, powerful presence was unnerving, but reassuring, too, in a way.

Now, he said, "I saw Bresler. I think he was sent to search up on the point and around the lighthouse."

Rebecca didn't really care about Rand Bresler. How could she, when all she could think about was the yawning hole in Mandy's family. She never lost awareness of the hollow place inside herself.

"Wow." Her feet didn't want to move. "I don't know whether to be relieved or disappointed."

"Go with relieved. There's a chance, if she was abducted, that she's being held alive."

Of course, he was bucking her up, but she suspected he didn't often bother with his detectives, so she should take it gratefully. "You're right." She summoned a smile. "Thanks. I'm hoping tomorrow morning—"

He frowned at her. "Did you stop for lunch?"

"Lunch?" Was she even hungry?

"Let's go get something to eat. We can talk about next steps."

An alarm flared. Sit across a table from him again? But what excuse could she make? And did she really want to head home, where she'd be alone?

"Why not?" she said, in defiance of any good sense.

*****

Will was glad to see that, because he and Rebecca had arrived after the usual lunch hour, the restaurant at Rand's Inn at Cape Trouble was empty enough to give them plenty of privacy. Neither of them had eaten here before. The Sea Watch Café in town, a favorite of Will's, only served breakfast and lunch and would already be closed for the day. The food here at the new resort was bound to be good, he figured; Bresler was the kind of guy to demand only the best.

After being seated in a corner booth where he could see the whole room as well as the rocky point and roiled surf, he and Rebecca glanced at their menus and ordered. Then he studied her.

"This getting to you?"

Her chin shot up and she pressed her lips together, making him expect a denial. She had to have worked hard to create a tough-as-nails persona to earn respect, especially in an agency where women were such a tiny minority. But after looking away, she met his eyes again and surprised him.

"In a way. Is the job always so…intense?"

Will thought about it. "No, a lot of investigations will feel routine to you in no time. You'll handle burglaries, theft from businesses, embezzlement, stolen cars." He shrugged. "A woman missing under mysterious circumstances isn't a norm here. And, yes, these past few years Burris County has seen more than its share of horrific crimes."

He nodded his thanks when the waitress brought their drinks, then returned his attention to Rebecca and the topic.

If Mackay hadn't warned him before Will took the job, he'd never have imagined this rural county had had a serial killer active for years. Or that shortly after Will took over as head of investigation, another killer began a series of shocking murders. That one still rubbed him raw, since the killer had been a rookie detective working in Will's unit.

And, yeah, that was the son-of-a-bitch who'd shot Rebecca.

"We have plenty of domestic abuse," she said, sounding sad. "Crimes against women. Stalking, rape."

"We do," he agreed. "You'll get those. Everyone handles a little of everything, but we also have some specialization within the unit." Seeing her surprise, he said, "For example, Dave Worley is good with a money trail. He has a degree in business, originally intended to go for a CPA."

"I had no idea." She offered a sheepish smile. "That's good, because I'm pretty slapdash with my checking account. I'm not sure you want me delving into an embezzlement."

A grin tugged at his mouth. "Duly noted."

"Sean?"

"I tend to give him the most serious stuff. He could step into the same job anywhere and earn respect." Tell her what he was thinking? "As I said, I'll pair you with him as much as possible. I don't want to stereotype by gender, but I'd like to see how you do with rape cases, child sexual molestation and the like. I suspect that a hurt woman or child will find it easier to talk to you than to Rob Britton."

Rebecca scowled for a minute, not liking to be assigned because of her gender, but then huffed out a breath. No, a woman who'd just been brutally raped would not feel comfortable talking to a beefy former jock with hands so big his fingers looked like sausages.

"I suppose I can't argue," she said after a moment. Her face lit with a smile that caused his heart to throw in an extra beat before he realized it was aimed at the waitress delivering their entrees.

While they ate — and his filet mignon was melt-in-the-mouth tender, the fries spicy — he got Rebecca talking some more about her volunteer work on the crisis line.

Not surprisingly, calls from abused women and teenagers with no family support were the most common. Suicide threats were the ones that sent a volunteer's adrenaline into the red zone.

"We don't hear as much from men," she said. "The male gene seems to keep guys from asking for help even when they're thinking about killing themselves." Her shoulders moved. "A couple of our regulars are men, though. One battles mental illness, and we seem to orient him. The other is an older guy, lonely and depressed." A shadow crossed her face, and he knew what she was thinking. "For someone like him, being willing to call means everything."

"He doesn't bottle it up."

"Until he explodes?" She averted her face, seemingly taking in the view from the sweep of windows, but Will wondered what she was really seeing. "We need a better way to identify older people who live alone and are at risk for depression."

"The senior centers—"

"Aren't the best. Oh, the one in Cape Trouble is okay, but North Fork?" She shook her head, her ponytail swaying. Will wondered if she knew how many tiny tendrils had escaped to soften the severe way she pulled her hair back. "They focus on sweet old ladies. I swear, what classes they offer are practically all crocheting, crewel-work and tatting. The aerobics class is the kind you do in a pink sweatsuit sitting in a chair."

Was it possible to work your heart muscle while sitting down? Will pondered. Almost immediately, he thought of a way. Funny, he wasn't sure he'd ever had sex in a chair. Car, yes, but he thought how well a recliner would work.

"Tatting?" was what he said.

Rebecca's cheeks had turned a little pink, which made him wonder what she'd seen on his face. "You know those doilies people used to put on the arms of sofas and chairs? Like crocheting, but using a thin thread?"

He summoned a vague picture of lacy white things with no known useful purpose. Safer to think about than sex with this woman.

"I can see why none of that would appeal to someone like Ed Brodsky."

"No." Her gray eyes clouded again. "I wish I could do more, but…"

"You're a good cop," he said quietly. "You reach out to people. You, of all people, have no reason to feel guilty you can't do more."

"No, but—" She shook her head and gave a smile that was a poor facsimile of the one she'd offered the waitress. And how sad was that? "How did we get off on this, anyway?"

"I need to know how the job is impacting my detectives," he said. True, but not *the* truth.

She didn't quite roll her eyes, but the impulse was apparent. "Well, I'm fine."

Will wasn't so sure, but he popped a couple fries in his mouth. While he was chewing, a thought came to him. "I remember hearing someone mention a group home for teenage boys in Cape Trouble."

"Jasper Beach, one of those big Victorians. The Elk Creek Home for Boys. Sean went there today. He knew it because Jason Payne's brother had lived there for a year."

Payne being the killer cop. "Right," Will said, details coming back to him.

"Staff is confident every resident was where he was supposed to be. They don't expect lights out at ten on a Friday night, but the staff do room checks."

Eventually, Will did ask what she intended to do first thing in the morning, and made only a few suggestions. He had a meeting he couldn't get out of, but then would join her for interviews. What he should do come morning was assign Holbeck to partner with her, but already knew he wouldn't. He missed actively participating in an investigation. Keeping his hand in was good, and Holbeck already had plenty on his plate.

When the bill came, he tried to pay it, but lost the ensuing skirmish.

"I let you Friday night," she said firmly, "but I was a little shaken."

A little? She was still brooding about what she perceived as her failure to persuade Ed Brodsky to give life another chance. Hearing those shots…that wasn't something she'd forget. Will even knew how she'd handle it: running herself ragged in the future to help every lost soul.

As they walked out, he said, "Get a good night's sleep."

Her gaze skated away. "Sure."

Will stopped in the middle of the parking lot. "Detective?" He congratulated himself for keeping this professional.

She looked defiant. "Lieutenant?"

"You're calling it a day. That's an order. No interviews, no canvassing, no going back to your desk to make calls."

"I had no intention of doing any of those things." A breeze off the ocean caught her ponytail and blew it across her face. She caught it with one hand, the raised arm lifting her breasts. Sweatshirt or no, he noticed.

Even so, he wasn't letting this go. "But you do plan to do something."

"My off time is my own," she said stiffly.

"Yes, it is. If you're going out with friends, that's fine." He gritted his teeth. If she said a date…

"On my way over here, Shelley called. She needed someone to fill in tonight. And since I missed Friday…" Rebecca let that trail off.

"You think you're in a state to deal with more people in crisis?" he asked gruffly.

Still clutching that ponytail, she glared at him. "Would you ask any of the men that question?"

His hesitation was fatal.

She snorted and walked away, already climbing into her Tahoe by the time he got his feet moving again. And…maybe it was just as well. Because the answer to her question was probably no.

*****

"Sexist jerk," she muttered during her drive inland to North Fork. Okay, maybe 'jerk' wasn't the right word, since he was trying to take care of her, but she couldn't let him and do this job. Thank goodness he lived in Cape Trouble; otherwise his huge SUV would undoubtedly have hugged her bumper all the way back to headquarters, where she switched to her own car.

She parked behind the modern brick building that held, among other things, the room set up for the crisis line volunteers. With the counseling center closed on Sundays, only one other car sat out here. Rebecca recognized it as belonging to Norm Snyder, a retired psychiatrist with a warm, disarming manner. Rebecca knew she wasn't the only volunteer who used him as a sounding board. She'd learned a lot from him.

The moment she let herself in the steel door, she called, "It's Rebecca."

A short man with a burgeoning belly emerged from the call center into the short hall. As always at the end of a shift, his white hair stuck straight up. In thought, he liked to tug at it. Today, he wore faded sweats. Norm swore he'd thrown away every tie he owned the day he retired.

"How'd it go?" she asked.

"Slow." He smiled beatifically. "It's a day of rest."

"I wish," she muttered.

"I heard about the missing woman." Sobering, he scrutinized her face. "You working that?"

"I'm primary in my fun new detective gig."

"Huh. You'll be good at it. Although you know my opinion."

She knew. Norm thought she should go back to school for a master's degree and put out a shingle as a counselor. He'd recommend her far and wide, he promised, with a puckish grin.

Even though she was struggling with aspects of what she did for a living, she couldn't see herself following his advice. Counseling felt too passive.

"I'll stay until you've poured yourself a cup of coffee," he said. "But before I forget, a man called asking for you today."

"Really?"

"He wanted to know when you worked. The voice wasn't familiar. I played dumb, said I don't know most of the other volunteers, sorry. He hung up on me."

"A few times, I've had people ask for a particular volunteer. Someone they'd talked to before."

He nodded. "That might be what this was. There was something, though." A frown still pulled his bushy white eyebrows together. "He sounded like he was smirking." Norm visibly shook off his concern. "It's probably nothing, but be extra careful when you go out to your car tonight."

"I'm a cop, Norm." She patted her hip. "I carry a gun."

Instead of smiling the way she'd expected, he said, "A gun doesn't do you any good if someone slips up behind you."

The unease any woman occasionally felt crawled up her spine, but she put some swagger in her voice. "Yeah, let him try."

"Tough lady." He shook his head. "Hope the phones stay quiet."

"Hope somebody who really needs help calls," she countered.

"You're right." He patted her shoulder. "Now, get your coffee so I can go home."

CHAPTER SIX

Seven of the nine detectives in the unit were at their desks this morning, which Rebecca hoped was unusual. Otherwise, if she ever wanted to get anything done, she might have to turn the front seat of her Tahoe into an office. As it was, she pressed the heel of her hand against her free ear to try to block out other voices. She was having enough trouble getting a read on Brian Vail, Mandy's ex and Sammie's father.

She was further distracted when Wilcynski walked into the bullpen, dressed entirely in black today. Black chinos, belt to hold his badge and gun, black, long-sleeved polo shirt. On the way to his office, he rapped his knuckles on Rebecca's desk, his dark eyes pinning her momentarily.

"When you get a break, I want to see you."

She nodded and said into the phone, "I'm not making an accusation, Mr. Vail. In a case like this, we always have to look at family and partners first. I'm sure you understand that. I'm asking you to help me confirm your whereabouts Friday night so I can cross you off my list, that's all."

"I went to a bar. Got shit-faced, took some girl home with me."

No embarrassment. *Some* girl, like they were interchangeable? *Mandy, what were you thinking?* Unfortunately, even smart women could be fools where men were concerned.

"Can you tell me the name of the bar?"

"Billy's."

"That's in Portland?"

"Where else?"

"And the woman who went home with you?"

"What about her?"

"She ought to be able to corroborate your whereabouts," she said with a lot more patience than she felt. "Her name would be helpful. A phone number would be good."

"Too late for the phone number. She was gone when I woke up. She left a number on a scrap of paper, but I dropped it in the toilet when I took a piss. Flushed it down."

Was he *trying* to be offensive? Yeah, she decided, he was. Because he didn't like being questioned at all? Because it was a woman asking the questions? Or because he was trying to distract her from the fact that he had no verifiable alibi?

"Her name?" Rebecca asked again.

"Courtney. That's what she said, anyway. We didn't exchange last names."

She asked whether he and Mandy had any kind of parenting plan set up for their daughter.

"Like...that says when I have to take her?"

Have to take her? "Yes."

"No."

Had he and she talked regularly? Yeah, mostly when she called to bitch because he hadn't sent money.

"I'm an artist," he said. "She knew that when we got involved. She was supposed to be using birth control." Anger simmered now in place of the studied indifference. "No way I can afford a kid until I make it."

She didn't point out that he was now Samantha's sole parent. Maybe he'd hand over custody to the Shaws without a battle.

Hanging up, she realized he hadn't once asked about Sammie. No apparent concern felt for Mandy, who had lived with him for a couple of years, from what her parents said.

Rebecca shook her head. She hadn't been dumb enough to fall for a guy like this, but she was pretty sour on men in general. Too bad Norm Snyder wasn't thirty or forty years younger. Oh, and single.

Holbeck was the only one to notice when she stood and started for their lieutenant's office. He mouthed, "Good luck."

She grinned and knocked lightly on the door Wilcynski almost always left partially ajar.

"Sir?"

"Sit down." He nodded at one of the straight-back chairs in front of his desk. They were probably discards from a principal's office.

"So, I just talked to—"

"Did you get any sleep?" he interrupted. The way he was inspecting her, she guessed the touch of makeup she'd used hadn't disguised the purple circles beneath her eyes.

"I'm fine."

"That's not what I asked."

Unblinking, she held his gaze. "Yes, I slept."

He let her see that he wasn't happy, but finally nodded. "Who have you talked to?"

"The lab called. The blood was human, and O positive, which is a match with Mandy."

"Her and at least a third of Americans."

He was still looking for reason to believe Mandy had taken off voluntarily, but he was also right. O positive was the most common blood type.

"I've set up appointments to talk to half a dozen people, starting with Mandy's parents," she said.

"You'd think the mother would have volunteered the information if Mandy had told her she was being stalked, but you have to ask."

"I just got off the phone with Brian Vail, the guy Mandy lived with before she came home."

"The kid's father." Wilcynski leaned back comfortably in his chair and clasped his hands behind his head.

The sight of a whole lot of muscles flexing threw her off her game momentarily, but she regrouped and said, "Right. Sounds like a creep. Didn't even ask about his daughter. Said Mandy was 'supposed to be' using birth control. God forbid *he* take any responsibility."

"I take it he's not packing to race over here because his precious daughter needs him."

"I think it's safe to say he'll sign away parental rights in a heartbeat, if it gets him out of paying child support." She couldn't help the disgust that dripped from her every word.

"Did he sound angry enough to want to kill Mandy? Say, because she deliberately got pregnant?"

Rebecca felt obliged to defend the missing woman. "We don't know that she did." When Wilcynski's only response was a twitch of dark eyebrows, she said, "No. He didn't want to be a father, and he holds Mandy responsible for screwing up. At the same time, I didn't hear any significant level of rage. I had the feeling she's pretty much out of sight, out of mind until she calls to hit him up for money."

"Nice guy."

Rebecca nodded. "The thing is, Mandy disappearing or dying doesn't get him off the hook for child support."

"In fact, if her parents were a different kind of people, social services would lean on him to take the girl, and if he refused they would make his life hell if he didn't pay that support, on time, no excuses."

"Put that way, I'm surprised he isn't over here joining the search."

Wilcynski cracked a smile. "Really liked the guy, did you?"

"I wanted to slap him." She sighed. "I know we have to take him seriously, anyway. Confirming his alibi is one of my first priorities."

"You're right. Why don't you get started on that now, make any other calls you need to. Give me an hour, and I'll be ready to go."

"I am capable of talking to people."

His hands dropped from behind his head and he leaned forward. "I don't distrust you, Detective. Now that I'm involved, I want to put faces to names, not depend entirely on you for impressions."

She nodded, probably woodenly, and said, "An hour sounds about right."

Marching back to her desk, she wished she could take a very short nap to prep for dealing with *hours* of up-close-and-personal with BJ Wilcynski. Sleep had been scant last night. She'd shrugged off the news that someone had called wanting her. Like she'd said, it happened. The six hang-ups during her shift were more disturbing.

Probably just somebody chickening out about going through with the call...but each time, she'd imagined she heard breathing, saw a smirk. Because he wanted to scare her, whoever he was.

She hadn't let herself freak out over it. Over and over, she'd said gently, "Please, talk to me," before hearing dead air. At the end of the shift, she'd only been a little more watchful than usual walking out to her car.

Some nights were better than others, that's all. Rebecca had no intention of relapsing to the scared little girl who prayed for mommy to come home, who refused to believe she wouldn't, who for months slept wrapped in a comforter in the closet in case *he* came looking for her, too.

Thank God Sammie was too young to feel the terror Rebecca would never forget.

If she ever caught herself huddled in a closet again, instead of confronting an intruder with a weapon in her hand, that was the day she'd hand in her badge and move to a gated community far, far away.

No, whatever creep had snatched Mandy Shaw should walk in fear of Detective Walker, not the other way around.

*****

"I can't think of anything like that," Vicky Shaw said piteously. She wrung her hands. "We were close. I think she'd have told me if anybody bothered her."

She and her husband had opted to take turns entertaining Sammie, currently wide-awake, active and whiny. Both adults, looking exhausted, said Sammie had begged for mommy at bedtime and woken screaming several times. They were praying for her to go down for her nap early.

As had been his practice so far, Will had sat slightly off to the side and let Rebecca handle the bulk of the interview, interceding only occasionally. She was skillful, he had to admit. Now she went down the list of Mandy's friends, asking Vicky to comment on each.

Of course, Mandy's mother openly detested Brian. Early in the relationship, Mandy had brought him for a visit once. He'd been plainly bored, borderline polite but not engaging. "Unfortunately," she said, "he's really good looking. Dark-haired, dark-eyed, brooding." Her gaze slid to Will, who willed himself not to react. "You know the kind."

Rebecca didn't look at him. Her "I do" sounded a little choked.

Vicky forgot about Will again. "After that, we saw him only a few times when we visited them in Portland. When she came here, it was alone, and later with Sammie, of course."

Yes, Mandy had dumped him, not the other way around. Vicky thought she'd been disillusioned for a long time, but had hung in there hoping he could be brought to see how important he was to his daughter. Then she found out he was sleeping with another woman. "When she gave up, that was it. He didn't seem to have the slightest interest in visitation."

The hand-wringing began to remind Will of a production of Macbeth he'd seen once.

His phone kept buzzing with updates on other investigations. Worley was on his way to Cape Trouble High School to speak to a couple of students aka possible vandals. Bet that would thrill the principal. Worley was experienced enough to have notified CTPD.

He tuned in to Rebecca's questions when he heard a name.

Carson? Such a nice young man, but... Will's attention sharpened at her hesitation.

"I don't think he's interested at all in becoming an instant father. Somehow, their outings never include Sammie, which limited how often Mandy and he saw each other," Vicky confided. "The Mount Hood expedition was typical. Why not drop all responsibilities and take off for a couple of days? He's very active and was always wanting her to go hiking or climbing with him. Mandy said they were having fun, but... I think she was looking around, too. She's ready to get married, really start a family."

She broke down, and her husband immediately appeared from the kitchen. He held her for a minute before leading her away. His soft voice was punctuated by her sobs.

Will used the break to think about Carson Crandall. Increasing irritation on Carson's part for Mandy's refusal to follow wherever his whimsy took him gave motivation for a fight that had gotten out of hand.

So far this morning, Will had gotten nowhere trying to identify Carson's supposed fellow climbers. What he'd learned was that the climbers' registration form was optional. If filled out, they could be dropped at a number of different sites. Timberline Lodge was the likeliest place for a climber taking one of the traditional routes to leave it, so he'd asked people there to look for a party with the names Scott had offered. No call back yet. Wilderness permits were mandatory, but "self-issued". Unless they got lucky, this was looking like a dead-end. If it came down to him being a serious suspect, they might find the park had cameras that would have caught his vehicle and license plate. A gas receipt coming home would be good, he thought.

Once Vicky was settled in the kitchen, Stuart rejoined them. He'd apparently heard at least some of what had been said, because without prompting he began to talk about the other guys in Mandy's circle. Scott Cardenas? Mandy said he hadn't changed since high school. Tim Spiva did seem to have grown up, but Mandy wasn't sure what she'd ever seen in him. He looked a little embarrassed. "This isn't the kind of thing she'd tell me, but I heard her talking to her mom. Tim has asked her out a couple of times since she came home, but Mandy said he didn't seem that bothered when she declined."

He fell silent for a minute, but not as if he was waiting for a question, so Rebecca only waited.

"Tim is an odd duck," Stuart commented finally. "But harmless, I'd swear. Just…maybe doesn't respond to social cues the way most people do. Tends to make people a little uncomfortable. Good kid overall, though." He shrugged. "I haven't talked to him in several years. Now that he's – what, twenty-four, twenty-five? – he's undoubtedly changed. Back then, he always had his head under the hood of a car. I was surprised when Mandy said he'd left the car repair place he was working for a job building decks, but maybe the money is better."

Will thought that was unlikely; skilled mechanics out-earned a lot of professionals. He made a mental note to follow up. Had Tim gotten fired from the previous job? Maybe didn't have a recommendation to take with him? Being an odd duck didn't make him a sociopath, but raised some warning flags for Will.

Stuart and then Vicky, after they switched places again, talked about Mandy's girlfriends, too. She liked some better than others, of course; there'd been petty quarrels, feuds, hints of resentment, sometimes over one of the guys. No surprise, since they had all taken turns dating within their circle of friends. That should be less true since Mandy had returned to the Cape Trouble area. Some of the old crowd had gone away for college and never come back, or met new people on the job. Still, the population of Burris County wasn't increasing, which meant a limited pool of potential mates within any age group.

God knows, Will couldn't help thinking, *he* had yet to meet a woman who pushed his buttons – except, frustratingly enough, the beautiful detective who worked for him.

When Rebecca asked, Vicky fetched her daughter's laptop. Will didn't miss the tremor in her fingers as she handed it over.

"You'll bring it back, won't you? I know she has lots of pictures on it."

"I will," Rebecca promised gently.

Mandy's mother had tears in her eyes when she closed the front door behind them.

Their next interviews were more of the same. This group of women sounded so damn young, Will started expecting his knees to creak when he stood up. Once he met Scott Cardenas, he felt even older.

Scott was "between jobs", he told them with a blithe shrug. They sat in his parents' living room, his dad currently at work and his mother grocery shopping, according to Scott. "I'm looking into taking classes spring quarter," he said, as if feeling he should offer some plan. "Finishing my AA might be good."

Will wondered how patient the boy's parents were feeling.

The boy's gaze hardly left Rebecca, who had a magnetism that drew everyone, not just Will. Being a guy, he kept giving her the once-over, but who could blame him? She'd worn those damn knee-high boots again.

The kid did seem genuinely shocked about Mandy's disappearance and scared for her. "It can't be one of her friends!" he burst out at one point. "We've all known each other since...since middle school. Elementary school."

"That's not true," Rebecca said. "I'm hearing about newcomers to the group."

"Well..." His forehead wrinkled. "I guess that's true."

"Have you and Mandy ever been involved?"

"Involved?" He looked blank for a minute, which Will was beginning to think was not an unusual state for him. Then, "Oh. Nah. I've thought about asking her out a few times, but...I don't know. She's really sweet, but she takes everything so seriously. You know? I like to have fun, but she's always checking her watch, worrying about what time she has to be home since she has to be up early for work." He finished with, "And she has a kid," as if that said it all.

He named a few guys who had dated her, or said they wanted to. "*I* think she needs someone who's older," he confided.

Will blinked. Maybe the boy was smarter than he looked.

"What do you think of Carson Crandall?" Rebecca asked, as if at random.

"He's one of the new guys," Scott said, as if just realizing it. Will downgraded him on the smarts graph again. Brightening, Scott added, "He's cool. We've been surfing. Hang-gliding at Cape Kiwanda, too. It was awesome, with the dunes and some serious winds."

"You ever talk about Mandy?"

He actually looked wary. "Oh, yeah, you know. Just the way guys do."

"Do you think he's serious about her?"

"Like...getting *married* serious?"

Rebecca kept a straight face. Will wasn't sure he did.

"Sure. She does have a child."

"Yeah, no. Scott talked about getting his pilot's license, and these trips he wants to take. Like climbing Mt. Fuji, or what's the one in Africa? I'd be on board, except I don't make enough money for shit like that."

"Tim Spiva? I know he and Mandy had a thing in high school."

"Yeah, everybody back then thought they'd stay together. Tim's intense. But he didn't want her to leave for college, and when she said she was going anyway, he broke up with her."

"Sounds like they're still friends."

He puzzled over that. "I don't know. They seem kind of awkward around each other. You know? Plus, she's with Carson, and I don't think Tim's really seeing anyone even though he brags he is."

Rebecca and Will exchanged a glance. She hadn't reached Jordan Torgerson yet, but in Will's opinion she'd become a priority.

Scott offered to make them sandwiches or something, saying he was sure his mother wouldn't mind, but Rebecca thanked him, claiming another appointment.

Once they reached the sidewalk, she said, "Do you think we'd have gotten peanut butter and jelly?"

"Maybe cheese and bologna."

"Speaking of..."

"Sea Watch Café?" he asked.

"Now, if the chef there offers a peanut butter and jelly sandwich, it would probably be fabulous."

In fact, once he'd found parking on Schooner Street, busy even in the off season, and they'd taken a table by the window, Will ordered the macaroni and cheese that was one of today's specials. He'd had it before here, and it wasn't anything like the kind he sometimes made at home out of a box when he didn't feel like really cooking.

They kept conversation light. The café was tiny, the tables too close together to allow for private conversation. He discovered quickly that Rebecca knew everyone. People kept stopping to say hello and eyeing Will curiously. Even the obvious tourists stole peeks at them, presumably because of the badges and guns both carried.

Their knees bumped a few times, until she angled herself in her seat so it didn't happen again.

She admitted to being a runner. "I use a treadmill at the gym more often than I like in the winter. Otherwise, sometimes I run on the track at North Fork High before work, and weekends on the beach, weather permitting."

"From the old resort?"

She nodded. "Most places are too rocky. Do you run?"

"Yeah, I've got to do something to stay in shape." Which was getting harder than it used to be, good reason to sound disgruntled. He signaled the waitress and ordered huckleberry cobbler a lá mode, anyway, which made Rebecca laugh even as she shook her head and said, "Nothing for me."

He admitted to working out at the same gym, although usually evenings, and enjoying racquetball and a good, hard game of basketball. She played in a recreational soccer league in spring and summer. He bet she was good. She moved like an athlete, light on her feet, balanced, and he couldn't imagine she minded a little physical contact.

Physical contact with her sounded good to him. Damn it.

He scraped his bowl clean and dropped his credit card on top of the bill. "Let me get this one. There'll be others."

Unlike yesterday, she didn't argue.

Tim Spiva was up next. Like too many of the others in this age group, he lived with his parents, which meant Bow Lake. Will looked forward to getting a feel for him.

He had to crank the wheel to maneuver the unmarked, department issue sedan out of what had become a too-tight parking spot, glad he hadn't driven his Suburban. Joining the slow traffic on Schooner Street, he growled, "Don't the tourists ever go home?"

"They used to. A couple years back, the chamber of commerce ran ads in magazines and persuaded some of those tourist publications like Visit Oregon to feature this 'undiscovered' gem on the Oregon coast. Tourism boomed, and the Rand Inn has boosted it some more. People enjoy beachcombing even in winter, when storms toss up interesting stuff." She grinned at his expression when they came to a complete stop as the car in front of them sat stubbornly waiting with turn signal on for another driver to laboriously back out of a parking spot.

He rolled his shoulders. "How'd the crisis line go last night?"

"Oh, quiet." There was something a little off in her tone. He turned his head to study her face. "As the guy who had the previous shift said, Sunday, day of rest."

"So you just sat there?"

"No, one of our regulars called, and I got a woman I've talked to twice before whose husband is abusive. I'm not the only volunteer she's talked to, either. We leave notes for each other. It's taking her time to work up the nerve to leave the creep. Last night, I could tell from her slurred speech that he'd hit her. She didn't want to talk about it, although she's admitted before to broken bones. But even though she says she's terrified he won't let her go, I get the feeling she's stopped as much by the difficulty of making it financially. They have two kids, his income is bare bones, which means he'll be paying child support at the lowest level, and she's never worked because, surprise, he didn't want her to."

"What do you tell someone like that?" he asked with honest curiosity. Thank God, he finally broke free of the bumper-to-bumper traffic and turned onto a quieter street. A few jogs, and they were back to the highway. Of course, the light was red.

"I tell her about programs available for women like her. Encourage her to think about returning to school. I've given her web addresses so she can check out some vocational training. At the library," she said wryly. "Naturally, they don't have a computer at home. Her husband wouldn't want her broadening her horizons. We've talked about the possibility of her leaving the area, too. She's afraid to let him have unsupervised visitation with the kids."

Will tensed. "He's hitting them, too?" When the light turned green, he took a left onto the coast highway.

"She says not, but I'm not sure I believe her. She thinks he would, if she weren't there to take the brunt of his temper."

"Jesus. You just sit there and *listen* to this? You can't do anything?" Too late, he heard how sharp that had come out.

"What am I supposed to do?" Suddenly, she vibrated with frustration and rage. "Violate policy? If I did, would you turn me in?"

After a glance in the rearview mirror, Will steered the car to the shoulder and braked before he let himself look at her. It was all he could do to unclench his jaw. "No."

"I did, all right?" Her knuckles showed white where she had the seatbelt in a death grip. "I ran her phone number at work. I know who she is. I know who *he* is. And this isn't the only time I've done that, all right?"

"Rebecca." Was that husky voice his? And, shit, he shouldn't touch her, but he was going to, anyway. He laid a hand on her shoulder, feeling vibrating tension and the underlying fragility of a woman's bones. "Do you ever talk to anyone about this?"

He'd seen cops crack because they had no one, or were unable to admit to being less than tough through-and-through. For a woman…if she didn't have anyone at home, would she dare talk even to a department psychologist?

"Who?" Her eyes were so dark, he wouldn't have guessed they were gray if he didn't already know. "My father, who hates me being a cop? Shelley, who'd drop me cold? One of my fellow deputies?" She let out the most pained laugh he'd ever heard. "My boss, who'll send me back to patrol, if *he* doesn't fire me? God, what am I *doing*?" Her head fell back, her eyes closed.

Fuck. This was everything he'd feared, and she'd worked for him for less than four full days. But he slid his hand around her nape and squeezed. When she didn't move, he began a massage, sliding fingers into her hair, finding every point of tension, kneading the rigid muscles tying her neck to her shoulders. He'd have liked to do more, but was already far enough out on a limb. He didn't say a word.

The tension beneath his fingertips eased slowly. A release of breath seemed to take anguish with it. Will took one more second to savor silken skin, hair like heavy satin, her warmth, and then he withdrew his hand.

After a minute, her head rolled and their eyes met. "I'm sorry. I don't know where that came from."

"Sure you do."

A tiny flinch acknowledged his accuracy. "I'm still sorry. Believe it or not, I usually keep it together. Just…once in a while…"

"It gets to all of us sometimes. Why do you think cops have such a high incidence of alcoholism, domestic violence, divorce?"

"You mean, I need a husband so I can go home and beat the crap out of him as a release valve?" she said with weak humor.

He felt his mouth curve. "Then I would have to arrest you."

They sat quietly for a minute. He started to say her name at the exact moment she said, "So, are you going to fire me? Send me for required counseling?"

"Fire you, no." What he should do wasn't as obvious to him as it would have been for any other officer under his supervision. "Would counseling help?"

"I…don't think so. I'm pretty self-aware, you know." Once again, charcoal gray eyes met his. "I really am fine. It's the women and kids that I struggle over. Sometimes, I want to go in swinging, that's all."

Will let himself smile. He wrapped his hand around her arm and squeezed. "Better do some weightlifting then."

He thought this laugh was genuine.

"Um…we're going to be late if we don't get moving."

The last goddamn thing he wanted to do was go talk to yet another over-grown teenager, but she was right. He put on the turn signal, checked his mirror and accelerated onto the coastal highway.

"This could all be a waste of time, couldn't it?" she said, her voice small.

If a complete stranger had picked Mandy Shaw up off the highway, she meant. "It could. That's the job. We untangle strings, follow each to the end. Most don't lead anywhere. It takes patience."

She was looking straight ahead now. Color had risen to her cheeks, telling him how self-conscious she felt. "I would have said I *was* patient."

"Negotiating, you seem to be. It's possible investigation isn't your niche."

"I want it to be."

Damn. Her muscles might have loosened, but his were tied in knots now.

"You're a woman," he said after a minute.

She turned a glare on him.

Will shook his head, even as he took the turn into the wooded neighborhood they'd left earlier. "All I'm saying is, you process things differently than most men do. In some circumstances, women cops tend to be more effective than men because they depend on their brain instead of brawn. Women officers I've worked with mediate, while too many men go straight to confrontation. Today you had friendly conversations. Nobody felt threatened. If I'd been there asking the same questions, the response would have been guarded if not hostile. On the flip side, because you're more sensitive to how people feel, react, you might be emotionally impacted in a way I wouldn't be – or maybe you're just letting yourself feel what I'd suppress."

All good theory, true as far as it went, but his gut said something was going on with Rebecca that went deeper than a usual response to the stresses of the job. In her case, of *both* jobs, one paid, one volunteer.

"I liked what I saw today," he said after a minute. "You're effective with people. Let's go on the way we are and see what happens."

"Thank you." Stifled.

"What's his address?"

She told him. Tim Spiva, it seemed, lived less than two blocks from the Shaws.

"Back to the crisis line shift," he said abruptly. "You didn't finish saying how it went. Hours of silence?" That indefinable something he'd heard in her voice drove him to keep poking at it. Maybe talking to the battered woman was what still bothered her…but he doubted it. She probably took calls from abused women every shift.

She glanced at him and away. "I had some hang-ups. Just breathing when I picked up." Her shrug looked staged. "We get those. People who want to talk, but also don't."

"How many is *some*?" he asked.

A little silence. "Four or five." Pause. "Maybe six."

Definitely six. "That doesn't disturb you?"

Spotting the right house number, he turned into the driveway. No sign of a car; either Spiva wasn't home after all, or he'd parked in the garage.

"I worry the caller may blow before she works up the nerve to ask for help, if that's what you mean." Her turn to be sharp.

"You so sure those hang-ups weren't someone trying to get to you?"

"Callers don't know who they'll get. We use only first names." She gazed straight ahead, at the closed garage door. He had the sense these were practiced lines. Because she'd used them during the night to reassure herself? "Most people have no idea where the call center is located," she added. "I'm just a voice."

No, once someone heard her voice, he would always know it again. Will would know it was her if she was whispering over a phone with a bad connection. But what could he say?

He made no move to get out of the car, and when she reached for her door handle, Will said, "Wait."

She went absolutely still, hand still outstretched, face averted.

"What you said earlier. About who you should talk to." His chest felt odd. Congested, as if his rib cage had shrunk. "I'm available. I can listen as a friend, without judgement."

That brought her head around in pure incredulity. "And I believe that the minute Tim lets us in the door, Mandy will pop out of the kitchen asking if we want coffee."

In other words, *When pigs fly.*

His voice came out a little scratchy. "We've already crossed a line, wouldn't you say?" He nodded at her expression of shock, then opened his door and got out.

CHAPTER SEVEN

Rebecca twisted in the front seat to don her navy blue raincoat, department issue. An umbrella would be way easier. It occurred to her that, now she wasn't in uniform, she could use one. Maybe. It would leave her with only one hand free, plus limit her range of sight.

With a sigh, she hopped out, locked and hurried for the lobby of an apartment complex in the part of Cape Trouble that lay east of Highway 101, where tourists rarely ventured but locals found businesses like auto repair, the hardware store, dry cleaners and septic tank servicing. Rain fell steadily, a gray, all-encompassing shroud not so different from the Oregon coast's equally ubiquitous fog, except she could tell already she was going to be wet to her knees by the time she made it under cover. Ugh. Nobody else lingered out here, that was for sure. Maybe Wilcynski's claim to be too busy to accompany her today was really an excuse to stay indoors, warm and dry.

She got lucky because a young guy was coming out just as she reached the door, and held it for her. Considerate, but not very security conscious. Inside, she shook herself like a sheepdog, then shoved back the hood and scanned a wall of mailboxes, recycling and trash containers for discarded mail, and two elevators. She was able to step into an elevator without an okay from any resident or use of a key.

On the second floor, she walked halfway down a long hall until she reached 226 and knocked. Jordan Torgerson had damn well better be here after all the trouble it had been to connect with her. This morning, Rebecca had made a fourth call to the young woman, for the first time using the phone on her desk rather than her personal phone. Jordan betrayed her dismay with her flustered response once Rebecca identified herself. Gee, you think maybe she'd been ignoring Rebecca's messages?

She heard footsteps and the door swung open to reveal the unexpected: a tall guy with almost-red hair and hazel eyes. What the hell?

"Carson," she said cautiously.

"Detective." Expression grave, he stepped back. "Come in."

Not moving, Rebecca said, "I understood this was Jordan Torgerson's apartment."

"It is, and she's here, but she called and asked me to be with her while she answered questions."

Why would she do that?

Rebecca entered behind him and took off the rain jacket, which was already dripping on the vinyl floor of the tiny entry. "Anywhere I can put this?"

"Oh, sure." He took it from her, looked around, and finally draped it over one of two chairs at a tiny table against the wall. Then he led her to the living room, where a pretty blonde waited, chin high and defiant.

"Ms. Torgerson?"

"I don't understand why you want to talk to me. I don't know anything!" She squeezed her hands together at her waist. "I left that stupid party *early*."

Wow, this was a lot of drama for nothing. Or maybe it wasn't for nothing.

"May I sit down?" Rebecca asked.

"Oh." Disconcerted, the young woman said, "Yeah," and plopped down herself at one end of the sofa. Carson crossed the small room and sat on the sofa, too, but separated by a cushion, sending a clear signal to Rebecca that he hadn't already replaced Mandy, at least not with Jordan.

Of course, that kind of body language could be a lie, too.

"First, let me ask why you didn't return any of my calls," Rebecca said, going for relaxed, friendly, only mildly puzzled.

Blue eyes widened. "It scared me, not knowing why you wanted to talk to me." *Duh.*

"You could have asked me."

"It just...freaked me out." She crossed her arms, pushing into the corner between armrest and back of the sofa.

Was Carson supposed to scoot over and take her hand? Let her huddle against him? If so, he'd missed the signal.

"Jordan, I'm trying to talk to everyone in Mandy's circle of friends. Particularly those who were at the party Friday evening."

"But I already told you! I left way early. Like eleven."

"I'm not arguing that you didn't," Rebecca said with patience she didn't feel. Nope, wouldn't tell the lieutenant how quickly her patience frayed these days. "What I hope is that, for starters, you'll tell me who else you saw at the party. Somebody must have seen something. I still don't have anything close to a complete list of who was there. If you can give me even a few additional names, that would be a help. They'll steer me to more people."

"Oh." She sat blinking, lips parted. What, had she expected to be cuffed? Rebecca to wave a truncheon she didn't carry? A Miranda warning? "Well." Jordan looked at Carson, who nodded what appeared to be encouragement. "I guess I can try to think who I saw."

She did, in fact, produce half a dozen new names, and admitted to having seen Mandy a couple times. She also didn't resist Rebecca's questions about her background. In fact, she seemed flattered to be asked to talk about herself.

Jordan hadn't graduated from high school here, which Rebecca already knew from Tim. Mandy was still in Portland with Brian when Jordan moved here with a friend from high school, who hadn't stayed. Jordan had, because she liked being near the beach, and was happy at the salon where she worked in North Fork. Rebecca didn't get the feeling she and Mandy had connected in any way, despite the shared group. It was pretty clear that Jordan lacked Mandy's level of maturity.

"Tim Spiva mentioned that you'd driven yourself," Rebecca threw out casually.

Jordan wrinkled her nose. "He was mad that I was leaving, but it's not like *he* has any say in what I do."

"I had the impression you'd been seeing each other," Rebecca said mildly.

"We went to a movie together. Once. And had coffee a couple times because we happened to run into each other. He makes it sound to everybody like we're really dating, and we aren't."

"Actually, he told me that what you've seen of each other is casual," Rebecca felt compelled to say.

She sniffed. "Well, I already called and told him to quit claiming I'm, like, his girlfriend."

"Bet that annoyed him."

"He was rude!" she exclaimed. "Like I was making something up."

The headache that had hovered all day sent a spear of pain through Rebecca's right temple. All she could think was, poor Tim. Why would he *want* Jordan?

"A last question," she said. "Why ask Carson to come here today?"

The pretty blonde squirmed. "I just wanted support."

Apparently a girlfriend wouldn't do. She'd needed manly support.

"I see." Rebecca tucked away the notebook on which she'd jotted the names Jordan offered, and rose to her feet. "Thank you for your cooperation, Ms. Torgerson. If I need to call you for confirmation of anything we spoke about today, I'd appreciate it if you would take that call."

She blushed. "I'm sorry. I will. I promise."

Carson rose with alacrity. "I should get going, too—"

"Will you stay for just a minute?" Jordan begged.

Rebecca saw his face. He really, really didn't want to, but after the briefest of pauses said, "Sure, I can do that."

Not feeling moved by the little girl *moue*, Rebecca shrugged on her still wet raincoat and, with a civil nod at Carson, left.

Downstairs, she stopped in front of the door. Rain still fell steadily. The sun hadn't set yet, but she'd swear dusk was already darkening the sky to dismal.

Wilcynski would want to know what she learned from Jordan, but he could wait until morning. Maybe one of the new names would lead somewhere…but Rebecca doubted it. Her mood was no more cheerful than the weather. Every day that passed lowered the chance they'd find Mandy alive, and they weren't an iota closer to figuring out what had happened to her. She'd heard dimming hope even in Vicky Shaw's voice when they talked earlier. Rebecca hated calling her at all when she had nothing meaningful to offer.

She took the plunge and ran out to her vehicle, jumping in and wrestling off the raincoat, but not quickly enough to keep the seat from getting wet. Double ugh. She fired up the engine and the heat, shivering at the cold air blowing from the vents. For an instant she felt incredibly isolated with her windows fogged up and the slanting rain beyond them.

It was nearly six o'clock now. The coast highway was her fastest way home, saving her from stopping at headquarters to switch cars. There, she risked running into Wilcynski. It wouldn't be the first time she'd taken the Tahoe home, since it had been issued to her personally versus it being a vehicle from the pool. On the other hand…the idea of being alone held no appeal. It wasn't so much that she wanted company as that she liked the idea of having people around.

A workout would feel good, she decided. So, okay, she'd swap out the SUV for her Subaru, and go to the gym. She might even eat out. Grab a gyro at the Greek restaurant in North Fork. That sounded better than anything she had at home, considering how long it had been since she'd grocery shopped.

Gas first, and a bathroom. Working, she never asked to use one at anyone's home.

Usually at this time of day, there'd be lines waiting at the pumps in front of the convenience store, but who wanted to stop if they could put it off? She squirmed in place as the attendant wearing head-to-toe raingear pumped the gas. As soon as he was done, she moved the Tahoe to a parking place and dashed in. The guy behind the counter hunched on a stool, barely glancing up from his phone as she rushed by. Obviously, *he* didn't want to be here, either.

Washing her hands, she made the mistake of glancing in the mirror. Her hair was now damp, her ponytail sagging and stringy. The foundation she'd used to disguise the purple bags beneath her eyes was history. As she stared at herself, droplets fell from her hair to her nose, then dripped into the sink.

She *definitely* did not want to encounter Wilcynski. Fortunately, there was no need for her to go inside at all. Switch vehicles, and she'd be gone. Once she was at the gym, who cared what she looked like?

She grabbed an Almond Joy bar on her way out, paid with change from her pocket, and went back out. A car had pulled in at the pumps, the attendant standing beside it hunched into his raincoat like a turtle while he waited for the tank to fill.

Once again, Rebecca had to wait while the defroster did its thing before she could back out. She used the interlude to tear open the candy bar and replenish her blood sugar.

The rain started to let up as she turned east on the winding highway leading to North Fork. She began to brood about her stalled investigation and whether she was at fault for the lack of progress. It was a red light blinking on her dashboard that yanked her back to the present. Her gaze flicked to it. The check engine light.

Rebecca frowned at it. Those did come on for no good reason sometimes, or only to indicate it was time for some routine servicing. Only, department mechanics serviced all vehicles even more often than manufacturers recommended. Wait. Hadn't she heard that it could come on if the gas cap hadn't been closed tightly enough?

But then she saw the temperature gauge, the needle in the red zone and still jumping upward.

The response to her foot on the accelerator didn't feel right all of a sudden. Was that fog clinging to her hood, or smoke seeping out? After a glance in the rearview mirror – no one behind her – she began slowing and finally came to a stop at a wide place on the shoulder, her hazard lights blinking. Engine off. She stared at the hood, not daring to blink in case she missed a flicker of orange.

Wonderful. A perfect cap to her day.

Two cars passed going the other way, neither even slowing.

She'd never had a sheriff's department vehicle break down before. Just sitting here wasn't productive. So how about calling for a tow? Of course, there was undoubtedly a specific tow company she was required to use.

Rebecca was digging in the glove compartment for instructions when bright lights reflected off her rearview and side mirrors, almost blinding her. Someone had stopped. Apparently, chivalry was alive and well.

Blinking, she straightened, aware that dusk was giving way to night. Even on a bright day, the forest growing close to the highway on both sides made this stretch of highway dark. Looking over her shoulder, all she could see was a car, the headlights keeping her from making out license plate or even the shape of people in it. Why hadn't the driver turned them off?

Apprehension raised goosebumps on her arms. So stupid – but no different than when she was the one walking toward a vehicle she had just stopped. She *had* to get past this.

The door opened. Damn. Did she meet a would-be rescuer with a drawn Sig Sauer? Or assume this stranger's intentions were good? What flashed into her mind was the news Wilcynski had passed on, about the ambush of a police officer. What if—

Headlights swept over both vehicles. Another car. No, a pickup. It had passed when the brake lights flashed red. A moment later, on a rush of relief she saw it backing toward her.

Behind her, the door slammed. She twisted in her seat to see that the car was pulling out. Weirdly, it swung in a U-turn and accelerated back the way it had come.

Meantime, her own headlights shone on a dark shape walking back from the pickup ahead of her. Her heart was still beating too fast. What was with the car that had taken off, not even passing so she could get a look at it? And the stranger approaching might not realize the Tahoe was a law enforcement vehicle.

Her hand dropped to her gun. Then she had a better idea and grabbed her phone. Wilcynski. He'd probably left for home by now, but... *Send.* It was ringing by the time a man bent his head to look at her through the window.

Carson Crandall? Appearing unexpectedly *twice* within twenty minutes or so?

Wilcynski's gruff voice came in her ear. "Rebecca?"

"Will you stay on the line?" she asked. "Just until I'm sure nothing is wrong?"

*****

Shooting to his feet, Will demanded, "What? Damn it, talk to me!" When she didn't immediately answer, he grabbed his coat and stalked out.

"Lieutenant?" a detective said to his back.

He flapped a hand, snapped, "Later," and kept going. Was that a murmur of voices he heard through the phone?

Urgency he didn't even understand had him out at his Suburban and warming it up by the time Rebecca spoke to him again.

"I probably shouldn't have called you, but your number was easy to find."

"What's the problem?" he barked.

She paused. "I broke down about halfway between Cape Trouble and North Fork. I haven't quite reached the viewpoint."

"You broke down how?" Gravel crunched beneath his tires until he reached the alley.

"The Tahoe overheated. Uh...Carson Crandall is here. I popped the hood because the engine is smoking. He says the dipstick shows no oil. There must be a hole in the oil pan."

Will had driven a lot of miles in his life without ever having a rock fly up and somehow punch a hole through metal, or the drain plug happen to fall out. And right when she was on a lonely stretch of road?

"Are you locked in your vehicle?"

Another brief silence. "I'm armed, you know."

"Don't care. I don't buy Crandall being there by chance."

"That was my first reaction," she said, voice low, "but actually it makes sense that he'd be behind me. He was at Jordan Torgerson's when I talked to her, and I left first. He lives in North Fork."

Will ground his teeth. "What's he doing?"

"He went back to his car. He says he'll wait here until a tow truck arrives."

"Until *I* arrive."

"What? You don't have to race to my rescue! I can get a lift from the tow truck driver—"

"I'm already on my way. Have you called for the tow yet?"

"No, I was trying to figure out who I'm supposed to use, and then this car pulled up behind me and—"

He interrupted again. "I'll do it. I'm going away for about thirty seconds to make the call. Then I'll call back."

It took a little longer than that, but she answered on the first ring. "Really, it's not—"

"I don't like coincidences," he snapped.

"Can I finish a sentence?"

Okay, he was overreacting, but he wouldn't be able to get a grip on himself until he was there, within touching distance. He took a deep breath. "Okay. What are you trying to say?"

"Nothing in particular, just..." She trailed off. When he managed to keep his mouth shut, Rebecca laughed. "I'll tell you about it when you get here."

"Five minutes." Maybe not even that, given the speed he was traveling despite drizzle and a wet road. Will made himself slow down. While he was at it, he made himself think.

He had quit functioning as her boss from the minute he saw her reaction to Ed Brodsky shooting himself. He hadn't managed to recover yet, and had a bad feeling he wouldn't be. He remembered thinking, *Get a grip or get a new job*, and realized that was about right. Or he could boot Rebecca Walker back to patrol. He didn't love the idea of telling her why. He could take advantage of what she'd said in confidence, despite the fact he'd feel like a scumbag. He grimaced, knowing he wouldn't be alone with that opinion.

For the first time in his life, Will had absolutely no idea what he should do...except that he wouldn't be making any decisions until he reached her now, found out what had alarmed her enough to call him for backup. Just Carson Crandall's convenient appearance? Will decided to reserve judgement.

Two sets of blinking hazard lights appeared through the mist and dark. He slowed down, braked and swung around to pull in tight behind Rebecca's Tahoe. After putting on his own flashers, he turned off the engine and walked forward, passing Rebecca and not stopping until he reached the driver door of the pickup truck. He planted a hand on the roof and bent forward as he would making a stop.

The window whirred halfway down. Crandall peered out. "Lieutenant Wilcynski? Good, she said you were on your way. I offered her a lift, but she said she'd rather wait for the tow truck."

"I'll stay."

"Then if it's okay with you, I'll get going."

Will stepped back. "Drive carefully." He couldn't make himself say something civil like *thanks for stopping* even if he should.

The pickup tail lights were receding by the time he walked back to the Tahoe. Rebecca had already opened her door.

With the engine off and no heat running, she had to be getting chilly, and he didn't like the way the windows had fogged. "Come on back to my car," he said, and walked away.

After a minute, her door slammed and he heard her footsteps. He tensed as an eastbound car approached, slowed down, then sped up. Even on low, the lights were blinding.

Once they were both in, he turned the engine back on and boosted the heater. "Okay, tell me what happened."

"It seemed fine when I started out—"

"No." He'd interrupted again. Well, fuck it. "Start with the interview."

Without the overhead light on, she was a dark figure beside him. He'd like to see her expressions, but maybe it was just as well he couldn't.

Voice very controlled, Rebecca offered a concise summation of a not very productive interview.

"And you think Crandall wasn't thrilled to be there," he said, reflecting on it.

"No, he tried to escape on my heels, but she was being helpless girl who needed big, strong man, and he was pretty well trapped."

Will wouldn't have had any trouble saying, *You're on your own,* but he wasn't the nicest guy around, either.

"I do think the timing is about right for him to be here. I stopped and got gas and a candy bar after I left Jordan's place. Took me, I don't know, ten minutes?"

He mulled that over. "You hadn't noticed the temperature gauge going up, nothing else wrong."

"No. Maybe a mile back, the indicator light came on. Then I realized the gauge was up in the red. When I saw smoke coming from under the hood, I pulled over."

"And Crandall came to the rescue."

"No." Her voice had an edge suddenly, the one he'd heard when she called in the first place. "Another car stopped first. Pulled in right behind me."

"That's why Crandall was ahead of you," Will said slowly.

"Right. The car just sat there. I'd swear the high beams were on. I couldn't see anything. Finally the driver side door opened. I don't think anyone had gotten out still when another set of headlights approached." She told him Crandall recognized her Tahoe and her in the glare of the headlights as he passed, so he braked and backed up. "He thought since I knew him, I might feel easier about him than a stranger."

The guy *was* a first responder, Will reminded himself. Stopping to help would be instinctive for him.

"What did the other car do?"

He didn't like her answer, and could tell she didn't, either.

"I was a little unsettled," she admitted. "It occurred to me—"

"That someone could have sabotaged the Tahoe in a way that would have you pulling over on a stretch of road with no houses or businesses."

"I couldn't help thinking of the Tillamook County deputy," she said softly. "But I was prepared."

He knew she was. But cops were killed all too often on the job, and they'd been prepared, too. The idea of the car hovering behind her, the pause, the lights on high beam, scared the shit out of him.

"You know, cars break down on all the time." She projected absolute confidence. "It's ridiculous to speculate about sabotage yet."

"Anticipating the worst is an occupational hazard." Good excuse for his panic.

Rebecca didn't say anything for a minute. Then, "I'm not a rookie."

Looking straight ahead, he didn't move. "I know that."

"I...appreciate you coming." She took a breath. "But...would you have come running if Sean had made the exact same call?"

Will wanted to lie. Damn, but he wanted to lie. "Probably not."

"Or any of the others?"

He clamped his mouth shut.

"You have to get over feeling protective just because I'm a woman."

"I don't know if I can do that," he said hoarsely. Hadn't she figured out that he wouldn't have reacted this way if she'd been any other woman?

"But...this will be impossible once everyone else notices you're treating me different than you treat them."

"I didn't want to promote you," he heard himself say.

"But you did because you were afraid I'd sue or something?" She sounded outraged, and he didn't blame her.

"I did because you have a hell of a record. You deserved it. The problem is mine, not yours."

He wanted to kiss her. Will knew she was attracted to him, too, but acting on it... They'd risk damaging both their careers. Risk? They *would* damage both their careers.

She stayed quiet so long, he didn't know how much longer he could stay still.

When she spoke, her voice was so soft, he barely heard her. "I don't know what to say."

"Jesus." He bumped his head a couple times against the headrest. "I deserve to lose my job. I'd fire anyone else who talked like this to a woman he supervised."

"Maybe clearing the air will help."

"Is that what we're doing?" The painful tension had knotted muscles he hardly knew he had.

"I don't know." She sounded unhappy, even bewildered.

He focused ahead. "We need to shelve this for now. Tow truck is coming."

She actually jerked. "Oh! I wasn't paying any attention! What is *wrong* with me?"

"Nothing." Will laid a hand on her forearm. "You've been professional from day one. I meant it when I said this is my problem, not yours."

The tow truck driver was maneuvering until he could back up to the Tahoe. Will opened his door to get out and help. The lightest touch on *his* arm stopped him. With the dome light on, he let himself look at her.

"No. I can't let you think that." Her voice was rich as always, steady. "Because it isn't just you. It's me, too. I...shouldn't have taken the job when you offered it."

"Rebecca."

"I don't want to be a coward," she said, then opened her car door and got out while he was still gaping.

CHAPTER EIGHT

Will stayed behind the tow truck pulling the Tahoe during the fifteen minute drive to North Fork. His silence had a brooding quality that intimidated Rebecca, making her wonder if she'd read more into what he had – and hadn't said – than he had intended. She was grateful when her phone rang five minutes along.

"Detective Walker?" a man said. "Detective Jantz."

"Thank you for calling." Jantz was the Portland Police Bureau detective who'd agreed to try to locate the mysterious Courtney, who had supposedly spent the night with Brian Vail. "Any luck?"

"Not so far. Just left the bar. Bartender worked last Friday, but he says the place was packed. He knows Brian was there for a while – apparently, he's a regular – but can't remember when he left. Doesn't know a Courtney, but that doesn't mean she wasn't there. The patrons all just shrugged when I asked. I probably went by too early, but I'm thinking I'll have better luck if I go by Friday night, anyway."

"You don't mind?"

"Nope. Had a beer and a decent burger." He sounded cheerful. "Friday night, I might make it a pitcher so I can hang around longer."

She chuckled. "Thank you again. Vail sounds like a jerk, but I'd be glad to cross him off my list."

"I understand. I'll let you know."

Dropping her phone in her jacket pocket, Rebecca said, "I told you a PPB guy offered to try to locate the woman who is supposed to be Brian Vail's alibi." She summarized.

Will nodded. "Good."

Occasional passing headlights let her see his frowning face and tight mouth. For all she could tell, he had forgotten she was there. Rebecca turned her head to look out the side window, first at dark forest and then at the businesses leading into the county seat. No, he was probably considering the damage she could do to him.

The tow truck stayed ahead of them until they reached the sheriff's department. When it backed up to one of the service bays that were part of the two story, concrete parking garage, Will continued in.

"Where's your car?"

He must have noticed earlier that her Subaru wasn't out back where she usually left it. Covered parking had real appeal on a rainy day.

"Second level."

His tires squealed as he took the sharp turn. Rebecca belatedly realized that he'd driven his Suburban again rather than his unmarked police car.

"There." She pointed, saying unnecessarily, "The Subaru." She had no doubt he knew what she and every other detective drove.

He braked right behind it.

"Well," she said awkwardly, "thanks again."

His expression was unrevealing, but he said, "Have dinner with me."

"What?" As in a *date*?

"We really do need to talk."

After a minute she nodded. What was he going to say? "How about Costas?" she suggested, as if him asking her to dinner was no big deal. "I've had a yen for gyros all day."

"I'll meet you there."

He was already parked when she pulled in a few minutes later. As they walked in, he rested a big, warm hand on her lower back. Nerve endings shivered all the way down to the soles of her feet. Rebecca had never realized how erotic that particular touch could be.

The smiling woman who seated them actually was Greek; she and her husband owned the restaurant, and he did most of the cooking. Both had thick accents. Every time Rebecca came, they complained about the rain. She'd never gotten a straight story about why they had immigrated or settled in the rainy Northwest instead of a part of the country with a climate more familiar to them.

This being a week night, there were only a few other diners – a family group in a big corner booth, and a couple by the window. Rebecca and Will took a booth far from anyone else, ordered drinks and looked at each other.

"Have you eaten here before?" she asked.

"Frequently. I'm not much of a cook."

"I enjoy cooking, but I only do it on my days off. Then I try to make a couple meals that each feed me for at least two nights." Embarrassed, she knew she was chatting just to fill the silence, but she couldn't seem to stop herself. "Usually when I get home, I just want something I can reheat quick."

"I feel the same," he said in that low, rough voice.

What other feelings did they share?

Their hostess reappeared to take their orders, then left them alone. A burst of laughter from the family group drew Rebecca's attention, but almost reluctantly she looked back at Wilcynski.

Will. From the minute she called him, he'd become Will in her mind. Would it even have occurred to her to call anyone else? No, only him. He threatened her in a way she hadn't wanted to acknowledge, but he also made her feel safe, an admission she wasn't any happier about. She'd never wanted to need a bulwark between her and the world, which had pretty much taken care of all previous relationships. Male cops might have issues with permanency, but there were plenty of women who found what they did, the badge, the gun, the uniform, sexy. Men didn't feel the same about a woman who carried a gun.

It was obvious that Will didn't love her being a cop, either. In his case, not because he felt emasculated by what she did, but because of his own over-developed protective instincts.

"Before you applied for the opening, I had almost decided to ask you out," he said unexpectedly. It figured he would jump right in. "I wouldn't have been your supervisor, I thought Alex would have cut us some slack." He paused. "Assuming you had said yes, of course."

She didn't know where he was going with this, what decision she would make, but she couldn't do less than be as frank as he was.

"I would have. I...noticed you as soon as you started." And she'd known he was watching her, known why.

"I've tried to avoid getting involved with fellow cops."

"Me, too," she said. "I mean, I guess I would have considered it if I met someone with another agency."

"I've been married," he said, startling her. "My wife was a paramedic. I worked vice at the time, then moved to homicide. We shared tales of blood and gore when we saw each other, which wasn't very often."

"Bet that was uplifting while you were throwing dinner together."

He gave that gruff, rusty laugh she'd heard so seldom. "Yeah, after a while I think we both realized we had nothing else in common." His shoulders moved. "Homicide didn't allow much of a life outside work, not given how often new bodies turned up. Compton, my last assignment, is a tough area."

He was opening up. What could she do but ask? "Do you mind telling me why you accepted the job here? It has to have been a huge change."

A nerve twitched in his cheek, but he didn't say anything for a minute. Finally he leaned back in the booth. "How about a swap? One story for another."

Oh, God. Rebecca was afraid her eyes had widened. What would he want to know about her?

She could lie.

No. Whatever else she did, she wouldn't lie. Not to him.

Heart pounding, she said, "Okay."

One of his hands had rested on the table top. Suddenly, he was tapping a nervous beat. His gaze dropped to his fingers, which went still.

"My sister was my only family. I'd begun to wonder awhile back whether Stefania's husband wasn't abusive, but later she admitted she was afraid of what I'd do if she told me. After she kicked the asshole out, she made me promise not to go after him."

Rebecca didn't have to ask if otherwise he would have. She nodded.

"He stalked her. Vandalized the house, her car."

No mention of children, thank goodness.

"She got a protection order. He violated it, over and over. Unfortunately, Stef lived and worked in the city of Los Angeles, but I was with the county sheriff's department and couldn't directly get involved. She got zero help from the officers who only occasionally responded, shrugged and said, 'What can we do?' He hadn't assaulted her since the divorce, had he? I confronted the son of a bitch several times. He complained, and my boss told me to back off."

Chilled, Rebecca knew what was coming. She hadn't missed the past tense he'd used from the beginning.

"He broke into the house. She called 911, then me. Even though I was half an hour away, I still beat LAPD. He'd shot her. I wanted to kill the first responders, who'd had two calls and chose the other one because Stef called all the time and nothing ever came of it."

"Oh, Will." Rebecca felt the tightness of his grip, and was astonished to see that she must have reached for his hand and he'd seized hers.

Grief deepened lines on his face, but rage also glittered in his eyes. "The bastard had killed himself, too. He'd defiled her by wrapping her in his arms before he did it."

She shuddered at the picture.

He made a sound that hurt to hear. Grief predominated now when his eyes met hers. "I was so angry. Angry at LAPD, and angry at my supervisors. I'd begged them to lean on their counterparts at the nearest station to Stef's home and workplace. I heard the same crap from them she got from the LAPD. I called the officers who had responded to her calls. I kept hearing, 'You know most situations like this don't amount to much. Your sister's smart, she's cautious, he'll lose interest eventually.'"

"They had to know how often the outcome is tragedy when a man refuses to let go."

He seemed to realize he was all but breaking bones in her hand and let her go, muttering an apology. The hand he scrubbed over his face trembled. Lieutenant Wilcynski, shaken, grieving. No wonder he hadn't wanted everyone in the department to know.

"I'm sorry," she said quietly. "So sorry."

Their food arrived, a gyro for Rebecca, a full meal for Will. She spread her napkin on her lap, but didn't reach for the gyro.

"I hear stories like this too often. I think…individual officers want to help, but we're so often overwhelmed. It might be different if we had more women officers, if there weren't still too many of the kind of macho men in the profession who knock their own wives around." Her own anger curdled, her appetite going missing.

"I agree," he said. "Except I've also seen women so determined to be tough, they're as bad."

He started to eat, and she did the same, sensing his need to retreat. Even so, after a minute she asked how he'd settled on obscure Burris County.

"You ever meet Adam Rostov?"

"The detective up here to find Naomi Kendrick?" Naomi was the amazing chef who'd started the Sea Watch Café.

"Right. He's a detective in Santa Lucia, which is one of the many suburbs that make up the greater Los Angeles area. He and I ended up working an investigation that crossed jurisdictions together, got to be friends during the couple months leading up to Stef's murder. He told me he wouldn't have minded staying up here, if Naomi didn't have to be in southern Californian for trial prep. She still owns the café, you know."

"I did, vaguely."

"He said if I needed to get away, I should call Alex Mackay. I got lucky, because he'd just encouraged my predecessor to retire."

"Taft. Rumor had it he plunked himself behind his desk first thing every morning and didn't heave himself out from behind it until five. Never went out to scenes."

Will's grin flashed. "Our esteemed sheriff had much worse to say about him. I don't think a few of the detectives are all that thrilled to have a boss who looks over their shoulder instead."

The way he looked over hers? No, his hands-on approach was just what she needed. Only the tension between them made it difficult.

"So what do you think, now that you've been here awhile?"

"I'm surprised to say I like it. There's plenty to keep me busy, I work for a sheriff I respect, and I might have a chance at having a life outside work here." His gaze rested on her as he said that.

As conflicted as she knew he was, she offered a twisted smile. "It's a theory."

"At least I've eaten half my meal without my phone once vibrating or ringing."

"But the job swallows you. I never shake off what I did or saw in any given day. You have fun with friends, and a part of your mind is somewhere else. You know what I mean."

"I do. But there has to be a difference between acknowledging the bad stuff and letting it consume you."

She set down the remnants of her now messy gyro. Wiping her fingers on the napkin, Rebecca said, "In a way, it's so frustrating. On patrol, at least, you get glimpses into people's lives, but you're never around long enough to *fix* anything." The passion in her own voice shocked her.

"Following through isn't usually our job. That's for social workers, counselors, foster parents, guardian ad litems, judges."

"I know that. I thought—" This sounded dumb even to say, but she went ahead anyway. "That as a detective I could dig deeper, make a bigger difference. Instead, I'm accomplishing absolutely nothing."

"We do dig deeper. You have been. But..." Will surprised her by hesitating. "Our focus is on finding the perpetrator. The only relief we offer the victim – or the victim's family and friends – is seeing that justice is done. Rebecca." He leaned forward, his dark-eyed gaze drilling into hers. "If it's the victims you most want to help, you're in the wrong profession."

She was so stunned, it was as if he'd struck her. Then she thought, no, it was like walking into a sliding glass door that her eye saw as empty space. Just...*wham.*

But this is what I always wanted to do.

She kept gaping. Stupid. What he said was so obvious, except she'd never seen her dissatisfaction that way. Any consideration she'd given to changing jobs had to do with this damn panic thing.

He was wrong. Arresting the bad guys so they didn't get away with the horrors they'd committed, that's what she needed to do.

She shook her head hard. "No, I'm just frustrated because I know exactly what the Shaws are going through." She was speaking with too much passion, but couldn't seem to dam it up. "I feel so useless!"

His gaze sharpened at her burst of vehemence.

Uh oh.

*****

She'd given him his opening. It was only one of many things Will wondered about this woman, but he suddenly felt sure she had been a victim in some way.

"Your turn," he said quietly. "Why'd you go into law enforcement, Rebecca?"

Her gaze slid away. "We're both done eating. We can't just sit here and talk forever."

"Sure we can." With a tip of his chin, he summoned Mrs. Costa. "Baklava and coffee for me. Rebecca?"

Now she looked at him, anxiety filling her gray eyes. "I'll have coffee, too."

"And a second baklava."

Mrs. Costa smiled, gathered dirty dishes and returned to the kitchen.

Rebecca protested, "I hardly ever eat desserts."

"You can afford them." With that lithe body, why would she worry about a few calories? Women. He shrugged. "If you don't eat it, I will. Or you can take it home with you."

Her magnificent eyes darkened. What had he said?

Instinct gave him an answer. *Home.* Where a killer had broken in and shot her.

Save that topic for another time.

For a moment, Will let himself take in the unreal fact that they were here together. Not as colleagues sharing a quick meal, but as man and woman. He didn't like to remember his sister's death, far less talk about it, but telling Rebecca had been easier than he'd expected. The understanding on her face, the way she'd reached for his hand to give comfort, neither were what he was used to. She was still skittish, but she'd agreed to have dinner with him, to talk.

Too bad talking about feelings was something he did so poorly. Maybe if he had done it better, he'd never have married Olivia. They'd have figured out in time what they were missing.

"If I tell you, you'll take me off this investigation," Rebecca said.

"Tell me anyway."

She searched his face with those haunting eyes.

"I think you'd find a lot of us went into law enforcement because of a tragedy," he said. "We hated feeling helpless. This is one way to gain control, to do what we couldn't then."

"Yes. Oh!" Looking startled, she summoned a smile and thanks for Mrs. Costa, who slid plates of baklava in front of them and filled their cups with coffee.

Once they were alone, Rebecca squared her shoulders. Her defiant expression matched her body language. "My mother was abducted, raped and murdered."

Oh, hell. So much explained in so few words.

Will swore. "How old were you?"

"Ten."

Now he reached across the table for her hand. "Tell me about it."

The story emerged haltingly. She came home from school one day and her mom wasn't there the way she was supposed to be. The house was locked, but she used the hide-out key to let herself in. Thinking it was weird Mom hadn't left a note or phone message, Rebecca called her dad at work, but he was out on a job site. His assistant promised to have him call the minute he got back in the office.

Rebecca's unfocused gaze told him she wasn't seeing the here and now. She'd hate knowing her childish self could be heard in her voice.

Then, all adult, she said, "As it turned out, Dad getting the message right away wouldn't have made any difference. Mom wasn't dead yet, but the police wouldn't have found her in time."

Jesus. Will clenched his teeth and braced himself to hear what he knew was coming.

"Dad called the police. He begged them to look for her." Rage made the jut of her cheekbones sharper, the gray of her eyes molten. "'No sign of a struggle, sir?'" she mimicked. "'You say your wife took her purse? Now, doesn't that suggest she left on her own and will be in touch in her own good time?'"

How many cops had said something similar? Most were right. The ones who were wrong…they had to live with the terrible consequences of inaction. Hiding his instinctive wince, Will understood how Rebecca had felt Saturday when he tried to put her off, scoffed at the idea of opening an investigation so quickly. You couldn't get more personal than this.

The story continued. Rebecca's father called everyone he knew, which included the mayor, who leaned on his police chief. By morning an investigator was talking to neighbors and friends.

"Two days later, an early morning jogger found my mother's body. I didn't see her, of course. Dad tried to hide how bad it was.

But once I was a cop, I looked at her file and read the trial transcript. Mom had been savagely beaten as well as repeatedly raped."

Now, Will saw only grief on her face.

"Dad had been uneasy for a while about a long-time friend of his. There was a time when he and his wife were over for dinner often. But Mom said this friend – Leonard Bailey – had propositioned her. Dad hadn't liked the way Leonard looked at her, touched her 'accidently'. A couple friends of Mom's told the investigator Leonard was making her really uncomfortable. But he was the county auditor, well known, married and had kids younger than me. He was supposed to be away when she disappeared, at a conference in Salem."

"A hop, skip and a jump away."

Her mouth curved sadly. "Yes. Well, it turned out he'd screwed up. Mom had scratched him, so they recovered DNA from beneath her fingernails. The investigator interviewed Leonard several times. He was starting to crack, I heard the detective tell Dad. Leonard was insulted to be asked for a DNA sample. Finally, the investigator persuaded a judge to sign an order. It was a match. They already knew he owned a hunting cabin on the Nestucca River. They found…evidence of her presence, what he'd done to her." She shuddered. "He was convicted." Expression stark, Rebecca really looked at Will again. "After a few months, we moved here. It was awful, being around people who all knew what happened. Dad had had his own architectural firm up there, but here he worked for someone else."

"Did you know the details at the time?"

"Dad tried to protect me, but I overheard enough to have a good idea." She gave a one-shoulder shrug. "I didn't know much about sex, and certainly not rape, but I understood being tied up and that she didn't have any clothes on and he did horrible things to her for about a day before he decided he needed to get home."

A pained sound escaped Will. "I'm sorry. I was afraid of something like this, but I hoped…"

"You hoped?"

He exhaled. "That it wasn't this bad."

"So now you know why I became a cop. If the police had launched an immediate search, if they'd believed Dad about

Leonard, they could have found that he owned an isolated cabin and gone there. They might have been in time."

Will didn't say anything. She was right – but moving that fast on an ostensibly respectable man with no criminal record would have been next to impossible. Suggesting an affair to a married woman was a long way from committing abduction, rape and murder.

"Only, now I know why they weren't in time," Rebecca murmured. Her thoughts must have echoed his. "I've had four days, and gotten nowhere."

"But you don't have multiple people telling you about a man who made Mandy uneasy, either."

She sighed. "No." Expression challenging, she asked, "*Are* you going to yank me from the investigation?"

"Of course not. It's only thanks to you that we got an early start on it. And you've done everything right."

"I wish we could get instant DNA results from the blood on her jacket."

Will didn't even comment on this pipe dream, not pointing out that the blood was most likely Mandy's. "If her abductor dropped it, that was surprisingly careless," he did say.

"She could have, I don't know, thrown it out of a car. If a wind caught it, would he have wanted to pull over and go looking for it? In the dark?"

"If she was capable of getting a window down, why didn't she open a door and throw herself out?"

Her brain was ticking; he could see an absorbed expression that had replaced the grief and memories. "It can't have been lost in the initial struggle."

"Again, not unless a wind whipped it away." Colburn hadn't found so much as trampled grass in the vicinity not explained by the volunteer who had spotted the coat.

"I've been thinking the jacket and where it was found suggests she was grabbed out at the highway," she said slowly. "Some passing motorist who stopped. Which means I'm *really* wasting my time." A frown wrinkled her forehead. "Only...what if that's why the jacket was there? To make us think that?"

"I've wondered," he agreed. "That's why I wanted you to keep on the friends and the ex." He hesitated. "Have you looked at the father?"

"Yes." She scrunched up her nose. "Fortunately, I was able to slide a few questions in without either of them realizing what I was getting at. Apparently, Sammie didn't feel good that night and kept waking up. They were afraid she might be coming down with something, but decided she wasn't sick enough to ask Mandy to come home."

"A decision they'll never forget."

"Unfortunately. Anyway, both Stuart and Vicky were home, no question."

"Okay." Having seen Stuart Shaw's ravaged face, Will hadn't wanted to think he could have hurt his own daughter, but sociopaths could fake just about any emotion with practiced skill. "If you had to go out on a limb and point to someone you've interviewed, who would it be?"

Rebecca went very still, clearly not eager to answer. Then she moaned. "Tim Spiva. I hate saying this, because he probably *is* just an odd duck. But...he has these mini-flashes of anger, which sit really strangely with his eagerness to help."

Thinking about the one interview he'd observed, Will nodded. "I didn't like the way he looked at you."

Her mouth twisted. "I didn't, either, but he's a guy. And...I'm realizing I need to find a more gender-neutral plainclothes uniform. Tim isn't the only one I've caught checking me out."

Will gave a rough chuckle. "I've done my share of checking you out."

She almost smiled. "Well, maybe, but I wasn't talking about you. Practically all the guys at least took a good look. Even Scott Cardenas, and if I didn't know better I'd swear he's about sixteen."

Now Will did laugh. "You do know that, at sixteen, a guy's hormones are raging? The subject of sex is humming in the background no matter what he's doing."

A tiny smile formed an almost-dimple in her cheek. "Diminishes with age, does it?"

"Men at my venerable age do occasionally turn their minds to other subjects." Amusement faded, leaving him disconcerted and, yeah, a little grumpy. "Lately…damn it, lately I might as well *be* sixteen again."

Neither looked away. He didn't breathe, and wasn't sure she did, either. He felt strangely exposed, as though he'd laid himself bare for her. And yet…she wasn't trying to hide anything, either.

He might have kept looking into those eyes forever if a footstep and cheerful voice hadn't recalled him. Mrs. Costa with the bill. Will tried to take a mental snapshot of Rebecca's face at that moment, so damn beautiful despite the day's stresses. Her lips had parted, and color warmed her cheeks. Her gray eyes shimmered.

He managed to get his wallet out of his back pocket and handed over a credit card, shaking his head when he saw Rebecca about to protest.

"Another time."

"You keep saying that."

Once again, he just let himself look. "I'm hoping there will be plenty more times."

Shock jolted her, but after a minute, she only nodded.

Triumph joined the tangle of other emotions that had taken up residence beneath his breastbone. So what sense did it make that he also wished he'd kept his mouth shut so that she still thought of him as the gruff, cold lieutenant?

CHAPTER NINE

During her drive home, Rebecca brooded about what had been said and not said – and what hadn't happened.

When Will walked her out to her car, her pulse raced and she felt tremulous with anticipation. And then what did he do but stand back and watch her get in, waiting until the engine started before nodding and saying, "Goodnight."

After all that, why hadn't he kissed her? All she had to do was think about his mouth on hers, his hands on her body, to have warmth pooling low in her abdomen and her skin tingling. Was he torturing her? Or having second thoughts?

Thinking about a shift in his expression after he'd paid, her guess was option number two. And could she blame him?

A chill told her she was having second – no, *first* thoughts, too. Sure as hell, she'd be the one who had to quit her job if they got involved. Not because he was more important, although of course he was, but because she'd have other options and he might not. Will was well-qualified to be police chief in Cape Trouble or North Fork, but Rebecca hadn't heard any rumor that Daniel Colburn was thinking of moving on, and Howard Lundy in North Fork never would unless he eventually got fired.

Beyond that…it would be a long commute to another county, and that was assuming a senior position opened up.

Rebecca knew Daniel would offer her a job in a heartbeat. Or…she could go back to patrol. That might work, except…wouldn't she come to resent giving up her ambitions for a man? Dumb question. Anyway, long range planning for what might be a quick fling was silly.

Could they manage a quick fling without anyone knowing?

And…oh, God, why was she wasting time thinking about a man when Mandy might conceivably still be alive, held captive by a maniac?

What was it Will had said about his marriage. *We shared tales of blood and gore when we saw each other.* Isn't that what he and she had done this evening? His tragedy, her tragedy, and the one they were investigating. For all she knew, he'd suddenly realized the same. What else could they possibly have in common?

She felt like a balloon that had just been punctured, hope trickling out the tiny hole. No more bobbing toward the sky for her. Instead, the all-too-familiar dread began to build when she turned onto her road.

Half a mile in, it narrowed and asphalt turned to gravel. Rebecca knew where every pothole was, weaving like a drunk driver to miss them. Occasionally everyone living up here went in together and bought a load or two of gravel, but they hadn't done it recently. She passed the few driveways. Homes were on five to ten acres minimum. Once, her headlights caught movement and she braked, waiting as a doe picked her way across the road and finally bounded into the forest.

At home, she pulled into a carport extending from one side of the log cabin, with its steep, pitched roof made of dark metal. Rebecca watched for any motion before she finally got out and hustled into the cabin. She'd taken to leaving blinds pulled so she didn't feel exposed in front of bare windows. Sitting outside on her porch watching for wildlife, enjoying the night air, wasn't something she did anymore. All these years in law enforcement, she had felt safely removed from being a victim. As Will put it, she had the control she'd lacked as a helpless kid trying to understand the horror that meant Mommy wouldn't come home. And if it could happen to Mommy, why not her, too? That part, Rebecca had never told her father.

The buoying sensation of hope had felt like a refuge from her constant awareness of how it felt to be a victim. Then, and more recently. Being shot had shattered any belief that she had made herself invincible. Telling Will her history tonight had made her realize what she'd gone through losing her mother had set her up for PTSD now. Nobody had diagnosed anything like that in her when she was a kid, but what else could she call the years of being afraid to fall asleep because she wouldn't hear someone climbing in her window or tiptoeing down the hall?

I already knew how it felt to be a victim, she thought bleakly. She wanted desperately to forget, but she might as well face facts. It wasn't happening. Never would.

Standing in the middle of her own living room, she listened to the sough of wind in the tall trees surrounding her cabin

I want a life, too, she thought. For a woman cop, relationships held special challenges. But…maybe that was partly an excuse. Maybe she'd been afraid to make herself vulnerable by trusting absolutely in someone else.

She wouldn't be going to sleep in the near future, so she did the same thing she had every evening this week: she took out her notes on interviews and read them over. She'd even drawn a sort of chart, trying to clarify who was where and when.

She hadn't been staring at it long when a buzzing began under her skin. Tim was part of her childhood, part of Mandy's, so maybe she'd given him an automatic pass. But verbalizing her discomfort with him to Will tonight had opened her to something she should have noticed.

Nobody had mentioned seeing Tim at the party again after Mandy supposedly left.

She tried to stay calm. She had mostly been asking who'd seen Mandy and when, so it was entirely possible the subject of his presence just hadn't come up. And maybe for good reason. Nobody seemed to really like Tim. Rebecca had the feeling he'd become part of the group back in high school because of his relationship with Mandy, and nobody actually *dis*liked him enough to say, "Hey, let's not tell Spiva about our plans, okay?"

And then she was hit by a thought so appalling, she got as far as grabbing her phone before realizing she couldn't blurt out what really was an unfounded suspicion. But she felt like a mechanical toy wound tight, ready to start spinning as soon as her thumb released the key. Jittery, even by her current standards.

If Tim had grown angry because Mandy refused him…how would he feel about Jordan Torgerson's call? The one where she told him to quit claiming she was his girlfriend.

The first thing Rebecca had said was, "Bet that annoyed him."

No, no. Mandy was one thing. He might have always believed she'd come back, that she was his for the asking. That made her different. He'd presumably suffered other rejections in the intervening years. Jordan's wouldn't be the first, and none of the others had driven him to homicidal fury.

Except…with her petite build, blonde hair and blue eyes, Jordan looked like Mandy. And her phone call sounded as if it had been unnecessarily scathing.

Picturing how the hysterical young woman would handle even a gentle suggestion that she be extra careful, Rebecca winced. That suggestion had to be made anyway. She just had to figure out how to do it without mentioning Tim Spiva by name.

And first thing in the morning, she'd run a background check on Tim before she started working the phones again, trying to find a witness who'd seen him late enough Friday night to let him off the hook.

*****

Rebecca had been on the phone all morning at her desk in the detective bullpen.

Will might not be able to make out what she was saying, but her warm, rich voice lit up every one of his synapses anyway. Concentrating on anything else had been an ongoing battle since she made her first call. By the time she finally rose from behind her desk and strode to Will's office, he was torn between slamming his door, backing her against a wall and kissing her until neither of them could remember their own names, or finding an excuse to yell at her.

She stopped in the doorway, all but vibrating with energy. "Lieutenant?"

He turned his desk chair as if just noticing her. "Detective."

It appeared she'd tried for gender-neutral garb this morning, without realizing she couldn't achieve that even wearing a Tyvek suit. The black slacks weren't form-fitting, he'd give her that, but draped nicely, while the crisp, button-up white blouse hugged her breasts and followed the curve of her waist. She'd pulled her sleek dark hair straight back into a knot at her nape, too, but the severe style only enhanced her delicate features and the perfect oval of her face.

"Come on in," he said.

She did, and sat down facing him, her expression odd. Will was painfully aware that any of the other detectives could glance their way at any time.

He cleared any huskiness from his throat. "You've found something new?"

"It's...more what I *haven't* found." She told him her reasoning of the night before, and said she had reached a dozen of Mandy and Tim's friends from the party. "I didn't want them to know my interest is in Tim, so I asked whether they'd seen a number of people later in the evening."

His brain finally clicked into gear. "Nobody saw Spiva after Mandy left."

"Nobody I've yet spoken to," she admitted. "And I may be totally off base, but—"

When she didn't finish, he said, "We can't get a warrant or make an arrest based on nothing but a gut feeling, but any half-decent investigator listens to his instincts. What do you know about him?"

The background check hadn't told her anything new. He'd had two speeding tickets, one when he was eighteen, the other a year ago. They were his sole contact with law enforcement. There'd been a string of jobs, which might hint at instability but wasn't all that unusual for a guy his age trying to find his niche.

Nodding when she finished with an unhappy shrug, Will asked, "What do you want to do next?"

"Talk to him again. Lean on him."

He nodded encouragement, able to tell she wasn't done.

"I'd like to tell Jordan Torgerson to take a vacation somewhere far from Cape Trouble."

His eyebrows rose. "Because he's interested in her?"

"Because she rejected him, and I suspect did it brutally." She told him what the petulant Ms. Torgerson had said about her phone call to Spiva, making Will inwardly cringe. Yeah, that would hit a guy where it hurt. "And she looks a lot like Mandy," Rebecca added. "Not their faces so much, but coloring, and they're similar body types." She wrinkled her nose. "Bad choice of words."

Rebecca had good reason to be devastated if and when the missing woman's body was found. Shaking off that thought, he said, "Even if you're right about Spiva, this is likely the first time he's done anything like this."

"Unless he drove to Portland or something. I didn't find anything searching Burris and neighboring counties that had enough in common with Mandy's disappearance to suggest a common perpetrator."

Will nodded. He had suggested that kind of search early on and found she'd already done it.

"Again," he said, "if Spiva did this, it's likely Mandy who triggered his rage. He might have been okay until she came back to town with some other man's kid. Even then he might have convinced himself he loved her enough to accept the kid. Think how grateful she'd be, how ready to fall into his arms."

"Only, she wasn't," Rebecca murmured. "She didn't."

"Right. But he's still coming to terms with what he did. Figuring out how to blame Mandy instead of himself. How likely is it that he'd move on another woman, one who pissed him off, sure, but doesn't actually mean that much to him?"

"Unless Jordan's resemblance to Mandy coupled with another rejection made him think he has to kill Mandy again."

"Assuming he has once already."

"Do you really think she's alive?"

No, he didn't. But that, too, was a gut feeling. "You've seen the cases where an abducted woman is held for weeks, months, even years." When Rebecca's lips parted, he raised a hand. "And we still can't rule out the possibility that she *chose* to disappear."

If Rebecca wanted to argue, she thought better of it. Instead, she nibbled on her lower lip. "If Tim did rape and kill her, what if he discovered he *enjoyed* it?"

Will's jaw muscles flexed. "Then we have to stop him before he grabs another woman."

His phone rang and he glanced at the number. "Hold the thought. It's the garage."

After he identified himself, the mechanic said, "Finally got to the Tahoe, and I don't have good news. The drain cap was still in place. The oil pan was punctured several times, best guess by a screwdriver. The oil ran out slowly enough to allow Detective Walker to drive several miles."

Rebecca never took her eyes off him.

"How long would it have taken to do the damage?" he asked, meeting her gaze with one that must be giving away his fury, judging by her widening eyes.

"Oh, no more than a minute or two for someone who knew what he was doing. I'd say this was someone who knows cars, except you can find out anything online these days. Pictures of the parts of the engine, even suggestions on how to commit sabotage." More briskly, he said, "We need to replace the engine. If you speak to Detective Walker—"

"She's sitting here right now."

"Tell her we're looking at a couple of weeks."

"I will. Thank you," Will remembered to say. He set down the phone very carefully.

"Why are you looking at me like that?" Rebecca exclaimed.

"Yesterday's breakdown?" he growled. "It was sabotage. Someone stabbed a few holes in the oil pan. Calculated damn well how far you'd get before the engine seized up."

She was suddenly breathing faster. "But...when? Who?"

"Where did you stop for gas?"

When she told him, he rubbed his chin. "They might have a camera. Did you ever take your eyes off the Tahoe?"

"Yes, I used the restroom. After I got gas, I moved it to a parking space before I went in." She hesitated. "Someone else arrived behind me. The attendant probably would have had his back turned after that."

"Anyone inside?"

"I'm not sure the clerk would have noticed a naked woman jumping up and down right outside the glass doors. He was bored, probably playing a game on his phone. Barely glanced at me when I paid for a candy bar."

Will squeezed the back of his neck. "Gas stations are generally well-lit, though. And given that there's always someone out there to pump the gas..."

"He couldn't have counted on being unseen. Especially at around five. If not for the rain, there'd have been a lineup at the pumps. That place has the lowest price in town. As it was...it's barely possible someone could have managed."

"You didn't stop anywhere else after that?"

She shook her head.

"Exactly where does the Torgerson woman live?"

"That would...make more sense. The parking lot wasn't well lit, and with the heavy rain I didn't see anyone but a guy who held the door for me. Total stranger who looked about eighteen," she added. "I dashed in, dashed out."

"He'd have had to do it pretty close to your departure, or you'd have run out of oil a lot sooner." Will couldn't believe they were calmly discussing this. He didn't feel calm. She looked as cool as a marble statue, and about the same color, too. He forced himself to say, "Crandall?"

"I don't see how. He was there before me, and still there when I left."

"But he could have followed you to the gas station."

"I guess so."

"Unless he was already following you, how would Spiva have known where to find you?"

Her forehead puckered. "I'll have to ask Jordan, but…I had the impression she'd just called Tim. She was anxious about talking to me, and thought it was his fault that I had any interest in her. She might have told him when our appointment was."

"We need to find out if the gas station and the apartment complex have cameras."

His voice was guttural enough, she was eyeing him warily.

"Um…what about the deputy who was ambushed? Have you heard any more about that? This seems…I don't know, more elaborate, but it could conceivably be the same guy."

"No. I'll ask for an update. But that deputy was lured to the ambush site. In your case, the perp would have had to notice by chance that your unmarked vehicle was in fact a police car."

"It's not that hard to tell," she said, with enough spirit he suspected she'd rather have been the impulse target of a random nutcase who hated police in general instead of someone after her in particular.

"In the driving rain? And if he attacked a deputy in Tillamook County, what's he doing here? And how could he know where you were going?" he said inexorably. "If you were with Cape Trouble PD, you'd have stayed in town and he'd never have gotten you alone."

He hadn't realized how stiff she'd been until her shoulders sagged a little.

"But Tim would have guessed that Jordan was my last interview, and that I'd probably be returning to North Fork. Although I almost didn't."

"What?"

"I thought about just heading north, going straight home."

"With it getting dark and the heavy rainfall, that might have worked for him, too."

"But if it's Tim, why *me*? If I weren't investigating, someone else would be."

"Because you're a woman?" And a beautiful one, at that. "It's remotely possible someone else has recently become obsessed with you."

She fought back. "What are the odds of that?"

He was sure as hell obsessed, but this wasn't the time to say so. "Not good, but what about all those hang-ups the last time you worked the crisis line?"

"Stalking a *cop*? It doesn't make sense," she objected. She clearly wanted him to agree.

"This kind of crime never makes sense to a sane human being."

"No." She closed her eyes for a moment, then fixed a gaze of such trust on him that his heart gave a hard squeeze. "What do we do next?"

At least she'd said *we*. He didn't want to let her out of his sight now that last night's fears had been confirmed.

"Talk to Ms. Torgerson. Then Crandall," he said. "Finish with Spiva."

"Why Carson?"

"Mandy might have said more to him than he's told us. Ditto Jordan. I'm especially interested in how much Crandall saw of the car behind you."

Rebecca's head bobbed. Her composure couldn't possibly go more than skin deep. "I should have already followed up with him," she agreed. "Jordan is probably at work."

"Why don't you call and find out, preferably without letting her know we're coming?"

"Yes, okay."

"Let me finish what I was working on, and we'll go."

Rebecca left his office looking a lot more subdued than when she entered it. His mood had done a one-eighty, too. Fear that she had become the focus of a crazy with rape and murder on his mind pushed everything else he felt onto the back burner. She didn't look anything like Mandy Shaw…but Rebecca was far more powerful, even threatening. Taking her down…that might sound like a real high to the kind of man who preyed on women.

*****

"I think she felt sorry for him." Carson Crandall stirred the huge pot of chili simmering on the stove in the firehouse. He'd seemed mildly surprised to see Rebecca and Will, but unperturbed, only warning that he would have to ditch them if a call came in.

When they first arrived, she'd asked about his background, learning that he'd started as a firefighter before training first to become an EMT and then qualify as a paramedic. At twenty-eight, he was older than she'd realized.

Having set the spoon down, he lounged against the counter, arms crossed. His expression was troubled. "I really liked Mandy, but we didn't do that much talking. Mostly, we had fun together, when she could get away. Between work and being a parent, that wasn't often. She saw other friends when I wasn't around, which was fine by me. Some of them seemed…" He grimaced. "Kind of young, I guess. Mandy was actually more mature than most of the others, but not that interested in looking for new friends, either."

"I take it your relationship with her wasn't likely to have gone anywhere."

He shook his head. "It was pretty casual."

"Would she have ended up back with Tim if you were out of the picture?" Rebecca asked.

She and Will had accepted cups of coffee from the apparently ever-brewing pot. They sat on the same side of the long table that separated the kitchen area from a motley collection of sofas and chairs facing a TV. She was very conscious that she brushed his upper arm every time she shifted on the bench.

At the moment, the three of them had the space to themselves. The firefighters were washing their truck, having returned from a call just before she and Will showed up. Carson had asked his partner to give them a few minutes of privacy. A young woman with a mop of dark curls, she'd cheerfully agreed, wrapped herself around the pole and slid out of sight.

In response to her question now, Carson shook his head without hesitation. "No, she told me once that she'd gotten to feeling trapped with him in high school. Didn't want to hurt his feelings by breaking up, and he didn't seem to notice she wasn't as into him as he was into her. College was the perfect escape."

Rebecca nodded her understanding. Will listened, expression impassive. Unlike Tim and some of the other people they'd interviewed together, however, Carson didn't make the mistake of forgetting Will was there. He spoke to both of them.

"She felt really uncomfortable when he hinted that he'd like them to get back together."

"Any insight into Jordan?" she asked. "Are you friends?"

"I wouldn't have said so." He shrugged. "We'd talked a few times, that's all. Truthfully, I don't think she much liked Mandy. She might have wanted to, uh..."

"Poach on Mandy's territory?"

"Something like that," he said, looking embarrassed. "Wouldn't have gotten her anywhere. There's a girl who'd be way more work than I want to take on. But yesterday, she sounded scared, and I thought why not."

Carson Crandall might enjoy an adrenaline high, might not be ready to settle down with one woman, but he would do what he could for anyone. He'd found the right profession, Rebecca thought.

She listened while Will grilled him about the vehicle behind hers after the breakdown, but Carson hadn't seen any more than she had.

She was about to thank him and swing a leg over the bench when Will stopped her with a hand on her thigh.

"I haven't had any luck finding the people you climbed with last Friday," Will said. "It's probably not important, but—"

"Oh, hey!" Carson's expression brightened. "I meant to let you know. I'd forgotten that they suggested I join them climbing Mount Rainier and one of the guys gave me his number. When I got around to cleaning out my pack, I found it." He pushed away from the counter to pull his wallet from a back pocket. A minute later, he found a scrap of paper he handed to Will. "Here it is."

"Do you want to copy it?" Will asked.

Carson grinned. "Already did."

"Very good. Thank you."

She and Will left just as firefighters started filtering upstairs, asking if the chili was done.

"Jordan? Or Tim?" he asked, when they reached the car.

"Tim, I think. From what Carson said, it's unlikely Mandy would have confided in Jordan. And we might have a better idea what to say to her after we talk to Tim."

"I agree. Unless she's here in Cape Trouble?"

"No, she should be at work in North Fork, too."

He had driven, which had saved the time it would have taken Rebecca to sign out a replacement vehicle. The reminder that she *needed* one... Not something she wanted to think about now.

Tonight? When she was alone at her little cabin in the woods?

She could stay with her father for a few days. He wouldn't mind. The down side, along with the lengthy commute, was that she'd have to explain why she didn't want to go home, and that would scare him. Bad enough that *she* was scared.

When Will started the car and cranked up the heat, she said, "Let me call the decking place and make sure Tim is working today before we make the drive."

He wasn't. The owner said he'd let Tim go. When she identified herself and asked why, he said, "Nothing to do with him. Just not much work to be done at this time of year. I shouldn't have taken him on at all, but I had a spate of late jobs and he had some construction experience. He knew the odds were I'd have to lay him off."

"Did he work yesterday?" she asked.

"No, I called yesterday morning to tell him not to come in."

Will had been watching her as she talked. When she stowed her phone at her waist, he said, "Fired?"

"Laid off. No work." She made a face at the drizzle showing in droplets on the windshield. "What a surprise."

"Then we try him at home."

"I don't have to give you directions this time."

"No." After backing out, he glanced at her. "How are the Shaws holding up?"

"Not well." She liked that he had asked, however gruff his voice. "Their son flew home. I'm sure his professors understand.

Mostly, I think it's the little girl who gives them reason to get up in the morning."

Will nodded acknowledgement.

Rebecca found herself remembering the first time her father, sounding broken, had said she was all that kept him going. Stomach tightening, all she could think was how terrified she'd been. Too young to hear anything like that. Because what if one day she *wasn't* enough?

We made it, she reminded herself. If she let herself get sucked into the past, lose her emotional stability, she couldn't do her job. Finding Mandy had become all-important.

So she took advantage of Will's silence and brooded on what to say to Tim, even tried to script how she'd start the interview. But thinking coolly became an increasing struggle, and she finally identified the reason.

The sensation gripping her chest wasn't so different from the dread she felt every night on her way home. Which was ridiculous. She wasn't *afraid* of Tim Spiva. She was the one in control. A cop, armed. Remember?

What she really feared was screwing up. The other interviews had been straightforward. This one would be anything but – and was out of her realm of experience.

She could ask Will to take over, except maybe this was like losing your virginity. Something you had to do once. Besides, Tim was fascinated by her, and she ought to be able to use that to compel him to say things he never would to a man.

All the same…she was really glad Will was with her. He'd stop her if she went too off-course, and his very presence made her feel safe.

Too bad she couldn't take him home with her.

Who says I can't?

Sneaking a sidelong look, she wondered what he'd say if she asked.

CHAPTER TEN

"I probably do know Mandy better than anyone else," Tim Spiva agreed. If he'd been a puppy, his tail would have been whipping and his body squirming with his eagerness to please Rebecca. "Even her parents. You know how it is. Nobody tells their parents everything."

He was a strange one, all right.

Will had chosen a seat off to the side, deliberately taking himself out of the picture. *Setting Rebecca up?*

No, damn it, analyzing how the guy interacted with her.

From the minute Spiva opened the door to them, he'd been riveted on Rebecca. Will had to fight with himself to let it happen. Rebecca would be rightly angry if he butted in. His practice was to let his detectives have free rein unless they screwed up. Rebecca couldn't be any exception, even if he wanted to smash the little creep's teeth down his throat.

"I do know how it is," she agreed, but with a deliberate coolness that had to annoy Spiva. "Given the years she was away, though…" She trailed off, her voice doubt-laden.

"We stayed friends, you know," he assured her. "We'd text, call each other. I knew things sucked with Brian." He said the name with loathing. "She wouldn't have stayed with him if she hadn't gotten pregnant. He probably did it on purpose. Stabbed holes in the condoms or something."

Stabbed was not the word most people would use to describe pricking tiny holes in thin latex.

Rebecca countered, "He says he didn't want her to get pregnant, that she did it on purpose to have a hold on him."

Spiva jumped to his feet, his face flushing with anger, his fingers balling into fists. "That's a lie! She'd never do that!"

Will readied himself to move fast, but then the guy spread his fingers with what appeared to be a deliberate effort.

"Uh, sorry." His face contorted with chagrin. "That guy just makes me so mad."

"I imagine you encouraged her to leave Brian," Rebecca said, sounding sympathetic.

"Sure. Everyone who cared about her probably did."

Will couldn't argue with that. He felt sure Mandy's parents had urged her a few hundred times to come home, where they thought she'd be safe. The irony had to be killing them now.

"She's been home something like six months, right?" Rebecca asked.

"Right." His head bobbed, his expression guileless.

"I have the impression you'd have liked to get back together with her."

Some squirming went on. "Yeah, but... You know. I mean, we could still be friends."

"Were you?" The question came out sharp.

The flare of rage came and went so fast, Will wouldn't have seen it if he hadn't been watching closely. Mini-flashes of anger, Rebecca had said. The next instant, Spiva looked like a kicked puppy.

"Well, *I* thought so. We did talk sometimes, but she went and got involved with another guy who didn't deserve her. I couldn't figure it out."

"Why is it you think Carson didn't deserve her?" Rebecca leaned forward slightly and her voice encouraged confidences.

"All they did was his shit," Spiva sneered. "Anything she wanted to do, he was too busy. Like Friday night, where was *he*?"

"You're the one who suggested he might have showed up at the party late."

The ingenuous expression returned. "Yeah, but if he did..." Simulated dismay widened his eyes. "That might mean *he* did something to her. Like, hurt her."

Instead of you? Will thought. There was something disturbing about the way Spiva said *he*, as if he were differentiating Carson from...himself?

"We don't know for sure yet that anybody did hurt her," Rebecca said, soothing.

"Guess you won't know until you find her, huh?"

Christ, was that a taunt? No way to prove it, but...

Rebecca froze, so still, she might have quit breathing. Her eyes never left that face, arranged to look boyish. "We might find other evidence," she murmured.

"What's that mean?" he demanded.

"You know I can't reveal details of the investigation, Tim." She studied him long enough to have Spiva twitching. "You can help me with one thing, though."

"Really?" He sat forward. Pavlov's dog. "Me?"

"Yes, we're trying to nail down where everyone was *after* Mandy left." She clicked her pen and poised it over a spiral notebook. "You can help by telling me who you saw when you went back into the house."

His excitement waned fast. "Oh. Wow. Ah... I was kind of wasted by then."

"You offered to drive Mandy home even though you were drunk?" Rebecca managed to infuse the question with disappointment.

"I mean, not that bad. Just...I kind of had a hangover the next day. Sucked, when I had to go to work."

"I hear you lost your job."

Anger tightened his features. "How did you hear?"

"I called looking for you."

"That guy's an asshole! I'm good. Better than those worthless pieces of shit he kept on." Calm replaced rage with startling suddenness. "But I don't need that job. It paid like crap anyway."

"Back to the party," she said briskly.

"Oh. Well, I'm trying to think. It seems like some new people showed up. Nobody I really knew. That's why I didn't stay long. I mean, once Mandy and Jordan were both gone..." He shrugged.

"How much longer did you stay?"

He shrugged. "Like fifteen minutes? Half an hour? I don't know. I had another beer, I remember that."

"Did you see Scott Cardenas?"

One person they'd confirmed was still there.

His brows wrinkled. "Yeah, I think so, but not to talk to. And Jen. I'm pretty sure I saw her." He went on. He was pretty sure he'd seen half a dozen people, but he hadn't actually *talked* to any of them. "You know, it was loud in there."

"I see." Rebecca scrutinized him for long enough to have his eyes narrowing. Then she glanced deliberately around the living room. "When will your parents be back, Tim?"

"They only left two weeks ago. They stay in Arizona all winter."

"Even for Christmas?" She sounded sympathetic. "Or do you plan to fly down there for the holidays?"

"Yeah. Probably. If I can afford to."

"They don't mind you living here? I'm assuming they're not expecting you to pay rent."

"Rent? My parents?"

There's a concept, Will thought drily.

"Why would they?" Spiva said. "Otherwise the house would be empty, which isn't so good."

"I seem to remember people here in Bow Lake keeping an eye on each other's houses." She slid that in like a stiletto. "Not much would have gotten by our neighbors."

His beefy hands clenched on the arms of the easy chair he occupied. "Nobody had better be watching *me*," he snapped.

"Really?" Rebecca did mildly puzzled well. "Don't you find it comforting to know people are watching out for you?"

He glared at her. "I don't like nosy people."

"And here I am, being nosy." She tipped her head to one side. "Do you not like me, Tim?"

He didn't blink in so long, Will wished he could see his pupils. Would they be reptilian?

"I don't like it when you act like you think *I* did something wrong," he said finally. "But I know you have to talk to everyone. And I want to help. I'll bet everybody says that, but they probably don't all mean it."

"Really?"

"A couple of people have complained because you keep coming back. Or they don't know why you were talking to them at all."

"Like Jordan?" she suggested.

"She was really freaked. She's kind of a little princess. You know?"

"Not really your type after all, huh?"

"I wouldn't want to waste a lot of time on her," he agreed, almost as if he were amused.

Rebecca let the silence grow just long enough to become awkward before she thanked him for talking to them and said, "Say hi to your parents for me. Tell them to think about us, stuck in the rain. Oh, and to wear plenty of sunscreen."

"Oh, sure." Spiva leaped to his feet, as eager as ever – although the way he let his gaze travel slowly over Rebecca as she stood up wasn't nearly as boyish as he was playing.

Will rose, too, and took a couple of steps closer, drawing Spiva's suddenly alarmed attention. Maybe he didn't like being loomed over; Will had a good five inches on him.

"Spiva," Will said with a dismissive nod. When Rebecca turned toward the front door, he rested his hand on her lower back in a way any other man would recognize as proprietary. Out of the corner of his eye, he saw Tim Spiva's reaction. He did not like seeing Will touching Rebecca. No, he didn't.

But he choked out a goodbye before closing the door behind them. Feeling sure he'd be at the window watching, Will kept his hand on her all the way to the car even though he felt as if he had a target between his shoulder blades. He even opened the passenger door for Rebecca, earning an astonished look from her.

Circling to the driver's side, he studied the house. No sign they were being watched, but his gut said Spiva was there somewhere, blinds parted just enough.

The brief interlude also allowed him to get a grip on emotions he shouldn't feel for a woman who worked for him. A woman he was currently partnering in what might well end up a murder investigation.

Right this second, he wasn't sure he cared. All he knew was that he wanted to order Rebecca to stay away from Tim Spiva.

And that would go so well.

*****

Rebecca watched as Will got in, buckled his belt and fired up the engine. Then he didn't move, just gazed straight ahead at the garage door. His big body looked tense, his expression brooding.

"What do you think?" she asked finally, bracing herself for a critique.

A storm brewed in eyes that had never looked darker. "I think he's as crazy as anyone I've ever met. He was trying to play us, but he couldn't keep it together when he thought you weren't convinced...or when you dented his ego."

Thankful he wasn't dismissing her impression of Tim, she said, "I noticed that. Odd duck is one way to describe him."

"I'd have said sociopath."

"We don't know." She could just see around the corner of the garage to a slice of the front window. Was Tim wondering why they hadn't left? "He could just be mad because we seem to doubt how much he cares about Mandy."

Will grunted. "He's obsessed with you."

A shiver traveled down her spine. "He might have a...a crush on me. Older woman he thinks is sexy."

"Don't take this lightly," Will growled. "It isn't that Torgerson woman he's thinking about. It's *you*. And he was off yesterday."

Rebecca gripped the seatbelt, hoping he couldn't see how tightly. "He drives a Jeep, and I'm sure that was a car behind me."

Powerful and intensely male, Will's hands flexed on the steering wheel, drawing her unwilling attention.

"What do you want to bet he has access to at least one of his parents' vehicles?"

Parents' vehicles. It took her a second to think about what he'd just said. "Did you see the concrete pad on the side of the house? It's covered."

"RV."

"I'll bet."

"Damn, I'd like to get a look in that garage."

"It would be bad if he saw you. And it's not like we can't check to see what's registered to his parents."

He grumbled but finally reached for the gear shift and backed the car out of the long driveway. "You can do it now, if you want, or wait until we get back to the station."

"He could have brought her here." Rebecca couldn't tear her gaze from the house. "Driven right into the garage." She swallowed. "She could still be there."

"Where's the brother?"

"Tim's brother? Um, Seattle, I think Tim said. Evan went to the U of O and must have graduated this spring. I'm pretty sure they were three years apart. Anyway, Tim said he got involved with a girl who is from Seattle, and he followed her there."

"It might be interesting to talk to this Evan. Get his take on his brother."

"Should I try?" That came out sounding timid. She cleared her throat. "I mean, what if he turns right around and tells Tim I was asking about him?"

"So what? I'm pretty sure he has the idea you might be just a little suspicious of him."

"The thing that bothered me most was when he said I won't know whether anyone hurt Mandy until I find her." Bothered? It had given her the creeps. "He almost seemed to think that was funny."

The steering wheel creaked. "He was taunting you."

Her initial excitement because she might have rattled Tim had faded. "And he might just be strange."

Aware the car was no longer moving, Rebecca realized they were at the stop sign facing the highway. "Are we going to talk to Jordan?"

"We are, but I want to see her apartment complex first."

"Really?" When he just stared at her, she gave him directions and waited until he took a left before asking why.

"If you remember where you parked, we might see an oil slick."

"Oh." Her stomach didn't like the reminder.

"As long as we're here, we can ask whether there are any cameras aimed at the lot, too."

Rebecca said defensively, "I was going to call."

He didn't say, *When?*

"It was getting dark, and the rain was coming down really hard. Even if a camera was pointed straight at my Tahoe, I doubt it'll show a thing."

"Can't hurt to look," Will said, almost mildly. Which didn't fool her.

Her thoughts reverted to the interview. "We don't have a single grain of evidence tying Tim to Mandy's disappearance. If only somebody had *seen* them leave."

"Let's find out what he was driving that evening. Somebody might have noticed the car, even if they didn't see a passenger or who was driving it."

"That's true." Rebecca straightened, energized again before she deflated. "I should have thought of that."

"You hadn't identified him as a suspect."

Her thoughts had moved on. "He wouldn't have let us in the house today if Mandy was there, alive."

"He could have had her trussed upstairs in one of the bedrooms." He paused. "There's no basement, is there?"

"Not that I ever saw, and I think I would have. I spent a lot of time there." No, she remembered seeing one of those openings from the outside allowing access to a crawl space.

If a decomposing body was in the house, Tim especially wouldn't have opened the door to them, she thought. If he'd killed Mandy, where had he dumped the body? Or had he buried it so deep, he was confident they'd never find it?

Or was she barking up the wrong tree?

"She still could have been grabbed at the highway, just because she was dumb enough to be out there alone in the middle of the night."

"That is a possibility, but one you have no way to pursue. Go with your gut, Rebecca." Will sounded grim. "Mine says you're right."

She managed a nod. "Left past Safeway."

When he turned in, she directed him to the area where she had parked yesterday afternoon. Despite the drizzle, as soon as they got out she saw the shimmer of an oil slick.

Will toed it with his boot. "Now we know. He had to have done this right before you came out or you'd have lost a lot more oil than this."

"Look. There's sort of a trail."

"Shit."

Chagrined, she said, "I should have noticed when I was at the gas station."

"Did you get out while the gas was being pumped?"

Rebecca shook her head. "Not then. After I got gas, I moved to a parking spot before I ran into the store. And, honestly, I barely glanced back."

"The attendant should have noticed."

"Except his raincoat had a hood, and a car was already pulling in on the other side of the pumps. Especially with the rain, it could have been quite a while later that he saw oil. I hope he saw it," she added. "Don't they dump sand on it, or something like that?"

"The gas station hasn't blown up," Will said tersely, and stalked around the building until he was sure there were no cameras. He was swearing when he returned. "Even dummy cameras might give a thief or rapist pause. How many single women do you suppose live in this complex?"

Of course she had no answer. She managed to mostly keep her mouth shut during the return trip to North Fork.

Jordan worked as a stylist at a hair salon that was new in town and looked to be aimed at a young clientele. The name 'Jazzy Cuts' was done in a swirly script, neon green against a color-streaked black background. As with most salons, right inside was a waiting area along with a display of hair products. The three stylists currently were all twenty-something, two with spiky, heavily gelled hair and multiple piercings. Jordan, who saw them immediately, had pulled her shoulder length blonde hair into a side ponytail that swayed as she swept up clipped hair from the floor around her chair.

Her alarmed gaze moved from Rebecca to Will, dropping to take in the gun and badge he wore at his waist before returning to Rebecca.

"You!" she burst out, ensuring that the other two stylists and their customers all turned to stare.

Rebecca smiled. "Sorry to interrupt you at work. I just need a quick word."

"Jordan? Are you all right?" one of the other stylists asked.

"I...sure. You know about Mandy Shaw disappearing. The police are still looking for her."

The weight she put on 'still' suggested the police were incompetent, but Rebecca let it go. Conscious of the audience, she said, "Why don't we step outside?"

"We have a break room."

"That's fine."

With Jordan less petulant, Rebecca became conscious of how delicate and pretty she was. No more than five foot three, which meant Rebecca, at five foot eight, towered over her. Jordan was the kind of woman who made most other women feel like whales.

She turned to face them as Will closed the door. "So?"

Rebecca took a moment. How to say this without pointing a finger at Tim?

"Are you involved with anyone right now, Jordan?"

"Not really. And what's *that* got to do with Mandy?"

"I suggest you stay in groups when you go out until we've identified Mandy's assailant." Seeing the flutter of lashes, she translated, "Figured out what happened to her. Made sure it wasn't one of the guys she knew who kidnapped her."

Jordan's eyes got bigger and bigger. Rebecca stole a look to see Will studying the girl with a clinical expression that would offend Jordan if she noticed.

"But...why *me*?"

Apparently, only bluntness would do. "Because you look enough like Mandy to draw attention from the same man."

Jordan let out a cry and took a step back. "You think it's someone I *know*?"

Rebecca inclined her head. "That is a possibility."

"Oh, my God." Her eyes darted around the small room with a microwave, table and chairs. "I don't even know what to do."

"Just be careful. Stick with girlfriends. Don't go out with any man for now. Don't let yourself be alone with a man, even one you consider a friend. Don't open your door without knowing who is on the other side. Take a look around when you walk out to your car from the apartment. Here, make sure one of your co-workers keeps an eye on you until you're locked in your car."

"Use common sense." His usual brusque self, Will must have lost patience.

"Oh God, oh God, oh God."

Rebecca sighed. "Jordan, there's no need to panic. All I'm suggesting is caution. We have no real reason to think you'd be a target. I'll also warn other petite, blue-eyed blondes in your circle." Were there any? she asked herself belatedly.

They escaped as soon as Jordan pulled herself together. The moment they were outside, Will exclaimed, "Good God!"

She felt bad for laughing until he caught her eye and grinned.

"Now you know why Carson was desperate to get away from her."

"She'd strain the patience of a saint," he muttered.

Rebecca chuckled again, but it didn't take long for her to sober. "I suppose we should go back to the station. I'll find out what vehicles Tim's parents own, and then...call some of the same people yet again, asking about the car instead of Tim."

"While you're doing that, I'll locate the brother," Will said. "Be interesting to find out how close they are."

"Okay." She offered a twisted smile. "Don't suppose you'd make a quick stop at a deli."

He started the car. "Took the words out of my mouth."

*****

Late in the day, Will waved Rebecca into his office. She walked in as he went back behind his desk and said, "Evan, I'm putting you on speaker. Detective Walker just joined me." He set his phone on the desk between them.

"Hey, Evan. Rebecca here. I was your babysitter, longer ago than I want to remember."

"And you're a *cop* now?"

"Yep. What about you? I hear you graduated from the U of O."

"Mathematics." There was a smile in the deep voice she had trouble imagining coming from little Evan Spiva, junior butthead. "I'm taking a year off before I go for my Ph.D. I'm working for a software company right now, though, so you never know. Maybe I'll get a brilliant idea for a startup and never bother going back to school."

She laughed. "Good luck with that."

"Lieutenant Wilcynski said you want to ask me about Tim," he said, sounding cautious now.

"Yes. I know this is really awkward for you. Did the lieutenant or your brother tell you about Mandy Shaw's disappearance?"

"The lieutenant did. I...don't really talk to Tim."

Her eyes met Will's. "Your brother was the last person to see Mandy. Because of that, I've spoken to him a couple times now. I'm getting the feeling he harbors some anger at her. I know he was the one to break up with her—"

"Only because she refused to stay around and said she was going to college. He thought breaking it off would make her back down."

"But it didn't."

"No, he was really upset."

"When he heard she was pregnant?"

Silence. "I feel really weird talking about him like this."

"Evan, let me put it this way. Mandy's father described Tim as an odd duck. I've gotten some...disturbing vibes from him. I guess what I'm hoping is that you'll help us understand Tim. Is he just socially awkward? Maybe unaware how people are responding to him? Or has he exhibited more worrisome behavior in the past?"

"He's... Man!" All they heard was breathing for a minute, then a heavy exhalation. "I'd tell you to talk to my parents, except they're kind of in denial about him."

"They did apparently feel okay with having him in the house. I'm assuming he has access to any cars they left behind, too."

"Yeah. I don't think he'd burn the house down or anything. But...I don't know. I used to be kind of scared of him. Not when we were young, like when you were around. It was later he got so intense. Weird about shit. Kind of...paranoid, I guess. Sure people were watching him when I could tell they didn't care about him. Once he thought I'd been in his room and he flipped out. Dad calmed him down, but later I found some stuff in my bedroom destroyed. The way he glared at me when Dad confronted him..." He went quiet again.

"So he had a temper he couldn't control."

A long pause ensured before Evan said, "That's the thing. He could. He'd...hide it. But that didn't mean he wasn't still angry."

She asked a few more questions. He became increasingly reluctant. At last Rebecca said, "Let me give you my phone number and email address. I have a bad feeling about what's happened to Mandy. If you can tell us anything else about Tim, please get in touch with me. It could really help."

He mumbled, "Yeah, okay," got a pen and presumably wrote down what she told him. "I'll think about it," he said, and did give her his dad's cell phone number.

When Will disconnected, they looked at each other again. The lines in Will's face had deepened. "Whatever he didn't want to tell us is bad."

She nodded, almost willing to bet Evan had seen his brother kill a neighbor's pet...or their own. Parents in denial might still find a reason to excuse that. Or they put him in counseling and believed him to be 'fixed'.

"Cars?" Will asked.

"Oh...a Ford Taurus, dark gray, and a blue Honda Civic."

"Either trigger anything?"

"I...think the Civic is too small. Plus, if they towed a car behind the RV to use while they're down there, it was probably the Civic." She took a deep breath. "It could have been a Taurus. You know Carson's best guess was a good-size sedan, too."

He scowled. "Rebecca..." Then he clamped down on whatever he'd been about to say, his glance toward the door hunted.

She jumped up. "I'll get back to my calls. Speaking of... Do you want me to call the parents, or will you?"

"I'll do that." He nodded dismissal, expression now closed. His "Talk to me before you leave" was abrupt.

She nodded and escaped, unable to look back to see if he watched her go or not.

CHAPTER ELEVEN

Late the next day, Will lounged in his office doorway, taking perverse pleasure in how industrious his detectives suddenly became. Only two were immune to his presence: Holbeck, who sat tipped back in his chair, his feet on his desk, seemingly doing nothing but staring into space, and Rebecca, who concentrated fiercely on a laptop open on her desk in front of her.

By now, Will knew how Holbeck worked. Right now, he was putting puzzle pieces together in his head instead of on paper or in the computer, as other detectives did.

Ignoring him, Will strolled between desks until he reached Rebecca's. He stopped right behind her, watching as she scrolled down what appeared to be a Facebook page belonging to... Curious, he bent forward. Tina Lynch. His gaze moved on to the multiple photos of groups of girls posing in skimpy clothing, their teeth gleaming white, their hair artfully tousled, their makeup perfect.

"Who the hell is Tina Lynch?" he asked.

Rebecca levitated and swung in her chair to look at him.

"And why are you looking at her page on the county's dime?"

Snickers came from a couple nearby detectives. She sent a glare their direction.

"Because she's my best friend," she snapped. "Why do you think?"

What he thought was that he'd been an idiot not to kiss her when he had the chance. Discover her taste, stroke a hand down her back, see arousal darkening her eyes and coloring her smooth ivory cheeks.

Getting cold feet was an unfamiliar experience for him. But, damn, he had to be sure before he made that move. This wasn't like starting something with any other woman. He needed to be serious – and to know she was, too.

"She's one of Mandy's friends," he guessed. Rebecca did not fit in with that crowd of plastic dolls.

She narrowed her eyes, but swallowed whatever irritation she felt. "Smart man."

Will reached for a chair behind a vacant desk and rolled it over beside hers, sitting so he could see the monitor. That put him so close to Rebecca, his knee touched her thigh and he could see the subtle lift and fall of her breasts when she breathed, the creamy skin on her throat and the tiny tendrils of dark hair escaping a bun.

He gritted his teeth and forced his attention back to the Facebook page. "Learn anything?"

"I'm sorry to say, Mandy is the first really discreet Facebook user I've seen in forever." Rebecca paged back, then scrolled down slowly so he could skim the missing woman's postings. "No bitching about her job or co-workers. No political postings, nasty or otherwise, no jabs about who is sleeping with whom, no whines about her parents being controlling."

Damn. He'd shared her hope that Facebook would open a window to the interactions among Mandy's group of friends – and especially her feelings for Tim Spiva.

"Photos?" he asked.

"Pictures of Sammie, groups of friends having fun, a few of her and Carson. I went way back and found some of Brian."

"Smoldering good looks?" he joked, remembering the way Vicky Shaw had eyed him while talking about Brian.

If Rebecca remembered, too, he couldn't tell. "Yes, in a sullen way," she said. "Not many smiles there."

"You read her friends' comments?"

"Of course I did," she said, sounding disgruntled. "'So cute!!!' 'Oh, I just want to hug her!!!' Did you hear the multiple exclamation points?"

Will laughed, because he had. Catching Holbeck's surprised stare, he pulled his face back into stern lines.

Apparently oblivious, Rebecca frowned at the laptop. "I've now checked out dozens of her friends' pages. Some of *them* should have censored themselves when it came to their personal lives, but none had anything bad to say about Mandy."

"Carson? Tim?"

She shook her head. "I suspect some of her girlfriends were jealous, because I saw a lot of Carson pictures. Tim appears in a few group photos, but references to him are rare and, with one exception, there only because he was part of a group that did something together."

"Emails?"

"Not many." Rebecca shrugged. "She was twenty-three."

He grunted.

"She didn't use Twitter or any other social media site that I found. I get the feeling she was pretty wrapped up in her daughter, her job and the friends here in Cape Trouble."

"Small world," he said thoughtfully, then let himself look at her. "Okay, who was the one exception?" As if he didn't know.

"Jordan Torgerson did not use the brains God gave her."

"Maybe He screwed up and gave an extra portion to the soul before her and then had to skimp," Will muttered.

Rebecca poked him with an elbow. And, damn, there he was smiling again.

She opened Jordan's page, going down to a post that opened with, *I cannot BELIEVE Tim Spiva is telling people we have ANYTHING going!!! It's not true! It will NEVER be true! So STOP!!!!*

"She wrote that the same day I first spoke to her. Follow-up to the nasty phone call, I guess."

"What a sweetheart."

Rebecca rolled her eyes. "There's a reason Jordan doesn't appear on Mandy's page. Not once."

Will sat back with a sigh. "That kind of post could make a guy a laughingstock. Not many would take it well. Aside from the cruelty, it's just plain stupid."

Rebecca did nothing but gaze at the laptop for a minute, then she shook her head. "I hope she can learn her lesson."

Jordan Torgerson might or might not develop some sensitivity if she had the chance. Will hoped she was following their advice. If not, they might find themselves hunting for two missing women, instead of one.

"Do Crandall and Spiva have pages?" he thought to ask.

"Carson does. He uses it to post photos from climbing expeditions, surfing, hang-gliding. He's gone skydiving a few times, too. Oh, and apparently, he's close to having a pilot's license. I guess his job isn't exciting enough," she said dryly. "I can't find a page for Tim."

"Which says something."

"Yes, it does." After detaching the cord from Mandy's laptop, she closed it. "Have either of Tim's parents returned your call?" Rebecca asked. "If not, I can try them. They'd probably remember me."

"I just spoke to his father. That's what I came out to tell you." Will squeezed the taut muscles at the back of his neck. "He wouldn't admit there was a thing wrong with his son. Tim is hard working, generous, a good son. Mr. Spiva told me Tim had called to tell them about Mandy's disappearance and was distraught. Sounding pretty hostile, he assured me I'm wasting my time looking at his boy."

Her forehead creased. "Do you think he believes that?"

"Versus trying to convince himself?" At her nod, Will said, "I think he's done a damn good job of convincing himself, but still harbors a few secret fears about his kid."

"I want in that house," she snapped.

He just shook his head. They had nothing for a warrant, and she knew it.

"I need to get out of here," she said suddenly. She yanked open a drawer, took out her handbag and shoved back her chair before he could move out of the way. The chairs crashed together, but she didn't seem to notice. Jumping up and tucking the laptop under her arm, she said, "I'll see you in the morning," and started toward the bullpen door.

"Detective," he said sharply, rising to his feet.

Her body quivered with resistance, but she stopped, keeping her back to him. Will was conscious of the complete silence behind him, a rare state with several detectives present. There was no nosier bunch than cops in general and detectives in particular. Only his knowledge of the audience had him holding onto a pretense of professionalism. Which meant he now had to come up with something to say to justify stopping her.

"Think about your next step," he said. "We'll talk in the morning."

She kept going.

*****

Rebecca sat at her kitchen table, adding to her notes and going over them all, again and again, until she quit seeing her own handwriting. Instead, she saw the pictures of Mandy from her Facebook page, pretty, laughing, always hugging or kissing someone. She saw Sammie's blonde curls and blue eyes, only the eyes were accusing. *You were supposed to find my mommy.*

She let out something like a dry sob and leaned forward to rest her forehead on her arms, crossed on the table.

Next step? If only she had the slightest idea. Will *should* take her off this investigation. She'd gotten nowhere. All she'd done today was spin her wheels, asking the same people questions they'd already answered. She hadn't tripped any of them up. Mandy Shaw was likely dead by now. In a couple hours, it would be midnight, exactly six days since she had vanished off the face of the earth. One hundred and forty-four hours. Too long.

Why *hadn't* Will replaced her? Did he still believe Mandy hadn't been abducted at all, that she'd stroll home one of these days? Maybe he considered this a dry run for a *real* investigation, if he ever trusted his new detective with one.

It came to her slowly: she should take herself off the investigation. He'd been right; she was too involved. She should have detoured through Cape Trouble tonight and returned the laptop to the Shaws, but she hadn't been able to face them. Tomorrow morning was soon enough, she'd convinced herself. By then, she would find the strength to see the despair in their eyes and offer comfort.

Wasn't that what she did working the crisis line? During negotiations?

No. The knowledge was bleak, but real. No. She always started out conversations with hope. More than that, *faith* – faith that she could make a difference for this one person. Where Mandy was concerned, she'd lost not only faith, but even the more fragile hope.

And this time, when she looked at Mandy's parents, at the little girl who'd have to grow up without her mommy, Rebecca saw herself, too, and her father. She might as well be looking into a mirror. She identified too much.

Am I really ready to give up?

She was still asking herself that as she double-checked window and door locks and made her way to bed, setting her gun and phone down next to the clock. Exhaustion had her stumbling and banging her shoulder on the bathroom doorframe. Rebecca rubbed her shoulder and climbed into bed. After setting her alarm, she turned out the bedside lamp.

And there in the dark, she understood something else. Maybe, despite all her noble words and intentions, becoming a cop *had* really been about feeling in control of her own life. Mandy's disappearance served as an echo that had her wanting to cover her ears and beg for silence. Feeling a failure as a detective ripped away any illusion she'd had that she could save this young mother. She hadn't felt so helpless since she was a child.

So what?

Stiffening, she heard a voice she recognized: the woman who was tough enough to succeed as a cop. It was a part of her who'd fallen silent recently.

Why had she been making this all about her when it wasn't? It was her job to do her best to find Mandy Shaw and arrest her kidnapper. Maybe she'd fail, but, by God, she'd *do* her best.

Both mad and disgusted with herself, Rebecca refused to be a quitter. That wasn't her. She'd bet every priest and minister alive had had a crisis of faith at some time or other, and probably most cops had, too. People who never suffered the slightest self-doubt were unlikeable egotists.

No, she still had no idea where to go next with the investigation…but it was her first, and all she had to do was ask for advice. Probably that's what Will had intended to offer when she had her fit of depression and walked out on him.

Her body relaxed and sleep tugged at her. Maybe, she thought drowsily, *he* had something to do with her recent sense of having lost control. She hadn't expected him, and didn't know what to do about him. Assuming she ever had any say in it.

His face hovered before her, harsh, male, his mouth held tight, his dark eyes hooded. And yet, she'd seen possessive, hungry desire in those eyes. She moved restlessly, wanting to touch, but he wasn't here.

*****

Snapping into instant wakefulness, Rebecca lay completely still, listening. A dream? It was possible. How many times in the last year had she flashed back to the shooting? But her instincts told her otherwise. She tried to breathe quietly, in through her nose, out through her mouth.

If she didn't hear anything in another minute or two, she'd make the rounds again—

Glass tinkled. *Yes.* That was what she'd heard. A window breaking, exactly as she'd heard it the night a killer tried to get to the young woman Rebecca had been guarding.

Now she rolled off the bed in a smooth, practiced move, reaching a crouch behind it. Her hand unerringly found her gun and she flicked off the safety. She had the fleeting wish for her vest – but it hadn't protected her last time anyway. Pain stabbed where she'd been shot, as if she needed the reminder. She didn't bother reaching for her phone, not when the closest conceivable responder would be at least ten to fifteen minutes away.

She'd left her bedroom door open and saw nothing but darkness through it. Damn it, had she slept through the motion-sensitive outdoor light coming on and then going off? Or had this intruder studied how to avoid triggering it? Her eyes burned as she stared without blinking.

Pushing herself upright, she eased her way along the wall to the doorway, glad her feet were bare. As she considered her options, she felt oddly calm. Hide? Try to scare him away? Or shoot the son of a bitch?

Her Subaru was in plain sight in the carport, a strong clue that she was home. Even so, she made the reluctant decision to go with scaring. What if she shot and killed a seventeen-year-old punk looking for electronic goodies to sell? She'd feel like shit, that's what.

And yet, the way her skin crawled, she knew whoever was moving silently through her house was no kid. Rage overcame the eerie calm. She *wanted* to kill him.

"I'm a police officer!" she called. "I'm armed, and I've called for backup." Then she crouched behind the bulk of her dresser, her Sig Sauer in a two-handed grip, pointed at the doorway.

The absolute quiet had her wondering if she'd imagined the sound of glass breaking. Maybe she *had* dreamed it. With PTSD, maybe—

A floorboard squeaked. She knew exactly where it was, a couple feet from her dining room table. She never stepped there.

Sudden anger flooded her. "I would love to shoot you," she said, almost conversationally. "Please. Come on down the hall. I'm waiting."

The same board squeaked. She heard a rush of footsteps, a tinkle of glass, a thud. He'd gone back out the damn window.

*****

The sound of his phone ringing jarred Will out of a deep sleep. He was disoriented only until the second ring.

"Wilcynski."

"Will? I mean, Lieutenant?"

Rebecca. Sounding calm, but whatever she had to say at – his gaze sought the clock – 1:08 in the morning wasn't good.

"What happened?"

"I had a break-in at home. I thought you'd want to know."

"Damn straight, I want to know." He was already out of bed and reaching for the pants he'd tossed across a chair. "You're all right?"

"Yes. Fortunately, I woke up when I heard glass breaking. I yelled that I was armed and had called for back-up. He took off. I got out to the front window and saw a man running toward my driveway."

"Is it clear up your way?" he asked in surprise. Here, he'd seen how dark the night was, with clouds covering what still wasn't much better than a crescent moon.

"No, he set off my motion-sensitive floodlight. I was really tempted to go after him, but—"

"Please tell me God wasn't that short on brains when he got to *you*," Will snapped.

"Thank you for your faith in me," she shot back, surprising him.

Despite the fear, a smile tugged at one corner of his mouth. "You were saying?" he asked, before shoving his feet into low boots and bending to tie the laces.

"I'd have been out in the open and he might have been armed. So, no, I stayed snug in the house and called dispatch. A state patrol officer was closest and is heading for the base of my road, but I think my intruder is going to have time to get away."

One way in, one way out. He didn't recall a single road turning off, either, even a dead-end one. Only driveways.

"We should check Spiva's house," he said.

"That kind of gives away our suspicions."

"Don't care," he said. "I'll head over there myself. I'm probably as close as anyone." In fact, he'd already grabbed his weapon, wallet and keys and was heading out the door.

"Thank you," she said, sounding meek for the first time in the conversation.

"I'll let you know," he said, and ended the call.

The Spiva house was dark. Will rang the bell and hammered on the door. No response. He went back to his Suburban, drove down the street and made a U-turn, finally parking two houses away from Spiva's. Turning off the engine and dousing lights, he waited. The neighborhood was remarkably quiet. With tomorrow being Friday – okay, today – most people were probably sound asleep. The parents would have to work, the kids go to school.

He kept checking his watch. Ten minutes went by. Fifteen. He straightened when headlights approached, but the vehicle was a pickup and continued past.

Another ten minutes, and he decided to give up. If Spiva had been the intruder, he hadn't driven straight home from Rebecca's. Will's limited patience was eroding. He should call her, make sure she had blocked the broken window and felt secure, then go home. She wouldn't like it if he showed up on her doorstep, but that's what he was going to do.

At least he knew his way.

Last time he'd driven up to her cabin in the woods, dawn had been breaking. He remembered the deep purple shadow of the long horizon over the ocean as he turned east into the foothills of the coastal mountain range. Above the trees, luminous shades of peach and orange peeked between tall, dark evergreens. Tonight...damn, it was dark up here. Once she discovered how vulnerable she was alone, unable even to see a neighbor's house, why had she still moved back to the cabin? He couldn't believe she'd just put the shooting out of her mind.

Will growled as the SUV bounced through potholes and made himself slow down. He'd noticed the cluster of mailboxes back before the road turned to gravel. A few driveways up here were marked with house numbers, but not hers, although a bear carved out of a stump was plenty distinctive. His high-beams pierced the absolute darkness that was her driveway, but when he reached the clearing, he saw that inside and outside lights were on. Somehow, he wasn't surprised that no marked car sat outside the cabin. She'd have refused any offer to send a deputy out to take a report. Of course, *she* didn't need anyone. Even thinking that irritated him, until he remembered how much of her doubts and fears she'd let him see. What mattered was that she trusted him.

He left the Suburban in front of her carport and walked up onto the porch. Blinds shielded every window, but she had to have heard the engine. Not seeing a doorbell, he knocked hard. "Rebecca!"

A deadbolt slid and the door opened. Will felt a punch at the sight of her, blocking the opening. She hadn't expected him, or she'd have gotten dressed.

Low-slung flannel pajama pants and a sacky T-shirt shouldn't have been sexy, but both were worn enough to cling to every curve on her strong, lean body. Dark hair tumbled over her shoulders and nearly to her breasts. He'd seen her hair loose only once, and that had been in the hospital, spread on her pillow around a blanched face and drug-hazed eyes.

"Are you going to let me in?" he asked, trying to decide whether she was mad or just bemused at his idiocy in running to the rescue again.

Without a word, she stepped back. That's when he noticed her bare feet, narrow and high-arched. Her toes were long, like her fingers. That, too, would fuel some fantasies.

Trying to throttle down his libido, he passed her and found himself in a warm, homey living room, rustic with the peeled-log walls finished to a soft sheen. Wood furniture gleamed, sofa and chairs were upholstered in rich colors. The wood stove sat cold.

"You hear from the state patrolman?" That was good. Businesslike. And he was damn curious, since he hadn't seen a patrol car waiting down there.

"No vehicle has emerged from my road since he arrived. A few minutes ago, he let me know he's been pulled away to another call." The warmth in her voice was muted. "The trouble is, it wouldn't have taken the guy long to make it onto the highway."

"Hard to speed around the potholes."

She made a face. "Depends on your motivation."

Will shrugged a concession. Damn it, he wanted to take her in his arms, but her stiff stance, crossed arms and expression didn't suggest an embrace would be welcome.

"Where's the broken window?" he asked.

"Kitchen." She turned and led the way. His gaze lingered on the swing of her stride and the sway of her hips.

The kitchen had the same rustic feel, without it being overdone. He felt comfortable in her home. It was the location he didn't like.

Right now, the chill air rushing in pulled him back to his reason for being here. Forgetting her décor, he crossed to the window lacking glass but for a few shards that made him think of icicles. The floor was clean; she must have already swept. Will glanced at her, to see that her crossed arms had tightened and her pupils looked too big.

Will frowned. "Once he broke it, he wiped any shards out of his way."

Her head jerked in a nod.

"Smashing the window must have made a hell of a racket."

She stared fixedly at the dark space where there should have been a reflection. "That's what woke me, except it wasn't as noisy as you'd think. He...taped the glass. He must have thought he could get it out mostly intact."

Will bent his upper body through the opening to see a large piece of glass lying on the decking. Masking tape formed a criss-cross that held together the two biggest pieces.

"That son-of-a-bitch cut the glass," he said incredulously.

She nodded again. Will straightened and faced her. "Isn't this the same window—?"

Finally, her eyes met his. "Yes," she said, voice low. "He must have been trying to cut out the glass to get in quietly, like Justin Payne did."

Will swore. Payne had been patient enough to get taken on as a detective with the county, in a perfect position to monitor the investigation into his own killing spree and use information known only internally – like the fact that Rebecca was providing a safe house to one of his projected targets. His attempt to make every single person he thought had failed his little brother pay in terror and blood had been big news at the time. His killings had been distinctive in several ways, starting with the letters drawn in blood at each scene. But reporters had glommed right onto another of those details: the neat way he had cut out a pane of glass to allow him entry to each home. Responding cops had found those panes of glass set against the house walls beside the windows.

The only reason Payne hadn't succeeded in killing Rebecca was that she'd been on guard, wearing a bulletproof vest and keeping her gun at hand – and had happened to be awake. If this asshole tonight had been as competent, Rebecca might be dead.

His heart contracted at the unthinkable possibility.

"Pack some clothes," he said roughly. "You're not staying here."

*****

Rebecca won the argument. Not because she was more stubborn than Will – she doubted that was possible. She thought his surrender had to do with her pointing out how it would look if anyone saw her coming out of his house first thing in the morning. From what Sean Holbeck had told her, the likelihood of that happening was excellent. Will had bought a house only a couple of blocks from Sean's, and at least three other deputies Sean knew lived close by, too. Chief Colburn and all *his* officers presumably lived there in town, too. Oh, and Sheriff Mackay lived in Cape Trouble, too.

Yes, Will had pushed for a hotel as an alternative, but she could tell he hadn't liked the idea of leaving her in a room that could be breached.

When he declared his intention to stay here, Rebecca quit arguing. The truth was, she'd known that, alone, she wouldn't so much as close her eyes for the rest of night. The worrisome part was that, while she might be able to get some sleep if any other cop had been here to stay the night, only Will's presence explained the comforting kernel of heat beneath her breastbone.

So now she was pulling pillows and a comforter out of the linen closet. He'd scoffed at her offer of the guest bedroom.

"With that window wide open, anyone could climb in. I intend to be right here to meet him."

"It would be nuts for him to come back." *Tonight*. But what about another night?

Will just looked at her with those dark eyes and a stubborn set to his mouth she already recognized. He'd been only slightly appeased to learn she'd already left a message asking for someone to get up here in the morning to fingerprint.

She returned to see that he'd already set his holster and weapon on the coffee table and was kicking off his boots. Arms full of bedding, Rebecca stopped between one step and the next, staring over the back of the sofa. Just like that, her pulse raced.

His feet were bare.

Not surprising, given his size, Will had big feet, something like a size twelve, and she saw a few dark hairs curling on his toes, too.

"You're not wearing socks."

For a moment, he didn't move. Then, very slowly, he turned his head until his eyes met hers. "I was in a hurry."

Rebecca couldn't look away, not after an admission so simple. So raw. Heavy stubble darkened his jaw. His hair was disheveled. She wanted more than anything to touch him, feel the texture of his unshaven jaw, the slick weight of his hair, the hammer of his heartbeat. She couldn't help remembering that she'd thought the same thing earlier, right before she fell asleep. She'd longed to touch him, but he wasn't there.

Breath shallow, knees weakening, she was slammed by the changed reality.

He was definitely here.

CHAPTER TWELVE

"Rebecca."

Will didn't know what he'd done to have her transfixed, but the glow in her eyes, her quick, shallow breaths and parted lips shot him to full arousal. At pushing forty years old, he shouldn't be able to go from zero to sixty so fast.

Her teeth closed on her lower lip and her lashes fluttered. "I— Here." One step and she dropped the bedding onto the sofa.

Fortunately, that had brought her close enough for him to capture her hand. "Please. Come sit down."

For a second, she strained away before some of the tension left her body and she nodded. Will took a chance and let her go. Instead of fleeing, she circled the sofa and sat down at the other end, sitting so that she faced him, one foot tucked under her.

"You didn't say about Tim," she said hurriedly.

The last thing Will wanted to talk about was Tim Spiva, but of course she needed to know. "He wasn't home. I waited. He didn't come home."

"You can't be sure he wasn't there."

"You're right, not if he parks in the garage. But I hammered on the door. I don't see how he could have slept through it. Besides, you and I both know this—" he jerked his head toward the kitchen "—was him."

After a moment, she nodded.

"I wish you *had* shot the little creep," he said savagely.

"You have no idea how much I wanted to," she confessed, voice barely audible. "But..."

When she trailed off, he finished, "You couldn't be a hundred percent sure your intruder wasn't a burglar."

"Either way, if I'd just kept quiet and waited until he started down the hall to shoot, it would have been murder."

"Legally, it would have been self-defense."

"But not morally. Especially since..." Once again, she trailed off, finally lifting one shoulder.

"Since?" he asked quietly.

Her eyes had darkened, and it wasn't desire he was seeing, not anymore.

"Since I felt so much hate." Her voice shook. "I wanted to kill him, and Jason Payne, too. And probably Leonard Bailey."

Leonard? The memory clicked into place. Bailey was the man who'd brutalized and murdered her mother.

His heart contracted. Holding out his hand, he said, "Come here," voice so rough he hardly recognized it.

She didn't move or blink or take a breath. He was about to give up and let his hand drop when she made a sound that hurt to hear and dove for him.

He pulled her into his arms and held her tight. Her position was awkward, since she was on her knees, but Will doubted she had noticed. She pressed her face against his neck and had managed to get her left arm mostly around his body. Her fingertips drilled into his back. Her right arm had ended up trapped between them, but she'd grabbed a fistful of his shirt and was hanging on tight. She shook with what he'd have taken for sobs if he had felt the hot warmth of tears on his neck.

"Rebecca. Sweetheart. God, you scare the hell out of me. When you called—" He broke off. Fuck. When he heard her voice on the phone, he'd feared he was having a heart attack. The problem was with his heart all right, but no cardiologist could help. It seemed he was ready to throw over his career for a chance with this woman.

He kept holding her, one hand moving up and down her back, circling, kneading, discovering how her taut muscles and fine bones felt beneath his fingertips. All the time, his damn heart kept feeling like a sponge being wrung out.

"It's okay if you were angry," he whispered. "If you were scared. Shit, I'm *still* scared."

She gave a couple of little sniffs, then pulled back. Her cheeks were dry – no tears, although he'd have understood if she cried – but the anguish in her eyes finished him off.

"What am I going to do?" she asked with apparent bewilderment.

"Right now? You're going to spend the night here on the sofa with me." He didn't know when he'd decided that, but it was non-negotiable. "Tomorrow, you'll call someone to come out and replace the glass. Then you'll have a security system installed."

She blinked a couple of times. "That didn't save Emily Holbeck."

No, Sean's next-door-neighbor and now-wife had been saved by the grace of God, if you believed in such things. In other words, by pure luck.

"They're not foolproof," Will conceded. "But most of the time, an attempted entry triggers the alarm."

Most of the time didn't seem to give her the reassurance he'd intended. And why would it? Even though any halfway decent security system would have gone off tonight, the way that window had shattered, her having one installed wouldn't satisfy him. He didn't know if he could sleep tomorrow night or any night, knowing she was up here by herself.

"Tomorrow," he said, "we'll go talk to Spiva. And you'll keep investigating. He's not smart enough to beat you, Rebecca."

"He has been so far."

"In six days, you've gone from arguing with me about whether we should open an investigation at all to narrowing down that investigation to a single suspect. That's damn good, Rebecca."

"But I can't prove a thing! Maybe he *is* just weird. Maybe the ex did it or some other guy in Mandy's crowd is a better actor. Did you ever think of that?" She was glaring at him by the end.

Will shook his head. "My instincts are telling me the same thing yours are telling you, and I've been an investigator for a lot of years."

She finally sagged, hardly seeming to notice that he was turning her, tucking her against his side with an arm encircling her. He rubbed his cheek against her head, the long, dark strands wanting to cling to his beard stubble.

"Have you ever been shot?" she asked.

Surprised, he went still for a minute. "Yeah." He cleared his throat. "Twice."

"Really?" Rebecca tipped her head to see him.

"Really. First time, I was a rookie. Pulled a driver over because his taillight was out. As I was walking forward, he stuck a gun out his window and fired off a couple shots. One got me before I could dive for cover."

"What was his problem?"

"Warrant for his arrest. We had a three strikes law in California. Of course, by possessing a gun in violation of his parole and shooting a police officer, he added two *more* strikes to the drug charge he thought he could evade. He's at San Quentin for twenty-five to life now."

"Oh." She rested her head in the hollow formed by his shoulder. "Were you hurt bad?"

"Nah. The bullet grazed my side, broke a rib. It left me with an impressive scar. I was young enough, it added a little swagger to my step."

Her tiny gurgle of a laugh encouraged him. "What about the second time?"

Remembering, he was quiet for a minute. "That one was bad. I was working Vice, and had been undercover for a couple months with an outfit moving cocaine from Central America. We planned a bust at a big sales conference, I guess you could call it. The other outfit was supposed to be made up of out-of-towners. Unfortunately for me, I'd arrested one of them. I'd have been dead if we hadn't been surrounded by cops. As it was, I was out of action for three months. Lost my spleen and had my kidney stitched up." Almost lightly, he said, "That's how I met my wife."

Rebecca nodded. The ensuing silence felt peaceful, but Will didn't make the mistake of believing it really was.

"Did you...I don't know, lose your nerve after that? Even for a while?"

Ah. He bent his head enough to press his lips to her temple. It was such a vulnerable spot, the skin so soft. "Of course I did. Anyone would have, except an excitement junkie like Carson Crandall," he amended. "No way I'd have admitted it when I was a rookie. I did the required counseling appointments, lied my way through them and was back in a patrol car two weeks later. I did okay during daylight when I could see who and what I was approaching. When it was dark, like it had been during that stop, I really sweated."

"You must have gotten over it."

This – being honest about the after-effects of either shooting – was a first for him. How he felt about this woman was a first, too, though. She needed his honesty, about this and everything else that came up.

"It took months." He thought about it. "Maybe a year. The second time, that was harder. A lengthy hospitalization and recuperation does that to you. Lots of time to live those moments over and over."

"Yes."

His arm tightened around her. "I knew I couldn't go back to Vice. I applied for a detective position and went to Homicide, where I stayed."

"It's supposed to be safer, isn't it?"

He shrugged. "Sure. No guarantees, as you're discovering. But most homicide detectives spend two-thirds of their time on the phone or computer." He huffed. "Most of *that* on hold or doing useless searches."

Her hair smelled really good. Not flowery or cloying. Lemon and some herb, he thought. Cheek against that sleek dark hair, he breathed in her scent and waited to find out whether she'd open up to him. She hadn't asked those questions out of idle curiosity, Will felt sure.

"I've...had some trouble with panic since I came back," she said finally, voice small and shamed. "It would have been bad enough if I were a man, but when you're a woman in a field dominated by men, you have to be even tougher. There was no way I could ever tell anyone."

"No," he murmured, a band squeezing his chest. He'd initially been attracted to the Rebecca who was confident and willing to challenge him. The more vulnerable woman he'd discovered had burrowed deep beneath his guard. Having her trust meant everything to him. To think he'd believed he was a loner.

"It hit me sometimes in situations that weren't anything like the shooting. You know. Walking up to a car I'd pulled over, or to knock on a door."

"Yeah." The electrical impulses zinging through him, the sweat soaking his uniform shirt, the way his heart had tried to beat its way out of his chest... He remembered, all right.

"The worst, though, is that I've never felt safe here at home again," she confessed. "I loved this cabin. I had it built. I could get out of my car and feel this peace steal over me. At night, I'd turn off all the lights and sit out on the front steps. Once my eyes adjusted, I could watch clouds moving over the moon, and deer coming out to eat the fallen apples from my trees. I put out dog food for the raccoons. Every so often, an owl would swoop out of the trees and snatch something out of the grass. Which sounds awful, but…it's just nature, you know. I felt like *part* of it. Now, I huddle behind locked doors and covered windows."

And now, a year later, any fragile sense of security she'd regained had been shattered, along with that window glass. *He* wanted to kill Tim Spiva himself, for doing that to her.

"But you stuck it out up here."

Her shoulders moved. "I kept thinking it would get better. Like I guess it did for you."

"You were attacked in your own home," Will said flatly. "That's different. We all need someplace we can feel safe."

"Yes." She fell quiet again, just for a minute, then said, "I shouldn't be telling you all this. I keep giving away stuff I haven't admitted to anyone." She sounded worried. "I don't know why."

"Sure you do."

"I don't!" She stiffened and started to pull away.

Not letting her go, he touched his lips to the top of her head again. "What I just told you? About being scared after both shootings? I've never told anyone before."

Rebecca quit moving, quit breathing, as far as he could tell. And then she looked up. "Is that true?"

His mouth twisted. "It is."

"You didn't even tell your wife?"

He shook his head. "She never admitted to any fears. I sure as hell wasn't going to."

Rebecca closed her eyes. When she opened them, he saw the sheen of tears. "Thank you," she whispered.

"Don't cry. Please don't cry."

"What?" She swiped at her face with the fact of her hand. "I'm not—"

"You are." He grabbed her around the waist, lifted and swung her around to sit astride his lap. And then he wrapped a hand around her nape and pulled her forward so he could kiss her.

For a startled second, she didn't react at all, even when he nipped her lower lip. Her eyes stayed wide. Just when he was thinking she didn't want this, she made an odd little sound, almost a whimper, and kissed *him*. Hard. Their teeth clanked, and he tasted blood, but his lip might have split open and he wouldn't have cared. Not when he could have his tongue in her mouth, hers tangling with it; not when her hips moved against him with urgent little jerks.

Will kissed her until he was seeing spots before his eyes, ripped away to take in air, and decided to pull off her T-shirt before he reclaimed her mouth. The resulting sight of her bare breasts, not large but perfect, froze him in place. He just looked for a long moment, taking in creamy skin, a long, slim torso, a puckered scar on her shoulder – and those breasts, high and firm, topped with small, dark nipples forming tight buds.

A groan vibrating in his chest, he bent her over his arm and closed his mouth over one of her breasts. He swirled his tongue and then sucked. Her fingers dug into his shoulders, her back arched and she tried to ride the erection straining at his zipper.

Will lavished attention on her other breast before burying his face between them and struggling to regain enough control to keep from flipping her onto the couch, stripping and mounting her. If only it hadn't been so damned long since he'd had a woman at all. He'd make this good for her if it killed him.

His chest working like an old-fashioned bellows, he sat up, lifting her with him. Her lips were puffy, one cheek red from the scrape of his stubble, her eyes heavy-lidded and dazed.

"Will?"

"Do you want this?" he asked, almost harshly, and braced himself for the worst.

For too long, she searched his eyes. And then she swallowed, nodded and whispered, "Yes. You know I do."

"Thank God."

"But...how can we work together—?"

"Can we talk about that tomorrow?" he said desperately.

There was another long look, and then she nodded. Her mouth even curved into a smile so sweet, his chest went tight again. "Yes."

*****

Surrendering to the unknown was unlike her. Rebecca had come to realize that, despite having gone into a profession considered dangerous, she lived a cautious life. "Can we talk about that tomorrow?" might translate into "You know you have to find another job now." But right at this moment, she just plain didn't care. Only enough of her native caution remained to have her flattening her hands on his chest to stop him pulling her close for a kiss.

"The only thing is, I'm not on birth control. And I don't have anything here."

His dark eyes burned. "I do. A few days ago, I stuck a couple condoms in my wallet."

"Oh." A surge of gladness and, okay, lust, had her grabbing the hem of his black polo shirt and tugging it up.

Will yanked the shirt over his head, captured her hands and spread them on his chest. "Touch me," he said hoarsely.

A mat of dark hair on his broad, muscular chest narrowed to a line disappearing beneath the button on his khakis. Rebecca looked her fill, dazzled and shaken. Slowly, she moved her hands, loving the hard planes of his chest, the way his skin quivered and muscles jumped. Her fingertips found his flat nipples, teasing as he watched her with that hot stare.

Then he wrapped his big, strong hands around her waist and stroked slowly upward, doing to her what she was doing to him. Exploring, arousing, until Rebecca groaned and leaned forward, desperate to press her breasts against his hair-roughened chest.

This kiss exploded, frantic, hungry. Now he gripped her hips and moved her up and down, rubbing her against the hard ridge that felt better than anything ever had before. They had to quit long enough to strip each other. The rest of him was as impressive as his chest: long, strong legs, dusted with the same midnight dark hair, lean hips, and a jutting erection that might have alarmed her if she hadn't been so far gone. They fell back on the couch, tangling, shaking. He stroked her, caressing her breasts and thighs, his fingers sliding into the slippery space between her folds.

"Now," she gasped. "Now. I need—"

The blunt tip of his penis was suddenly there, where she wanted it. Rebecca arched up, only to have him exclaim, "Fuck. I forgot the condom."

He rolled her and groped on the floor. Cloth rustled, there was a small thump, a ripping sound and he somehow got the thing on despite her attempt to help. And then, God, he was between her thighs and pushing inside her. The pressure, the fullness, shocked her, even as being filled felt so good she cried out.

He moved in and out, thrusting hard and deep until she heard herself making indescribable sounds as her fingernails bit into his back and buttocks. Will hooked an arm under her knee and lifted her leg, which seemed to let him go deeper yet and left her splayed and utterly vulnerable.

The need tightened inside her until she thought she'd die if it didn't spring free. She dug one heel into the sofa cushion and pushed upward to meet every thrust, each rapturous jolt pushing her higher until all that agonizing, exquisite tension exploded. Rebecca bucked, calling his name.

With a fierce last thrust, Will came, too, his big body rearing above her, a guttural sound escaping his throat.

"Rebecca," he whispered raggedly, his weight coming down on her.

She wrapped her arms and legs tightly around him and held on, needing this closeness as much as she had the passion that preceded it. Needing to believe that whatever sacrifices had to be made would be worth it.

*****

After Will staggered off to the bathroom to get rid of the condom, he turned out lights as he returned, leaving on only the front and back porch lights.

He rubbed his scratchy cheek against her much softer one, stretched out and arranged both of them until he was comfortable and could tell she was, too, then murmured, "Now I can die happy."

Head pillowed on his shoulder, Rebecca snorted. "Oh, good. That makes me feel safe."

He laughed, feeling amazing. Like he could bound over the tallest building in Burris County in a single leap – although he'd rather wait to do it until he'd slept for a few hours snuggled up to Rebecca. Despite the lethargy, the pull of sleep, he made a last assessment. Gun – a reach away. Outside lights to make any intruder think twice. And the second condom on the floor also within easy reach.

He smiled, feeling her body easing, her breath evening out, and let go.

What was left of the night was no exception to the rule: he never slept deeply. The first time he came fully awake, the absolute darkness had changed to a pearly shade of gray that could be dawn – or could just be the average overcast day. He listened, but if rain fell, it was softly, not dinging off the metal roof. Of course, there was no bedside clock. Will considered digging his phone out of his pants on the floor to find out the time, then thought, *screw it*, and fell back asleep.

The next time he roused, the quality of daylight hadn't changed to speak of. He discovered Rebecca had somehow turned over, so that her head now rested on his upper arm and instead of being tangled together, they were spooned, her firm butt pressed to his groin. Will was even less interested in the time of day.

After lifting an arm from the quilt, he discovered how chilly the house had become. The furnace had been running when he first awakened, he was sure, but of course cold air was pouring in the window that lacked glass. He shut that picture out of his head, not yet ready to deal with the threat to Rebecca. That long, slender, silky, feminine body, though, was another matter.

He brushed her hair aside and strung kisses along her neck, nipping the muscle that ran between neck and shoulder, then soothing any sting with his tongue. Her grumbly sounds changed to squeaks and sighs as he savored the chance to explore every dip and curve, from her breasts to her hips, the jut of her hipbones, the soft nest of curls, the wet heat they protected.

Reaching behind him, he found the condom and managed to get it on without lifting the quilt and freezing them both. Then he went back to playing with her until her hips rocked and she struggled to turn over. "This is good," he murmured, and slid into her, the pleasure bringing an "Aaahh" from him and a whimper from her.

Tender and slow ultimately became hard and fast, Will pulling her to her knees and taking her ruthlessly from behind. She shattered first, him following. Once again, they sagged to the sofa, both breathing hard, hot enough not to need a quilt anymore.

"If I had another condom," he said, nuzzling her nape, "I'd suggest we share a shower. As it is—" He gave an exaggerated sigh.

Rebecca reached back and patted his hip. "Something to dream about." She was quiet for a minute. "What time is it?"

"I have no idea," he admitted. "I figured we were entitled to a late start."

"Yes, but—" already her voice had tightened "—I have a lot to do."

"Yeah." His mood didn't quite crash and burn, but close. He did correct her. "*We* have a lot to do."

Still, neither of them moved for several minutes. He soaked up the pleasure of holding her, her scent, her utter relaxation against him, before groaning and heaving himself to a sitting position.

"If you let me use the bathroom first, I'll put coffee on while you shower."

"Okay." Freed by his move, she wriggled to a sitting position, too, grabbing the quilt as she did. "Brr!"

"No shit."

By the time he was mostly dressed, she'd scuttled toward her bedroom. Will eyed his boots, regretting the lack of socks, but sticking his feet in them anyway.

No surprise, it was even colder in the kitchen, and the sight of that damn broken window depressed his ebullience further. Along with everything else, he and Rebecca would have to have a serious talk about where they were going as a couple. Because she was right – they couldn't work together *and* sleep together. He, for one, voted for sleeping together. On the other hand, making those decisions ranked well below finding evidence to allow them to put that cocky little asshole, Tim Spiva, behind bars.

One thing Will did know – if Rebecca insisted on coming home tonight, she wouldn't be alone.

He found coffee in the refrigerator, and was turning around when the bright green numbers on her microwave came into sharp focus, startling him. 11:15. He was certainly entitled to take a day off, as he'd intended to take last Friday before Mr. Brodsky raised his rage and depression to the next level. Will hadn't told anyone he wouldn't be in today, however, so people had to be wondering.

He started the coffee and then took out his phone, leaning against the counter as he tapped in his voicemail password. When the pleasant female voice told him he had four messages, he groaned.

He was still listening when Rebecca appeared, shiny hair that looked like it might still be damp braided down her back and dressed in the black slacks and white shirt she had convinced herself made her appear sexless.

Holbeck had had a break in his investigation; it seemed yesterday's deep cogitation had produced results. Worley wanted input on whether he ought to go to the high school today to make his arrests, or wait until the three boys who had vandalized the organic farm got home and their parents were present. Sheriff Mackay wondered where he was. The last message was a quick, "Call me," from Rey Mendoza, a detective with North Fork P.D. Will had worked with him on several investigations now, and had gained a great deal of respect for him.

Rebecca had apparently been searching for window glass companies, because next thing he knew she was talking to one. She ended the call and said, "If I text him the size, he says he'll be here in about an hour."

Will nodded. That was prompt.

"Not a lot of choice in home alarm systems companies. I think I'll just go with the one based in Cannon Beach that Emily and Sean chose."

Leaving her talking again on her own phone, Will stepped out the back door and contemplated damp, gray forest while he returned Mackay's call. His boss trumped even his detectives, never mind a detective from another police agency.

"What's up?" he said.

"Tillamook County arrested a suspect in the shooting of the deputy up there. It was an ambush, all right, but they think the wife hired this guy to kill him."

"Another loving relationship."

The sheriff grunted. "Apparently there have been domestic violence calls to his home. He was on probation at work. Rumor has it the wife has a lover, besides."

"Say, the guy who knocked off her husband for her?"

"They're looking into that."

Movement caught Will's eye and he tensed, then relaxed as a doe stepped out of the woods, head turning, and cut across the lawn.

"You aren't coming in today?" Mackay asked.

"I probably will. I'm currently up at Detective Walker's place. She had a break-in during the night." Will told him the details, up to his own arrival here. He might have to make true confessions, but not yet. "She's scheduling someone to put in an alarm system. I'll probably wait with her until someone shows to replace the window glass, then we intend to talk to Tim Spiva. My gut says he abducted Mandy Shaw. I've had the sense that he's intrigued by Rebecca, which makes me more than a little uneasy. You know this is on top of the sabotage done on the department Tahoe this week. Spiva had the perfect opportunity to do that, too."

They talked about it for a minute, Mackay seemingly not suspicious of his lieutenant's deep interest in his one female detective – whose first name Will had just carelessly used.

He was about to return Worley's call when behind him, Rebecca said, "Coffee's ready. I poured you a cup."

It would taste good, but he realized he felt better rested than he had in longer than he could remember. Energized, even.

When he told Rebecca so, she chuckled and stood on tiptoe to kiss his cheek. "Ditto. I hardly recognized myself in the mirror this morning, with no bags under my eyes."

He kissed her with more intent, the whole thing getting serious enough that her cheeks were pink and her lips swollen by the time he reluctantly lifted his head. Damn, he wanted—

No condoms, he reminded himself. Not to mention people depending on him. And workers scheduled to show up in something like forty-five minutes.

He settled for coffee, and continued returning calls while Rebecca scrambled eggs and popped what looked like a whole wheat bagel into a toaster, a second already sliced and waiting to go in.

After talking to both his detectives who'd left messages, he and Rebecca sat down to eat. She'd produced some homemade raspberry jam to spread on the bagels. This tasted a lot better than his usual oatmeal or cereal. It was sad to be at an age to need to think about watching his cholesterol, but his paternal grandfather had died of a massive heart attack at sixty years old, so he'd started paying attention.

He told Rebecca what was going on with the other two investigations as well as the news from Tillamook County, thinking that being able to talk about things like this was the one thing he had missed after his divorce.

"I wonder what Rey wants," Rebecca said finally.

"You know him?"

"In passing. Daniel Colburn and Sean both think highly of him."

He relaxed at the character references, refusing to let the warmth in the way she said 'Rey' spark anything close to jealousy. Good God.

Pushing his plate away, he said, "I'll call him and find out."

"I hear someone coming." She stood, carrying both their plates to the sink. "Looks like the guy here to take fingerprints."

"Good." Will scrolled to Mendoza's number and touched 'send'.

After only a couple of rings, the North Fork detective answered. "Lieutenant, thanks for getting back to me. I have something that may concern you."

"Yeah?"

"We got a call a couple of hours ago about what looks like an abduction." The detective sounded tense. "Young woman. Her co-workers say you were there talking to her a few days ago."

All those nicely relaxed muscles knotted with new tension. "Shit," Will said. "Not Jordan Torgerson."

CHAPTER THIRTEEN

"Shit," Rebecca heard Will say. "Not Jordan Torgerson."

She turned from her view out the window to meet turbulent dark eyes.

He listened for a moment, then said, "We begged her to be careful. How the fuck did she put herself at risk?" Then he frowned. "Wait. She lives down here. How could she have been snatched from the hair salon?"

Rebecca realized she'd clapped her hand over her mouth to hold in a shocked cry. She didn't like Jordan, with her little girl act and self-centered view of the world. But extreme immaturity didn't mean she deserved the kind of horror she must be facing. Nobody did. And Jordan, of all people, lacked the fortitude trauma would demand of her.

Rebecca had missed part of the conversation, because Will was setting his phone down on the table. Expression grim, he said, "Someone's knocking."

"What? Oh." She hurried to the front of the house, letting a crime scene investigator in and escorting him to the kitchen. Will and he exchanged nods and a few words. The guy set to work immediately to dust the glass and any other likely surfaces.

Rebecca whirled back to Will.

"What happened?"

"She took a break, stepped out back to have a cigarette. Rey says an alley runs behind the businesses on that block. No windows on any of them looking out at where she stood. When Jordan's next client arrived, another of the women went out to get her. Saw a half-smoked cigarette smoldering on the pavement and Jordan's phone six feet or so away. She ran around the building screaming her name, then called 911. Once the responding officer understood that Jordan was involved in another investigation, he called for Mendoza. They discovered blood and a blonde hair on the cinder block wall where she'd have been standing."

"I can't believe this."

"I can," Will said, with an angry snap to his voice. "Spiva went for *you* and struck out. What do you want to bet he's been watching Jordan, too? Really pissed, he drove up to North Fork and hung around until that idiot girl stepped out *alone* into the alley, which she probably does half a dozen times or more a day. He drives down the alley, brakes, grabs her, bashes her head against the wall and throws her into the trunk. According to Mendoza, there are no security cameras. Why would anyone pay attention to a car turning into an alley or emerging from one?"

"Did she just drop her phone?"

"Maybe, but he said there are scratches consistent with it skidding over the asphalt and bumping up against a Dumpster. It may have gone flying out of her hand, or he tossed it. He's obviously wise to the GPS capability of smart phones."

Yes, given that Mandy's had never registered in any way after her disappearance. Her phone might be on the ocean floor, or washed up somewhere on the rocks. It could have been hammered into shards. It, like Mandy Shaw, was undoubtedly dead.

Rebecca swallowed. And now Jordan—

Another knock.

This time it was a stocky, graying man from the glass company. She escorted him to the kitchen, where he spoke to the CSI guy, studied the window and went out back to get his tools and maybe the new glass.

Had she ever had so many visitors at one time before?

She touched Will on the arm. "Do you want to go ahead and get started?"

"I'll wait," Will said tersely. "Let's go out in the living room."

She nodded and followed him. From the front window, she saw two men appearing from the back of a white van, carrying something that looked like a hair dryer and other tools. She obviously had to stay until they'd finished.

"Would Tim have taken her to his parents' house, do you think?" she asked.

"You mean, is he brazen enough to do that? I wouldn't be surprised. But we still don't have enough to justify a warrant."

"I know, but—"

"We talk to him. We ask him to let us walk through the house. If he refuses, we call the parents again and ask for *their* permission.

Say we just want to eliminate their son so we can focus our investigation elsewhere."

"You make it sound so reasonable, but if they've spent years in denial, they're likely to get mad at us for daring to suspect their poor, good-hearted boy of such a heinous crime."

"Possible. Even likely. We can also call the brother again and beg him to talk his parents into agreeing."

The smiling, sexy, relaxed man of this morning was gone. He'd resumed his cop face, unreadable but for simmering anger. Did he regret the night with her? The things he'd admitted to feeling, the tenderness and urgency in his kisses and touch? Even the possibility opened a gaping hole inside her, as though she'd lost something essential to her very being. Or maybe Will had been filling the hollow left from her mother's death, but it turned out he didn't want to.

Just as bad was an ominous awareness Rebecca didn't really want to confront, not yet. Only, it was awfully hard to ward off not only the remembered fear from last night, but also what Will had just said.

Spiva went for you *and struck out.*

If he'd been able to remove the glass he cut out without it breaking so that he could enter the house quietly, or if she'd had her bedroom door shut so that it muffled sound, or just been more soundly asleep, *she* could be the one held captive right now. To be restrained and unable to fight back, to suffer through a rape or beatings or being cut—

Nausea swept over her, followed by the prickles of rising goosebumps.

She would know exactly what her mother had suffered in her last two days of life. And thinking about what her father would go through horrified her as much as imagining what could have happened to her – and *was* happening to Jordan Torgerson.

"I don't like whatever you're thinking," Will growled, gripping her upper arms and looking down at her. His hard face was no longer impassive; worry and tenderness transformed the storm in his eyes and the set of his jaw and mouth.

Rebecca bent to rest her forehead on his chest. In response, he wrapped his arms around her, enclosing her in the security of his sheer size and solidity. *Look at me*, Rebecca thought in bemusement. So fiercely determined to take care of herself, to be invincible, and now she craved a man's protection, his strength. How the mighty are fallen, she thought wryly.

But...maybe this could be a two-way street. Last night, Will had needed her, too, and she still believed it hadn't only been for sexual satisfaction. And always taking care of herself hadn't been working out so well this past year, had it?

Will kneaded the back of her neck in silent support.

"I'm scared," she finally murmured. "Mostly for Jordan, a little bit for me."

He kissed her head but didn't say anything.

Rebecca drew a deep breath and straightened, offering him a crooked smile. "I'll go see if I have a new window yet."

*****

Ten minutes later, they were on their way, Will having persuaded Rebecca to leave her own car behind. The argument had taken most of those ten minutes.

She was scheduled to handle the crisis line tonight. "If I have to cancel, I will, but we might have hit a brick wall by then. In which case, I'd as soon have something useful to do as not."

"Fine," he'd said, even though it wasn't fine. "I'll drive you there and pick you up."

She was a cop; she was armed. He dug in his heels and told her she wasn't spending the night alone, either. Eventually, she threw up her hands and gave in, but wasn't a happy woman. What he couldn't tell was whether she was secretly relieved, or genuinely mad.

Probably both, he thought with faint amusement he was careful not to let her see.

She called the Shaws during the drive to let them know about Jordan, asking them not to share the news with anyone else yet. Will listened to her say, "Yes, I think this has to be related to Mandy's disappearance," and, at the end, a very soft, "I wish I could."

"They know, don't they?" he said, as she put away her phone.

"Yes." Rebecca looked straight ahead through the windshield, although probably not seeing the scenery. She cleared her throat. "Tim first?"

"Best chance to shake him up."

Today's rainfall was barely a mist, but necessitated keeping the wipers on. Driving along the coast highway, Will had occasional glimpses of a sullen ocean and crashing waves. They'd been damn lucky last Sunday to have a break in the weather for the search.

There wouldn't be a similar search for Jordan, he reflected. She could be anywhere by now. Brooding, Will wondered where Tim Spiva had stowed her, if not at his parents' house.

By concentrating on Spiva, were he and Rebecca making a mistake? He thought of that old saying his mother used often – stowing all the eggs in one basket.

Yeah. They might be making that mistake. But he didn't think so.

"You haven't heard back from the detective trying to verify the ex-boyfriend's alibi?"

"No. He'd decided his best chance of finding someone who could identify the girl who went home with Brian was by hanging out at the bar tonight, in hopes there are Friday night regulars. I assume he'll call late, or in the morning."

"Good." Damn, he couldn't feel optimistic about the fate of a woman abducted a full week ago. And Spiva wasn't likely to have bothered with Jordan if he still had Mandy available.

"We know Tim doesn't own any property in the area," Rebecca said suddenly. "But he could have access to a friend's place, or even a vacant cabin or house. We should have been tailing him."

Will had had the same thought, except the sheriff's department was chronically short on manpower. "He'll be watching to be sure he isn't followed if he has Mandy and now Jordan stashed somewhere else." He frowned. "You checked to be sure the parents don't own any other property?"

"Of course I did!"

Slowing, he put on his turn signal. The Bow Lake neighborhood was just ahead on the left. "I wonder if Colburn could spare someone to help."

By the time he passed the house where she'd lived, he saw out of the corner of his eye that Rebecca was rigid.

"*I* might have had a chance of taking him down," she said suddenly. "Jordan doesn't have a prayer."

"What?" He swerved to the curb and braked. "You're blaming *yourself* because you didn't trot along with him last night?"

"Not...exactly."

Not exactly. Jesus. "Then what?"

"Just—" she turned a troubled gaze on him "—I didn't foresee this, and I should have."

"Didn't foresee it?" Will repeated her words in disbelief. "Who was it who insisted we warn Jordan? Because you did foresee Tim's interest in her?"

"But we knew he was fixated on me. That's how you put it, right? So why didn't we try to set him up? We had the chance to trap him, and we didn't take it! And now he has her," she said desolately.

"Rebecca." He'd never felt more sure that she wasn't cut out for this job. She'd never learn to separate herself emotionally from the victims. "First, no one could have predicted that he'd react this fast and go for another woman. Second – you're talking about setting a trap, with *you* as bait. That happens a lot in fiction, not so much in real life, and for good reason. What if he was enraged enough to kill you immediately, instead of snatching you? I'm not setting you up when the possibility of screw-ups is high. So get it out of your head. You hear me?"

After a moment, she nodded, although he wasn't convinced he'd really dented her stubborn need to save everyone else, whatever doing so cost her.

He drove the last couple blocks in silence, pulled into Spiva's driveway and cut the engine. Then Will laid a hand over one of hers. "Hey. Take some deep breaths. You can't afford to let him get to you. Last time we were here, you played him just right. Flattered him one minute, undermined him the next. Let's go in there and rattle this vicious little punk."

Rebecca nodded, turning her hand to hold onto Will's, perhaps unconsciously. "Got it. It's just..." She took one of those deep breaths, and her voice steadied. "I was remembering something he said, too."

Will turned in his seat to look at her, not liking her tone. "What?"

"You were there. He said Jordan was a little princess."

"I remember."

"It was after that. He said he wouldn't want to waste a lot of time on her."

"Oh, hell." Will hadn't registered the significance then, but he remembered, all right. "He was smirking."

"I just figured he'd lost interest in her." The heaviness in her voice was akin to horror. "Now— What if he kept Mandy alive for days, but he gets bored with Jordan really fast?"

His fingers bit into her hand, but he made sure she was looking into his eyes. "You've got to put this out of your mind. You don't know that's what he meant."

Her head bobbed. "Yes. Okay."

He had to free his hand to undo his seatbelt. By the time they met on the walkway, Rebecca had composed her expression to resolute and relaxed her body language. There she was, the crisis negotiator, projecting confidence and caring, whatever she felt inside. Will murmured, "You take lead. He reacts to you in a way he doesn't to me. I'll intervene if I think I have to, but you did fine last time."

She nodded stiffly.

After ringing the doorbell, Will listened to the *bong* deep inside and wondered if Jordan was hearing it, too.

The door opened promptly. A burst of canned gunfire accompanied Tim, who gaped at them. "You want to talk to me *again?*"

Rebecca dipped her head. "We do."

"Well, uh, sure." He backed away, not seeming as cocky today. Taken aback? "I was just eating. You know. And watching a movie."

Will flicked a glance at the screeching car chase on the big-screen TV. An open pizza box sat on the coffee table along with a roll of paper towels and an open can of beer. Would his mommy be dismayed to find out her darling son wasn't using a coaster?

"I'd appreciate it if you'd turn off the TV," Rebecca said, still sounding pleasant.

"You sound..." He hesitated.

She raised her eyebrows.

"Like you think I've done something!" he burst out.

"The TV."

"Oh. Yeah." He found the remote on the floor in front of the sofa and aimed it at the monster television. The sudden silence had Will bracing himself.

"Do you mind if we sit down?" Rebecca asked.

"Huh?" Tim shifted his weight, his hands knotting and unknotting again, the way they had the last time they were here. "No. I mean, sure. Go ahead." He dropped onto what was likely the same cushion where he'd been sitting when they rang the doorbell.

Will sat only a few feet away on the sofa, Rebecca on an upholstered chair facing them. Tim's gaze slid sidelong at Will. *I'm making him uneasy. Good.*

"So—" He jumped to his feet. "You want coffee? Or...not a beer, I bet. But something?"

"Thank you. No."

After a moment, he subsided, managing to increase his distance from Will in resuming his seat.

"First," Rebecca said, "I wanted to thank you for trying to come to my rescue the other day. When my Tahoe broke down."

Seeing shock on Spiva's All-American face, Will almost smiled. *Smart.*

"How did you—? I mean, what are you talking about?"

"Wasn't that you? I thought how nice it was of you. Then it turned out I had a second knight in shining armor when Carson stopped, too. I'd have been in trouble without him."

Truer words had never been spoken, Will thought.

And oh, yeah, Spiva's expression darkened. "I don't know what you're talking about."

Rebecca looked puzzled. "I was so sure that was you. Driving one of your parents' cars, I figured."

The muscles in his jaw balled. "Wasn't me."

"I see." She leaned forward. Her gray eyes glinted like steel. "We weren't all that surprised when Jordan was abducted this morning. You hinted as much, didn't you, Tim?"

His shoulders hunched, and Will could feel him wanting to leap up again. "I don't know anything about that, and I don't like you talking to me this way." If he was trying for hurt bewilderment, he failed. There was a darkness in his voice that transformed what he'd said into a threat.

Rebecca challenged him with her gaze. "No? Tim, you have an obvious link to both missing girls. That makes me...uneasy." She paused. "Fortunately, there's something you can do that would help us cross you off our list and turn our attention elsewhere."

He tried to hold out, but couldn't. "What?" he finally asked.

"I know you're insulted at the idea we might be looking at you for something awful like this. I regret making you feel like that. But we can take care of it easily. We'd just like to do a walk-through of this house. Not such a big deal." She infused her voice with some humor. "If you've dropped dirty clothes and empty beer cans everywhere, I won't tell your mom and dad, I promise. Of course, you're welcome to accompany us."

"That's bullshit!" He exploded to his feet.

Will rose to his as fast. Operating on instinct, he lowered his hand to the Glock at his hip.

Rebecca stayed seated, her expression registering faint surprise. "Why would you mind, Tim?" She studied him. "Didn't you tell me you'd do anything at all to help us find Mandy?"

"You won't find her here!"

"No?" Still cool as a cucumber, she asked, "What about Jordan, Tim? Where will we find her?"

"You're treating me like shit, and you don't even know what happened to either of them!" His head lowered like an angry bull's. "I want you to go. I shouldn't have let you in. I was trying to be *nice*."

"Why won't you just let us walk through?" Rebecca asked. "No sweat for you, right? You can erase our suspicions, just like *that*." She snapped her fingers.

Spiva jerked. "I don't have to, and I won't. You need to leave."

Rebecca shook her head. "I'm really disappointed in you, Tim."

"Yeah, well, I'm disappointed in *you*. I thought we were friends, sort of."

Sure he did.

"So you're throwing us out."

"Yes!" he yelled. "If you don't go, I'll call Dad, and he'll call his lawyer!"

"Your dad." Will went for a musing tone. "Good idea, Tim. Glad you thought of it." He lifted his phone. "I have his number in here. After all, they own the house, don't they? *They* can give us permission to search."

Alarm suffused his face. His body flexed and bulged, like one of nature's odd creatures designed to swell to appear more dangerous. "Get out! Now!"

"Sure." Will let Rebecca go ahead of him, then scrolled calls until he came to Gregory Spiva's phone number. "Yeah, here it is."

On the porch, both turned to face Tim, who had suddenly, eerily, calmed down.

"If you do that—" he nodded toward Will's phone "—you'll be sorry."

His voice, deep and growly, raised the small hairs on the back of Will's neck. "Are you threatening a police officer?" he asked.

"You don't even know if a crime has been committed, do you?" Tim Spiva smiled. "Come back and talk to me if you ever find either of their bodies, why don't you?" The door closed quietly in their faces. The dead-bolt slid home.

"Call," Rebecca said urgently.

Scowling and walking to the driveway to be sure he was out of earshot of the house, Will did. Three rings. Four. Five. Then a man snapped, "Is this Lieutenant Wilcynski again?"

"Yes, it is, Mr. Spiva. I'm calling to ask you to give permission—"

"Forget about it!" Spiva senior snapped. "My son is on the phone with his mother right now, shocked to find himself under police suspicion of hideous crimes! I told you Tim isn't capable of anything like that, but you didn't listen to a word I said, did you? Tim is a good kid who sometimes doesn't understand how people see an expression or something he says. I suppose," he said grudgingly, "that he might have a little of that Asperger's thing. If you can't tell the difference between that and—"

"Mr. Spiva," Will interrupted, "did Tim tell you that a young woman he recently dated has now been abducted?"

"He says he's told you they weren't dating, that she's just a new addition to that group of friends. There's not a reason in the world for you to connect him to her! Leave us alone."

Dead air.

Beside him, Rebecca stared at the house. "She's in there." Her voice cracked. "I can't believe this. He could be killing her right this minute."

*****

Rebecca didn't care whether anyone saw her and Will eating together that evening. She had no appetite anyway, and couldn't remember what she'd ordered or why she'd bothered.

She had begged Will, insisting there had to be *something* they could do.

He had tried, she had to give him that. He'd called Tim's brother again, having to leave a message.

"This girl could die anytime. Tim is taunting us, saying we can't do anything until bodies are found. The only way we can be certain we're wrong about him is if we can search your parents' house. They've dug in to defend their belief that he's a good-hearted, misunderstood boy. If you can persuade them to change their mind, you might save a young woman's life."

She'd felt drained after that, not knowing whether Evan would even listen to Will's plea, much less take action. Or whether he *could* influence his parents.

Colburn had agreed to put an officer in front of Tim's house, the police presence so conspicuous neighbors would be wondering about it. A deputy would take over in the early evening.

Then Will had gone to talk to the sheriff, who promised to make calls to a few judges he considered most likely to grant warrants on thin evidence. An hour later, he walked into the detective unit later, shaking his head.

When Will came out of his office, Mackay said, "I came the closest with Parsons, who conceded that Spiva's link to the two women is compelling, but he said he needs physical evidence or at least convincing testimony that Spiva has demonstrated a pattern of violence. He said essentially the same thing the father did: people on the Asperger's or autism spectrum can present in unsettling ways. They say the wrong thing and never know they have."

"This son of a bitch is sneering at us," Will said tautly. "I know the difference."

He and Rebecca worked the phones, talking to anyone and everyone who had known Spiva from high school on – teachers, coaches, employers. There was almost always a hesitation, and it became clear nobody felt comfortable with him, but Evan was the only one to hint at a vicious temper.

Evan didn't call back.

Now, sitting across the table from Will at Costas, Rebecca said, "What if we claim we heard a woman scream? Given our suspicions, wouldn't that qualify as exigent circumstances?"

"Sure." In his growl, she heard the same frustration she felt. "But what if we find no woman inside? Even if Tim's our guy, he could be holding the women elsewhere." His intense gaze didn't let her look away. "Rebecca, we can't do anything that won't stand up in court. How would you feel if he ended up walking, and probably smirking, because we violated his rights?"

Rebecca made herself nod. She wanted to be mad that he was able to maintain a self-command that eluded her, but also understood she might be falling apart if not for this man and the very unyielding quality that made him someone she could trust completely.

I'm seriously falling for him, she realized, with shock she didn't need on top of everything else happening. How was it possible? She'd hardly known Will until this past week – until then, he'd been Lieutenant Wilcynski, a fascinating, sexy but distant figure – and she'd been sure she disliked him after their initial encounters.

But she'd spent more time with him in a week that she would in several months of a typical dating relationship. She'd already been deeply in trouble by the time Will insisted on feeding her last Friday night, after Mr. Brodsky killed himself. *One week ago, right now.* Another wave of unreality hit her. That day, she'd seen beneath the aggressive personality, the arrogance of a big man able to cast most people into his shade, to the rock he really was. His steady gaze had kept her going when she thought of faltering. He'd picked her up after what felt like a failure and put her back together, offering unstinting praise she hadn't even known she needed. And since then…he'd come running every time she needed him.

And, God help her, she'd never felt anything like she had in his arms on her living room sofa.

"I never called Shelley," she said numbly.

"Then call her now."

A young waitress bustled up with their dinners. Rebecca looked down to see that she'd ordered exactly what she always did: a chicken breast gyro with feta. At the sight, her stomach growled, making her realized she'd never even *thought* of lunch.

"Eat," Will said brusquely. "You can't be effective on the job if you don't take care of yourself."

"I haven't so much as seen a treadmill all week."

"Me, either. But let's start with food."

Her first bite tasted so good, she began gobbling. Guilt assailed her when she swallowed the last bite and wadded up the wrapper, but she tried to block it. Will was right.

"I can't cancel on Shelley this late." Wise decision or not, it wasn't as if there was anything else they could do tonight except go watch Tim's house – and someone else was already doing that.

Of course, Will's dark brows drew together. "Damn it, Rebecca, that's the last thing you need!"

"No, I can do it. It'll be good for me. I know I've...expressed some fears to you, and maybe seemed weak, but have I failed on the job in any way?"

He kept frowning at her, his eyes as dark as bitter espresso, but after a minute he sighed. "No. I don't think I said so, but you did everything I asked and more in talking to Tim. You're good with words." He moved his shoulders as if alleviating tension. "No, it's a lot more than that. Just hearing your voice, I feel my mood lifting. I suspect you have that effect on most people. I think you could convince damn near anyone to do anything."

She might have started to blush at the first part of his speech, but the end... Dismayed, she said, "You make me sound manipulative."

Shaking his head, he set down his own gyro and wiped his fingers. "Not you. Even if you're trying to persuade someone toward a goal – and you must do that during a negotiation – you're thinking about what's best for them, not only the hostages if there are any. Intentions count."

"I could go evil."

He smiled, just a little. "Not you, Rebecca."

Will asked some questions about the crisis line staffing, probably just to distract her. She explained that shifts typically ran four hours, that the line was unmanned from two until six in the morning, and that poor Shelley had to do a lot of filling in. Many volunteers did a couple shifts a week, including her, and others, like the retired psychiatrist, might do five or six. "I think he's bored," she added. "A lot of people who work in social services throughout the county step in. We all want to help *before* something really bad happens."

She wasn't surprised by Will's interest. For one thing, a lot of the people who called in would eventually bump up against a police agency, most often as victims.

When they arrived at the counseling center, she directed him around back. When he pulled in next to a car she didn't recognize, Rebecca said, "I'll see you at ten," and reached for the door handle.

"I'm walking you in." No give.

Rebecca rolled her eyes. "I'll look like a kid being walked to her classroom."

He flashed a wicked grin. "I could kiss you goodbye. Would that help?"

She was still smiling when she relieved the current volunteer, a guy who she had crossed paths with a couple times. Doug Vaughn looked like a college student but was actually an assistant D.A., which meant he had a law degree and almost had to be at least twenty-five. Even as he eyed Will, leaning comfortably against the wall as if he was a fixture, Doug told her about a couple of calls and they went over the log.

Ear tuned for the ring of the phone, Rebecca poured herself a cup of coffee and returned once Doug was gone to find Will prowling through the small, windowless room.

"Place makes me claustrophobic," he growled.

"Your office isn't any better. The day you interviewed me, I felt as if I was locked in a cage with a tiger."

He laughed, and as usual her heart soared at the sight of Will happy.

"Tell you the truth, I don't love my office, either. Why do you think I leave the door open most of the time?"

Very sweetly, she said, "To encourage your detectives to think they can pop in anytime? To remind them you're there?"

"Yeah, that, too." His mouth quirked. "Doesn't hurt for them to know that I've got my eye on them, too."

Rebecca laughed, too, even as she shook her head. "You need to go away. I can't have you sitting here listening when I get a call."

"Fine. I'm going to the health club." He sobered. "I'll have my phone with me at all times."

"Me, too."

"Good. Don't let anyone in without knowing who it is first."

She rolled her eyes. "Adult, here. Cop."

"Armed. Yeah, yeah." Big, warm hands framed her face just before he kissed her until she lost awareness of time and place and duty. When he lifted his head at last, they stared at each other. His eyes smoldered. Hers were probably dazed. Will nodded and left her there, suddenly feeling chilled and very alone.

It was probably just as well the phone rang.

She cleared her throat a couple of times before she picked up the receiver, wanting to be sure her voice wasn't so husky, she sounded like a woman who'd just crawled out of bed.

"Crisis line," she said. "My name is Rebecca. How can I help you?"

"Oh, goody!" a man said. "I thought you'd be there. All by yourself, now that your boss finally left."

Tim Spiva. Who had somehow evaded the surveillance team and managed to follow her and Will – and must be outside the building right this minute.

Her stomach clenched in dread and she turned her chair to look at the closed door. If she stepped out into the hall…would she still be alone?

CHAPTER FOURTEEN

No, ridiculous. The outside door is locked, Rebecca reminded herself, to quell the icy sensation. The outside *steel* door is locked. The door she was staring at, the one separating her from the counseling center, hall and break room, was steel, too, and should also be locked. Except…she suddenly didn't remember doing so after Will left.

She leaped up and hurried to it. God, she hadn't locked. She flipped the deadbolt, closed her eyes and concentrated on pulling herself together. *This is what you do.*

"Why would you care whether the lieutenant stayed or not, Tim?" she asked in a tone of unconcern.

"I don't like him" was the sharp reply. "He thinks you're *his*."

She reached for her own phone.

Should she rile Tim by admitting that she and Will did have a relationship? No; it was none of his business.

"I don't like the idea that you're following me," she said.

"Who said I am?"

"How else would you know Lieutenant Wilcynski brought me here?"

"Maybe I just happened to drive by."

Rebecca's skin crawled because he sounded so pleased with himself. "There's a police officer sitting in front of your house. How did you leave without him seeing you?"

"I parked somewhere else. It's none of that cop's business if I leave or where I go." His tone darkened. "You shouldn't have put him there, Rebecca."

"That sounds like a threat." She began typing a text.

Tim on—

"It's a fact," he said.

—phone. Is here or near.

She sent it winging on its way, praying Will hadn't gotten as far as the health club, wasn't in the middle of getting undressed.

"Why did you call me here, Tim? You have my own phone number."

"You're alone there. I like knowing no one else is listening. It's just us."

"I can't tie up the line to chat. Someone may be trying to call who really needs me."

"How do you know *I* don't?"

Revulsion spilled into all her other emotions. "We hardly know each other, and you seem to be trying hard to disturb me. Why would you do that?"

"Being nice didn't get me anywhere, did it? You lied to me last Sunday. You said you weren't going to be searching, but you did. With *him*."

Her phone vibrated and she looked down even as she answered, "Only police officers were permitted to enter vacant houses."

On my way. Patrol unit dispatched too.

"Did you really think Mandy was in one of them?" Suddenly calm, Tim sounded only curious.

"No," Rebecca said, "but we had to look."

"She might be now."

She tensed.

"You know, like musical chairs. Stay one hop ahead of the cops."

"Is that why you called? To tell me where Mandy is?"

He laughed. "Why would I do a dumb-ass thing like that?"

"Mandy trusted you. You were friends."

"We *weren't* friends," he snarled, in another instant mood swing. "She cut my heart out. So why would I care what happened to her?"

"You said you did. That you wanted to help."

"You lie. So can I."

Will believed he could get anyone to do anything. *So try.*

"We still need your help," she said, projecting warmth with all she had. "Do you know how scared her mom and dad are? Have they ever been anything but nice to you, Tim? And what about her little girl? She needs her mommy."

"You called the cops," he said suddenly. "Bitch. I just wanted to talk."

"What do you mean?" But she could hear the siren through their phone connection.

"You shouldn't have done that," he whispered, and was gone.

Even so, she said, "Tim?" But the quality of the silence told her the connection had been severed.

Not two minutes later, someone hammered on the back door.

*****

"It's pitch dark up here," Will complained, blinded except for the narrow slice of the night illuminated by his headlights. They swung across the front of her cabin, then, as the driveway curved, lit up the carport, plunging the cabin once more into darkness. "You can't even see lights from neighbors' houses."

Rebecca's rejoinder was quick and predictable. "City boy."

He knew she was trying to convince him she was fine, but *he* wasn't fine. He was angry, and scared, and fighting a familiar sense of helplessness. He had done everything he could think to do for his sister, and she'd been brutally killed anyway. If that piece of scum got to Rebecca—

He wasn't letting her out of his sight.

All he did now was shake his head. "You have a nutcase obsessed with you, and we've just isolated ourselves on the side of a mountain at night."

"This time, if he breaks in, I *will* shoot him."

Not if Will saw him first.

"I usually leave some lights on," she admitted.

He saw that she, too, was looking toward the cabin. Once he turned off the engine, they both sat in silence for a minute. He, for one, was waiting for his eyes to adjust. There had to be *some* light.

Her phone rang. She answered, saying, "Thanks for calling."

All Will could hear was the rumble of a man's voice. Rebecca listened, said, "We have our eye on someone local, so I'm not surprised, but it's good to eliminate him as a possibility anyway."

When she ended the call, she said, "That was Jantz."

The Portland detective trying to verify Brian Vail's alibi. "And?"

"He got lucky. Courtney something-or-other came into the bar tonight. Someone pointed her out, and she agreed that she'd spent last Friday night with him. Jantz had the impression she was there looking for the creep."

"One detail cleared up."

Rebecca sighed. "The back door is closest."

"Okay. Let me grab my duffel, and you can lead the way." While he had the back hatch open, Will also pulled his gun. If Rebecca noticed, she didn't comment.

A minute later, they were inside. She immediately turned on the back porch and kitchen lights. When she opened her mouth, he shook his head. In her ear, he murmured, "I'll do a walk-through."

Unlikely Spiva would think she'd come home alone. Still, he might be foolish enough to believe Will would just drop her off. If so, he was in for a surprise.

But no one was here. Relaxing marginally as he closed her closet door, Will holstered his Glock and walked back to the living room. "Where is he?" he said.

"Not here, I take it."

He still carried plenty of tension. "Not inside, at least."

"Why wouldn't he have gone home?" she asked.

"Because he thinks you might have been taping the conversation, and what he said was enough to enable us to get a warrant?"

"And yet, it wasn't," she said, with understandable bitterness.

"Mackay might yet find a judge who'll sign off." He crossed the room and took her in his arms. Her body stayed stiff. Not rejecting him, he thought. She was wound up, and he couldn't blame her.

"He's crazy!" she burst out. "Really crazy. Why would he call me like that?" She sounded as if she were begging, and for an answer he didn't have.

Will only shook his head and ran his hands over her back. She wouldn't like knowing that every time he touched her, he was struck again with her relative physical fragility. When he first joined the sheriff's department, he'd seen her laughing and swaggering with the other deputies, and assumed she was tough. She had to be, in one way, to have seen and done what she had as a cop for nine years. But she could be hurt a whole hell of a lot more easily than he could, and yeah, that scared him.

"Can we have a fire?" he asked.

"What?" She lifted her head, expression startled. "Oh, sure."
Then she smiled. "City boys don't know how to start fires, do
they?"

"This city boy has camped and built beach fires, so I imagine I
can figure it out," he said drily.

"I can do it quicker. Um...do you want to sleep out here
tonight? Or in my bedroom?"

He thought about it while she knelt in front of the cast-iron
stove and wadded newspapers from the pile beside it. They'd be a
lot more comfortable in her bed. Maybe too comfortable. If Spiva
hadn't known where her room was, he did after she'd called out last
night. He could smash the glass and shoot into the bed faster than
either Will or she could react.

"Out here." He crouched beside her. "I like sleeping with you
on top of me."

She glanced sidelong. "That's good." Her voice had become
husky. Sultry, however unintentionally. "Because I liked sleeping
on top of you."

He was hard, just like that. "You had to say that," he muttered,
wincing a few times as he rose to his feet.

Her laugh was the sexiest sound he'd ever heard. He'd never
have forgiven himself if he hadn't managed to buy a pack of
condoms at a convenience store when he stopped for gas.

Flames flickered inside the stove, then leaped eagerly from the
newspapers to devour kindling. She took her time, carefully placing
larger pieces of split wood and sawed branches.

"You cut your own wood?"

"My dad helps. I don't have a chain saw, so every so often he
brings his up here. I have ten acres, and all of it's wooded except
this clearing. So far, I've kept myself in firewood just from downed
trees and branches. I let them dry for a while, Dad cuts them up, I
split 'em."

"Pioneer spirit."

"You're not burning wood to save on your electric bill?"

"I'm thinking about it," he admitted. There was something
about a wood fire. The heat felt different, and the woodsy, smoky
smell conjured memories of his family gathered around a crackling
bonfire when they camped in the Sierras.

Long ago and far away, he thought.

Apparently satisfied, Rebecca closed the stove door. A glass inset let them still see flames.

Deciding to bide his time, Will took a shower while she made coffee. He put on sweatpants and a T-shirt, and, remembering her reaction last night, left his feet bare. He padded down the hall to find her curled at one end of the sofa, cradling a steaming mug in her hands. His coffee waited on the coffee table. Personally, he'd just as soon have turned out the lights and made love to her by firelight, but she'd positioned herself in a way to suggest she wasn't ready.

Taking his cue, he sank down a couple of feet from her and reached for his cup.

"We're risking our jobs here, you know," she said after a minute.

"I do know." He kept his gaze on the fire, although he was plenty aware of her. "Why do you think I held off?"

"Held off?" She gave him a look. "What, three or four days?"

A grin tugged at Will's mouth. Okay, they'd only worked together for a week now. No, eight days, none of which either of them had managed to take off.

"I did a little better than that," he said mildly.

She gave a small snort.

"Come on." He turned his head, meeting her eyes. "You were hot for me, too. You can't deny it."

Rebecca was honest enough not to argue. "No, but I knew getting involved with you was stupid. Unless, I don't know, this is just a quick fling you're hoping no one learns about."

Annoyed, he clunked his cup down on the table. "That's what you think?"

"I don't know!" Distress was there. "That's what I'm asking."

"Rebecca." He moved just enough closer to be able to take her hand. He set their clasped hands on his thigh. "If I hadn't been serious about you, I'd never have started this. I was hit hard the first time I saw you. I told myself what I was feeling was lust." This was more than he'd meant to say yet, but he pushed himself to go on. "I hadn't hooked up with anyone since I moved here. I decided to make myself look around. You were off limits, but there had to be other women who'd be interested."

A muffled sound came from her.

Will grimaced. "Trouble was, I didn't see anyone who interested *me*. Maybe because I kept catching glimpses of you. Even in that ugly damn uniform, I could tell how long your legs are, and you have this natural saunter, like a model on a runway."

"I do not!"

"Sorry, but you do. Every time you walk down the hall, I see guys turning to stare. It's all I can do not to punch them."

She gaped at him. "I haven't had that many men I work with ask me out."

"Maybe because most of them were afraid of you," he said, only half joking. "Or smart enough to know they risked losing their jobs."

"So why didn't *you* keep your distance? Or is it because Lieutenant Wilcynski is more important than a mere deputy, newly become detective. It's me who'll have to quit if we go anywhere with this, isn't it?" she challenged him, not quite hostile, but close.

Of course that's what she'd been thinking, he realized; she had worked nine years as a cop in a rural county, where women on the job were unlikely to have been accepted readily. Her reality had been facing down conscious and unconscious bias.

"No," he said. "What we'll do is make decisions together. I'll start looking for another job in the area."

"I could get one more easily than you can," she said slowly, her expression wary.

"That's true, but you have a history with our department that I don't. I'm the newcomer." He hesitated, hoping she wouldn't take this wrong. "You do need to think about whether this is what you want to keep doing, though. I'm getting the feeling you may be at a crossroads."

She crossed her arms tightly, holding herself in. "Because I admitted to some PTSD."

"No." How to say this? "Because I think you need to emotionally invest yourself in the people you're helping. As a cop, you can't afford to do that beyond a point, or you'll burn out."

The gaze she fixed on him held desperation. "Is that what's happening now?"

"Damn it, Rebecca." Will couldn't take the distance she'd established. He scooted over and tugged her into the circle of his arms. "No. What's happening is some panic disorder because of the shooting, mixed up with a first investigation that echoes a little too closely the way you lost your mother. What's more, it's a frustrating one involving people you once knew. On top of that, the man we think is the killer has attempted to grab you. Twice. You show me a cop who would stay cool under that much pressure, I'll show you one who is either pretending for all he's worth or so cold-blooded, we don't want him wearing the badge."

Rebecca studied him for a long time before she sighed and let her head drop forward to his shoulder. He closed his eyes in relief, savoring that gentle weight along with the warmth of the fire and the fact that she had as good as said she wanted to pursue this relationship, too.

Hell, he was past the idea of pursuing it, which implied something that was just out of reach. He was already involved. He'd swallowed the hook, and she could reel him in any time. So, okay; he was holding back a little to give Rebecca time to get on board. She was getting hit from a lot of directions right now. He'd be an asshole to push her too hard.

Uh huh. Wasn't that what he'd been doing? Putting her on notice?

Maybe, but because they worked together – and he was her supervisor – they didn't have the luxury of dating for three months before they made any decisions. Especially with her in danger. He wouldn't be able to hide his twenty-four-hour-a-day bodyguard services for long.

Rebecca was the one to finally wriggle a little, separating herself from him enough to look at him. "I can't believe we're having this talk."

"Yeah." He cleared his throat. "I know this has come out of nowhere."

She shook her head, then nodded, then shook her head again. And finally laughed, if weakly. "It did happen fast. And there's so much I don't know about you."

"Like?"

"Oh, your childhood, your parents, why you went into law enforcement, your favorite color or movie or book—"

"Do people have favorite colors?"

This chuckle appeared genuine. "Of course they do. Mine is red. Look around you."

He turned his head, for the first time taking in details unrelated to security: the huge framed photograph of bare branches and fallen leaves, the small pillows on the sofa, one of which she now clutched on her lap, the rugs scattered on the hardwood floors. And he saw that, along with the warmth of wood, it was her use of red and rust and yellow, with hints of orange, that had made him aware her place was a lot homier than his.

"Those ceramic canisters on the counter in the kitchen are red," he said. Glossy red. A teakettle on the stove was, too, and he vaguely recalled noticing something copper hung above the burners.

"Favorite color: red."

He kissed the tip of her nose. "Got it."

"What about you?"

"I wouldn't wear it, but I have to say I like the red in here, so I'll go with that, too."

"Hey, we're compatible," she teased. "No need for further discussion."

She got up to add some wood to the floor, then snuggled up to him again as if she didn't want to be anywhere else.

"My parents," he said after a minute. Yet another thing he didn't talk about, but he was honest enough to realize that might be why his marriage flopped. One of the reasons. She didn't share, he didn't share. They might as well have been roommates with benefits. What he wanted with Rebecca was out of his experience, but part of it had to be letting the other person see the crap you usually kept buried deep. She'd exposed a lot of hurt. His turn.

"Things were good until I was about ten. At least from a kid's point of view. Then my parents started fighting. Really ugly. Looking back, and judging from what I heard, I think my mother had an affair." He shrugged. "My sister Stef and I huddled together. She was a couple years younger. I was afraid later that she'd married an abusive man because on an unconscious level that's what she expected. I don't know."

Rebecca reached up and gripped his hand, instinctively offering wordless comfort. That contact, bare skin to bare skin, was even better than having her pressed against his side.

To get it over with, he jumped to the ending. "My father killed her, then himself."

"Oh, Will," she whispered.

"He was thoughtful enough to do it when Stef and I weren't home. Maybe he thought gunshots would have a neighbor calling for the police, but, as it happened, everyone who lived close enough to hear was at work or school."

"You found them?"

Hearing the horror in her voice, he rubbed his cheek against her head. "Yeah. Thank God it wasn't Stef. She went home with a friend that day. At least she didn't have to see."

"Thank God *I* didn't have to see my mother. Why didn't you say, when I was telling you how I lost her?"

"I just...don't." Old emotions felt like rocks in his chest. "Most of the time, I don't think about it. It happened something like twenty-five years ago, you know." Actually, a little more than that, he realized.

"Then you're at least thirty-five?"

"Thirty-eight. Thirty-nine in March."

Rebecca nodded. "Even so..."

"Even so, you never forget."

"No." She was quiet for a minute. "He wasn't a cop, too, was he?"

"No. I wouldn't have followed in his footsteps. I hated him for a long time. Hated her, too, when I got old enough to understand what she'd done. Being exposed to that kind of violence, though, has an impact on your decisions."

"The destructive power of a gun."

"Something like that." More like losing the ability to trust. Will didn't waste much time analyzing his motivations. Sometimes, it was better *not* to know shit like that. His view of the profession underwent a seismic shift by the time he'd been on the streets a year, anyway. Now...he could hardly remember the boy he'd been.

Rebecca swiveled enough to look at him with those disconcertingly perceptive gray eyes. "What happened to you and your sister? You stayed together, right?"

"Yeah, an aunt and uncle took us in." He shrugged. "They had two kids of their own, so it wasn't ideal, but they were good to us. I stay in touch with them and my cousins."

"You're so confident. How can you be?"

That uncomfortable pressure in his chest pushed him to lighten the mood. "Guess it came naturally." He let a wry smile form.

"Stef used to call it bossy. I don't think I've ever been the best liked in any crowd, but I always end up giving the orders."

"Now, that I can believe." Rebecca had relaxed into quiet humor. "But *I* like you best."

The simple way she said it, her patent honesty, hit him hard. Baseball bat to the chest. When he could form words, he said roughly, "I like you best, too."

Her mouth curved into a smile that glowed. "Then I guess we're good."

"To hell with the job?"

"To hell with the job," she echoed in a whisper.

His control snapped, and he took her mouth with searing intent.

CHAPTER FIFTEEN

After the most extraordinary night of her life – and that was saying something after the previous night – Rebecca woke up slowly, reluctant to open her eyes. If it had been a dream, she'd just as soon stay asleep, thank you.

She realized she was alone, but cozy. Will must have tucked the quilt around her when he got up. So...where was he?

Her nose twitched at the smell of brewing coffee. And was that bacon?

"Rise and shine," he called from the direction of the kitchen. "Breakfast is almost ready."

Except for her mom and dad, nobody had ever cooked breakfast for her before. She smiled as she swung her feet to the floor, clutching the quilt around her. The house wasn't quite warm enough for her to want to make a naked dash for her bedroom.

"I'm up," she called back. "Getting dressed."

It didn't take two minutes to pull on her current working wardrobe – still no chinos or polo shirts – and pull her hair back into a ponytail. Will had already dished up when she reached the kitchen.

Not to be sexist, but she wished she'd actually *seen* him cooking. 'Domestic' was not a word that went with big, brawny and intimidating.

"This looks fabulous," she said, plopping down in front of one of the full plates. She was starving, and feeling way happier than she should be given what Jordan was going through and how the Shaws must feel as they waited for news and that she herself was probably soon going to be out of a job.

"Thought the smell of breakfast cooking would sweeten your mood this morning." Was his expression watchful?

"You already managed that."

He grinned. "Ah. If I'd known that, I wouldn't have bothered." Her wrinkled nose didn't seem to dampen his good humor.

Rebecca ate half her breakfast before she was able to make herself think again about Jordan and Mandy. Then she set down her fork and looked at him. "I have no idea what we should do today."

His jaw tightened. "I do. We're going to talk to neighbors. With it being weekend, we should have a good chance of catching most of them at home. Just because the nearest neighbors didn't see Tim come home last Friday night doesn't mean they won't have things to tell us. He seems to take offense easily. Did he strike back at one of them? Did anybody see him torturing an animal? Maybe Tim's mother confided in someone over coffee about her son's troubles."

Rebecca felt a different kind of energy tingling all the way to her fingers and toes. "Yes! I should have thought of that."

Will shook his head. "We've been a little busy, and, hey, this is your first investigation, remember?"

"Yes, but—" She wanted to jump up, but instead grabbed a piece of toast slathered with butter and jam and went back to eating. He'd gone to so much trouble, she could finish her meal.

They cleared the table together. It was weirdly smooth, as though they'd done this kind of thing together dozens – hundreds – of times. *I want every morning like this,* she thought. *Every evening. I want to spend every night in his arms.* The depth of her longing could have frightened her, but she wouldn't let it. Not today. She had to trust he'd meant the things he said.

She left him still loading the dishwasher while she brushed her teeth and paused to lower the thermostat. A phone rang – his, she knew right away. The call might not have to do with Tim or her; he did supervise seven other detectives and their investigations, after all. But the minute she entered the kitchen, Will turned, his gaze locking on hers.

"Evan," he said, "I'm going to put you on speaker again, since Detective Walker is with me. Is that okay?" A moment later, he set the phone on the table. "Can you hear me? Good."

Rebecca pulled up her chair. "Hi, Evan. Thanks for calling. Did you talk to your parents?"

"I tried. They wouldn't hear anything I said." Anger boiled in his voice.

The frustration in Will's dark eyes matched her feelings. "We appreciate you trying," he said. "Maybe you got through more than you think you did."

"I doubt it. They've never been willing to hear a bad word about him. But that's not why I called. I thought of something."

Rebecca straightened in her chair. "Something?"

"The Robinsons live directly behind us. Unless they've painted it, the house is tan with sort of pink trim."

She thought she could picture it, except the trim was more of a soft peach. "I know that house," she said.

"See, the Robinsons and Mom and Dad are good friends. He – Lloyd – retired last year, and they went to Arizona, too. Rented a house because they don't have an RV, but they all went jeeping together, hung out. You know."

Jeeping? But she wasn't about to interrupt. He was talking faster and faster, as if this was important.

"They had Tim watch over their house, too. Water plants. Make sure no big branches fell on the roof during storms. That kind of thing. I don't know for sure if they are going south again this winter, or if they've left, but..." He hesitated.

"It's possible Tim has access to another empty house," Will said.

"Yeah."

"If they're in your parents' confidence, are they likely to refuse to talk to us?"

"I bet Mom and Dad never say anything bad about Tim, even to them. There's no way they'd admit the cops have been calling them because they suspect him of abducting a woman."

"Any chance you'd have their cell number?"

"Unless Lloyd's changed carriers, I do have it. Lloyd and Judy were always Tim's and my backup if we couldn't reach Mom or Dad."

"Didn't they have kids?" Rebecca asked. "I don't think I babysat for anyone named Robinson."

"They moved in there later. When I was eleven or twelve, something like that."

Will wrote down the phone number, then said, "Evan, you did the right thing calling us."

After a short silence, he said, "Will you let me know? If this helps?"

Rebecca leaned forward to bring her mouth closer to the phone. "We will. I promise."

When he was gone and she and Will looked at each other, her heart thudded.

"Call. Hurry."

He pushed the phone toward her. "You do it."

"Me?"

His thick dark eyebrows rose. "You are primary."

She didn't think she actually was, but wasn't about to argue. Turning the napkin Will had used as notepaper, she dialed.

The phone rang four times before a voice said, "Lloyd here."

Rebecca introduced herself and said that Evan Spiva had given her his name. She asked permission to put him on speaker and explained that her lieutenant, also working the investigation, was with her.

He agreed, but said, "What's this about? Did someone break into our house?"

She started with Mandy's disappearance, which clearly shocked him.

"I know the Shaws. They're nice people. What about that cute granddaughter?"

"She's safe with them. Samantha is one reason we're sure Mandy didn't just take off. From what everyone tells us, she would never have left her little girl."

"No," he said gruffly. "No, I can't imagine."

She didn't tell him about her own close calls, but explained that the second missing woman had recently begun dating Tim. "She broke it off with him in a pretty insulting way. The fact that both women link to Tim drew our attention to him, and, to be frank, he's behaving strangely. He told me to come back and talk to him once we find the women's bodies, for example. I asked his permission to search his parents' house, and he refused. Unfortunately, they also refused." She paused. "Evan tells us that they are really protective of Tim, completely unwilling to consider him as troubled. I don't know what they've told you—"

"Not much." He went quiet for a minute. "Tell you the truth, Judy and I have wondered about him. There have been rumors in the neighborhood—" He broke off. "But he seemed to be holding down a job fine, and Gregory and Ann had such confidence in him, what could we say?"

Will bent closer to the phone. "Can you tell us about those rumors, Mr. Robinson?"

"I'd rather not," he said, obviously uncomfortable. "They're good friends."

"I understand." Will sat back, the lines in his face having deepened. "Just so you know, Tim has recently been fired from two jobs in succession."

The decking job had qualified more as a layoff, but Rebecca wasn't about to comment. "The reason I'm calling," she said, "is that Evan tells us it's possible you asked Tim to watch over your house again this year."

She read the small, ensuing silence as appalled.

"We did."

"It's possible that, if our suspicions are correct, Tim has held both young women captive in his parents' house. However, now that we know he has access to another house—"

"Oh, my God." His swallow was audible. "You think he could be using *our* home?"

"That is possible," she agreed. "What I'm hoping is that you'll allow us to do a walk-through to be sure that isn't the case. I know it could cause some awkwardness with the Spivas—"

"We're law-abiding people, Detective Walker." He sounded shaken. "You absolutely have our permission. I sure don't want *him* to ever step foot in our place again."

"It's important that you don't contact him or let the Spivas know we've called or about anything we've said until we've completed the search," she said urgently. "Please."

Voice tight, he said, "We were supposed to get together with them today, but I'll call and make an excuse. My stomach has been acting up some. I'll make it sound worse than it is."

"Thank you."

"We have a hide-out key," he added brusquely, telling her where it was. "You'll call as soon as you know something?"

"We will."

Not a minute later, she and Will were hurtling down her driveway. Not much for praying, she did this time.

Please let them be there. Please let them be alive.

*****

The crime scene van pulled in just as Rebecca came around the corner of the house holding up a key. Thank God it had been where Lloyd Robinson said it was. If Tim had known there was one, sure as hell he would have taken it. Seemingly, the Robinsons *hadn't* told him, thinking of it as a backup in case Tim let them down or lost the key they'd given them.

"If he's here, he'll be looking to see who pulled into the driveway," he murmured to Rebecca. They'd agreed not to knock. They were going straight in.

She nodded and pulled her gun, as he already had.

She slid the key into the lock, turned it, and opened the door. Will burst through the opening, Glock in firing position. "Police!" he called.

They cleared the first floor, seemingly reading each other's minds. When they reached the kitchen, he eased open the cabinet beneath the sink with one finger and nodded toward it. The trash can overflowed with fast food wrappers, beer cans and more. Not likely the Robinsons hadn't emptied it before they left.

A glance into the utility room told him it, too, was empty – but the washer lid was open.

"Now, why would he do laundry *here?*" Rebecca murmured. Her eyes were bright with energy, rage and what Will suspected was hope.

He went up the stairs first, taking them two at a time, then flattened his back to a wall and listened. When he heard nothing but silence, he waved her up. Working together again, they started with the first room on the right, which appeared to be a den. She slid the closet open and shook her head.

Beyond ensuring it was empty, they skipped the bathroom. The CSI team would go over it. The last room on the right appeared to be the master bedroom, and both it and the second bathroom were pristine. Tim wasn't spending the nights in their bed just because he could.

Across the hall, empty sewing room. Linen closet – no room for anyone to hide.

The last door was closed. Will didn't let himself feel anything beyond the familiar tension and sharpness of focus.

He gingerly turned the knob using the hem of his shirt so as not to leave fingerprints – or mar the ones there. Then he shoved open the door and Rebecca flew in with weapon ready.

"Oh, thank God," she whispered. "Jordan."

Will stepped in, holstering his gun. A barely recognizable Jordan Torgerson lay spread-eagled, tied to the bedposts, her mouth duct-taped, her face and naked body bruised and bloody. But her eyes were open – and tear-filled.

*****

Seeing extra bedding piled on the shelf in the closet, Rebecca immediately grabbed a blanket to cover the girl. Will tore off the duct-tape in a single, ruthless, ripping motion that left her skin red and inflamed, but she gasped for air through it.

He pulled out a Swiss knife and neatly sliced each of the ropes halfway between her wrists and the bedposts. Keeping the knots intact could be important to compare to any found with Mandy. Leaving Rebecca to comfort a now-sobbing Jordan, Will called for an aid car and summoned the CSI team.

When it became apparent Jordan couldn't lower her arms to her side, Rebecca gently kneaded the frozen shoulder muscles until she was able to slowly move them to what would be a more comfortable position once the spasms let up.

"Jordan." Rebecca bent over, waiting until the young woman really looked at her. "Have you seen Mandy?"

Her face convulsed again, but she also shook her head.

"Has Tim said anything about her?"

She curled into a ball, the sobs escalating.

It seemed like an eternity until the medics arrived, maneuvering a gurney into the bedroom. Thank goodness, Carson wasn't one of them. A minute later, with a rattle and kind words from the EMTs, she was carried out. Not moving, Rebecca listened as they progressed awkwardly down the stairs. By the time she heard them outside, she'd managed to turn her gaze from the open doorway back to the bed with its blood-stained sheets. Anger bubbled, boiled, so corrosive, it spilled acid into her mouth.

When Will came through the door, she said, "I should have shot him when I had the chance."

"Killing someone stains the soul."

"I don't care."

"I know." He wrapped his hands around her upper arms and bent forward to kiss her forehead. Somehow he must sense that she couldn't let herself lean on him right now. The anger made her strong.

"Did you call Mackay?"

"I did. He'll let us know the instant he gets the warrant. We'll want to be ready."

She nodded. "Let's see if anything of Mandy's is mixed in with those clothes." The small heap in a corner had drawn her attention while she comforted Jordan.

"We need photos first." Will went out in the hall and spoke to someone, who then followed him into the bedroom. He looked only vaguely familiar to Rebecca.

He nodded to her. "Detective Walker. I'm Marc Brunner." He glanced at Will. "There's blood in the sink and bathtub. Not much to the eye – he must have thought he'd rinsed it away – but it's there in enough quantity to suggest there was a hell of a lot."

Rebecca's stomach turned over, but she nodded.

Brunner snapped photos of the pile of clothes, then spread out what was there with a gloved hand.

Rebecca's muscles locked. "There are two pairs of panties."

"Christ." Beside her, Will stared. "There are."

"We'll get DNA off of them." Brunner said matter-of-factly.

Rolling his shoulders, Will said, "All right. Detective, let's get over to the Spivas' house."

When they pulled up in front a minute later, she saw the patrol car still at the curb. They parked and walked to the driver side window as the deputy rolled it down. "Lieutenant. Rebecca. Uh, guess I should call you detective now, shouldn't I?"

Not for long, she thought, but only said, "Rebecca is fine." She nodded toward the house. "Any activity?"

"Nothing. I've been here since my shift started at seven. I haven't seen lights, motion." He shrugged. "Either the guy went on a bender and is dead to the world, or he isn't here."

"Okay." Will told him what they'd found at the Robinsons', and explained that they were waiting for a warrant. In fact, his phone pinged right then. "I want you to wait out here. Watch for a rat jumping ship."

The deputy, older but solid, said, "Gotcha."

Another marked car rolled to the curb just then. "Backup," Will said briefly. "We'll have to break in the door if Spiva doesn't let us in."

Rebecca had the sinking feeling that Tim wasn't, in fact, home. They rang the doorbell. Will hammered on the door. Straining, Rebecca heard nothing from inside.

They went around back, and found the kitchen door had a glass pane. Will tapped it with the butt of his gun, snapped on some gloves and reached inside to unlock and let them in.

This time, the four of them cleared the house, Will and she taking the upstairs, the pair of deputies the downstairs.

Tim wasn't home. About all they learned was that he was reasonably neat. The hall bathroom could use a scrubbing, but he must take out the trash and he did put his toothbrush and toothpaste away in the medicine cabinet. He didn't make his bed, but dirty clothes more or less made it into a hamper. A cursory search found no weapons of any kind.

His parents' Taurus was in the garage; the second bay sat empty.

Staring at it, Will said, "Where the fuck is he?"

At least he didn't have to ask how Tim had escaped the house with a cop sitting in front, since Tim had told her he'd taken to parking some distance away. With lots so big in this neighborhood, going out the back door and making his way through wooded yards without being seen wouldn't have been difficult.

Rebecca wished she could answer his question. Instead, she put into words what he was thinking. "Is he close enough to know we've gone into both houses and that Jordan is gone?"

"I'd bet on it," he growled. "I've already put out a BOLO on the Jeep."

That meant Tim would have to be careful, but reality was that in a sparsely populated county like this, patrols were spread thin. She made a mental note – check what vehicles the Robinsons had left behind, and whether Tim could have gotten his hands on keys.

Will walked the perimeter of the garage, returning to the door into the house and Rebecca without, apparently, having spotted anything of interest. All he said was, "He won't want to enter Cape Trouble or North Fork."

"No." Although who knew what Tim would do? His behavior had become increasingly irrational. Already crumbling, he would be enraged that Jordan had been taken from his control, and to have his parents' house no longer a refuge would have to shake him. Would he try to flee for Mexico? Call and beg Mommy and Daddy to bail him out? Or...?

It was the 'or' that stumped her. No, she didn't think Tim would flee. His ego wouldn't allow him to admit defeat. If he could find a new bolt hole, he might try to snatch another woman.

Me?

Between one blink and the next, she saw Jordan, naked, bloody, debased, but the memory enraged her. She had no room left for fear.

"Let's walk through both yards," she said suddenly. "I can see him laughing at the idea of burying Mandy so close to her home."

Will's gaze narrowed. "Let's."

*****

Spacing themselves about ten feet apart, they walked from the street fronting the Spivas' house to the street fronting the Robinsons', back and forth. They detoured only when necessary, to circle trees and the occasional large rhododendron. Either the Robinsons or a previous resident had planted perhaps a dozen, skillfully enough that they almost appeared native. Will wasn't a gardener, but he guessed they'd be beautiful in bloom.

He dragged a large, fallen fir branch to one side to be sure its placement wasn't deliberate. Tipping back his head, he could see where it had broken off. He'd just dropped it when Rebecca said in quiet voice, "Will."

He turned sharply.

Sitting on her heels, she said, "The ground looks disturbed here."

She was right. The distribution of fir and spruce needles and wet, rotting leaves was supposed to mimic the surroundings, but subtly failed. The ground was slightly higher, too, the earth too soft when Will toed it with his boot. The dimensions of the raised soil were a dead giveaway. He winced slightly at his unintentional pun as he studied what wasn't quite a hillock, roughly six feet by three feet. Perfect dimensions for a grave. Generous, even, given that Mandy Shaw had been a small woman.

He glanced at his watch. A cadaver-sniffing dog would have found Mandy's body even quicker, but it had taken the two of them only half an hour.

"Given a couple of months, the soil would have settled. She might never have been found."

"No." Mostly, what Rebecca's face showed was pity.

Given the stir the official vehicles must be causing in the neighborhood, he was surprised Stuart Shaw hadn't showed up to find out what was happening. Thank God he hadn't. If neither of them had cause to go out, they wouldn't have to stand by as their daughter's body was uncovered.

As much as Will hated notifications, he wished he could leave Rebecca out of this one, but knew it to be impossible. As hard as it would be on her, the Shaws would need her compassion. He couldn't imagine the news would truly shock them, however hard they'd been trying to hold onto hope.

He took out his phone and called Brunner, who said, "We need more manpower."

"I can dig. Let me see who else is available."

Holbeck had wound up his most pressing investigation yesterday and was probably at the paperwork stage. He answered his phone on the second ring. "Lieutenant?"

When Will explained, he said, "I'm on my way. You want me to bring tools?"

"I'll have Brunner call you."

After speaking to the CSI team leader, he called Mackay. "Looks like we found a grave at the back of the Robinsons' property."

The sheriff swore softly. "What do you need?"

"Nothing right now. What we don't have is Spiva. He's not home, and if he gets anywhere near, he'll see the activity here. His absence makes me nervous."

They briefly threw around useless ideas about where they might find him. When Will put away his phone and looked at Rebecca again, he saw that she'd risen to her feet and was talking on her phone. From her side of the conversation, she was getting an update on Jordan's condition.

When she was done, she said, "They've had to sedate her. The attending confirms she's been raped, from the damage probably multiple times. He believes the attacker wore a condom, but he did recover some semen. He guesses the assault was vicious enough to tear a condom."

With the woman not aroused, her vaginal passage would have been dry, too, increasing the friction. Hard not to remember that pathetic young woman crying, "Why me?"

"Has anybody tried to notify family?" Rebecca burst out.

Hating to see her distress, Will said, "I asked Worley to try to determine where she's from. Let me check my texts." Half a dozen had arrived. He scrolled down to Worley's, aware Rebecca was close enough to read it at the same time.

JT from Roseburg. Parents on way.

"Oh, thank goodness," she breathed. "I'll bet they take her home as soon as she's released, and she never comes back."

"She'll do better at home," he agreed. "She needs to talk to us as soon as she's able, though, and be prepared to testify in court."

"Her fragility will go over well with the jury," she commented. "That is, if she can avoid saying anything too spiteful."

"I think we can count on the DA to coach her," he said drily.

What he wanted was to wrap Rebecca in his arms, say the kind of soft things he'd never been known for, share his strength and maybe draw some of hers. But already Brunner was returning, and Holbeck would be here soon. Others would inevitably gather. He and she needed to maintain the façade, little as he liked it.

As soon as the drama of Tim Spiva's arrest was over, Will intended to sit down with Mackay and start putting out feelers for a new job. He wished Rebecca would examine her own heart, because he thought being an investigator would eventually damage her, but he had to be sure she knew he didn't expect her to make the sacrifice.

Ten minutes later, Holbeck and Britton walked around the Robinsons' house. Both carried shovels, Holbeck also hefting what looked like a gardening bucket that probably held smaller tools.

Britton nodded a hello. "I thought you could use some more help."

"Thanks," Will said briefly. Now they could trade in and out, and with luck Rebecca wouldn't feel obligated to take turns digging. Brunner watched like a hawk as they labored, sweating despite the damp air on the typically misty day. He would eventually go through the dirt they flung onto a pile with a sieve so as not to miss any tiny piece of evidence.

Rebecca watched in complete silence, never looking away from the growing hole, her face as still and pale as marble.

When Holbeck said, "The soil's more compact," they abandoned the shovels in favor of trowels and brushes.

Moments later, they all saw the jut of a human shoulder. Before, they'd spoken occasionally. Now, they worked in complete silence.

Naked, slashed in a dozen places including her throat, she lay on her side, the position of her limbs awkward. Spiva had just dropped her into the grave, Will realized, his anger cold. He hadn't offered her even the respect of dressing her, arranging her body or covering her face. He'd just shoveled the soil back on her, probably gloating because he believed no one would ever find her. It was easy to imagine him savoring and hugging to himself the knowledge that Mandy's grave was less than two blocks from the home she'd never see again.

Stepping back, Will laid a hand on Rebecca's back, not caring if anyone saw. She leaned into it, her small give telling him she needed the closeness. He couldn't forget her reaction to Brodsky's suicide. He knew her; she'd feel as if she had failed Mandy.

For a moment, they both watched Marc Brunner. Having taken over, he now crouched in the hole, gently brushing the earth from the young woman's face with the care her killer hadn't given her.

Rebecca's sigh felt like defeat.

"We need to tell her parents."

CHAPTER SIXTEEN

Yellow crime scene tape draped from bush to mailbox, continuing around the corner. Rebecca stood outside the Spiva's house, her ever-present frustration spiking. Beside her, Will made a slow turn, his cold gaze sweeping their surroundings. He hadn't said that he thought Tim was watching them, but his anger and non-stop vigilance spoke for him.

Reality was, twenty-four hours after they rescued Jordan, Tim Spiva had eluded all efforts to find him. Will's mood had deteriorated, as had his language. He'd stuck to Rebecca like glue. They had spent the previous night at her cabin again, but when she kissed him and slipped her hand beneath his T-shirt, he had stepped back.

"Don't tempt me. I can't get distracted tonight."

Incredulous, she'd gaped at him. "You really think you'll be blind and deaf to the rest of the world if you're making love with me."

"Yeah." He tipped her face up, his own expression softening. "That's what you do to me."

She'd been oh-so-tempted to stomp off to her bedroom and leave him alone *and undistracted* on the sofa, but…the lure of spending the night tangled up with him, her head on his shoulder, her hand over his heart, had her huffing out an unhappy breath and shoving more wood in the fire. Sad to say, distraction was exactly what *she'd* needed. There was so much she didn't want to think about.

Now, they went in the house, following voices upstairs to Tim's bedroom. Marc Brunner turned.

"Good, you made it. Let me show you what I found."

All the dresser drawers had been removed, but one sat upside down on a clean white sheet on the bed. The bottom looked like the typical, thin sheet of a cheaper wood, but Marc lifted the drawer enough so that they could see there were two bottoms. One fit in the groove typical of dressers of this era; the other had been tacked on lower.

"It stuck when I tried to pull it out," he said. "I figured the bottom was warped. You know how that happens. But then I took a closer look."

His hands encased in gloves, he turned the drawer back over and gently worked the original bottom out.

What had been the narrow space within held two bras, one a serviceable white, the other skimpy, pink, polka-dotted and lace-edged. Rebecca didn't have to be told which was which. The glint of silver drew her gaze to the white bra. A delicate chain had been wrapped around it. Marc lifted it enough that they could see the origami crane 'folded' out of sterling silver.

"Mandy's," Rebecca said softly. "His trophy."

Banked rage in his dark eyes, Will said, in a voice that was nearly guttural, "No jewelry for Jordan."

"She was wearing some. A toe ring and earrings."

"He might have been waiting to take those until she was dead."

"How's she doing?" Marc asked.

Rebecca had to take a slow, deep breath before she could answer. "Physically, she's not in bad shape. Severe bruising, a broken cheekbone, two cracked ribs and two broken fingers. Bent backwards. Three long cuts that will leave scars." Her own voice came out hoarse. "Emotionally..." She shook her head. "She hasn't been able to answer questions. She's curled into a ball, either crying or withdrawn so far she doesn't even respond to a voice. She wasn't a strong personality. Coming back from this will be slow."

"That he's keeping trophies..." Rebecca hesitated. "It suggests he'll go on killing, doesn't it?"

"That would be my take," Marc agreed.

Will growled, "And we still don't have any idea where that piece of shit is."

"If he's still around here, he'll pop up." Marc again.

This growl was wordless. Will swung around and walked out, the crime scene investigator looking after him.

"Anything else?" Rebecca asked.

"That was it."

"Okay. Thanks." She followed Will, finding him already standing beside his big Suburban, his gaze again raking the street and neighboring houses.

"I want to drive through Jasper Beach."

Her surprise changed to understanding. "All those vacant houses."

"The ones we've already searched."

She understood; Tim might think they wouldn't go back.

They spent an hour driving up and down the streets in the shabby enclave, bumping over potholes, gravel crunching beneath the tires. Every so often, he'd pull over and they walked around cottages that had to be seasonal rentals.

Finally admitting defeat, Will said, "I need a cup of coffee."

She left the choice of where to go to him, not surprised when he drove to the Sea Watch Café. It being a weekday, he was able to park close by.

"We should grab some lunch while we're here," Rebecca said, although she wasn't hungry. Still, her eye had gone to the folding whiteboard out front listing the day's specials.

"You're right," Will agreed.

"Why don't you order for us?" Rebecca suggested. She stopped on the sidewalk. "I'll take that split pea soup and you know how I like my coffee. I want to look at the pretty pictures for a minute, maybe talk to someone."

Realizing she wasn't with him, Will turned. His eyebrows rose when he realized she wasn't looking into the window of a gallery, but rather a real estate office.

"You won't need to buy a place."

Because he fully intended she would move into his, he meant. He'd never be comfortable living in the middle of the woods. Maybe she should be annoyed at his assumption, but wasn't that a logical step? And the truth was, she *wanted* to live with him. Sleep with him every night. They had a lot of decisions to make, but that wasn't a hard one for her.

"I just want to get an idea of prices. Maybe talk to someone for a minute."

Unless she was imagining things, his eyes warmed. Then he surveyed the street, every parked car, every pedestrian, before he nodded.

"Street's busy enough, it ought to be safe. Don't take long."

Rebecca saluted. "Yes, sir."

A smile might have been tugging at his mouth when he continued on to the café. Rebecca opened the door, the attached bell tinkling, and went into the real estate office, sandwiched between a high-end gallery and an antique store.

Photos of houses and land for sale were posted in the windows, both facing in and out, and the walls displayed more. A small hall likely led to a couple of offices at the back. She heard voices coming from one of them. A smiling woman came down the short hall toward her.

"How can I help you?"

"I'm thinking of selling," Rebecca admitted. "I mostly wanted to compare my place to others for sale, maybe take home a couple of those booklets." A stand held several editions that advertised local real estate.

"Are you leaving the area?"

"No, I—"

The bell tinkled behind her and a rush of cold air swept in. The Realtor looked past her and Rebecca began to turn. The slow transformation to shock on the woman's face triggered adrenaline, and Rebecca reached for her gun.

Something hard was jammed against her neck.

"Surprise! *I* came to see you this time, Rebecca," Tim said, sounding weirdly gleeful. "Turn slowly. I need to lock the door."

Seeing no alternative for the moment, she did. His long arm reached out and she watched him flip the deadbolt. Cars passed on the street, but no heads turned. There was no one on the sidewalk to look in and see what was happening.

Will. Come to check on me. Hurry.

Tim deftly removed her Sig Sauer from her holster. She heard no clunk to suggest he'd set it down. *Stuck it under his waistband,* she thought. If he turned at all…

"You!" he snapped, in an entirely different tone. "Stand next to her."

The Realtor, a woman who appeared to be in her late thirties or early forties, followed his order. She seemed shell-shocked.

"Pull down the blinds," he snapped.

Rebecca looked back through the window and found herself staring into the eyes of a man who, gaping, had come to a stop right outside. She jerked her head just slightly. *Go!*

His eyes widened and he broke into a run.

"No way to cover up the glass pane on the door," Tim mused, sounding unconcerned. "Oh, well. The offices don't have windows, do they?"

Rebecca's mind cleared. Oh, crap – there were other people in the building. Not giving herself time for second thoughts, she yelled, "We're being taken hostage! Run out the back door. Now!"

"Fuck!" Tim wrapped a thick arm around her throat, squeezing, and tried to turn her fast, as she resisted. Pain stabbed as he twisted her.

But she heard a babble of voices, then the slap of feet.

"Stop!" he bellowed, so close to her ear, she winced involuntarily. He wrenched her around to face the back.

Three strangers had reached the door at the end of the hall. Unlocking, opening it seemed to take forever.

Out of the corner of her eye, Rebecca saw movement. She flung out her arm and knocked Tim's just as he fired his handgun. No, too late. Blood blossomed on the back of a man's white dress shirt, but somehow they all fell through the opening before he could take aim again. One of them had the presence of mind to yank the door closed behind them.

"You fucking bitch," Tim snarled. "I might even have been *nice* to you."

That was almost funny, but she managed to keep her mouth shut. She'd counsel any hostage to avoid angering the HT. Her first priority had to be calming everyone down, especially him. *No, me first.*

Delay was her goal, now that somebody had seen them and, please God, called 911.

The other woman had begun to whimper. Rebecca didn't blame her. Deep in her psyche, she was doing the same. She'd never imagined that she would be the helpless one. But any display of fear on her part would feed Tim's ego and his form of crazy. He didn't rape and kill immediately; he was driven to humiliate, to degrade women. He wouldn't be satisfied if he couldn't push her into begging.

Yes, she thought, satisfied with the analysis. And then she made a vow: he would *never* see her afraid, no matter what he did to her.

"Move." He shoved the woman, who stumbled into a wall, then Rebecca, and they started down the hall, not stopping until they reached the back door. "Lock it."

The Realtor's terrified gaze slid sidelong to Rebecca, but once again she did as he asked.

The door appeared to be steel, the lock a dead-bolt. Assessing possibilities, Rebecca thought even the SWAT team would find entry through it to be a challenge. Unless someone on the outside had a key, of course. Like the Realtor who'd fled.

Tim looked over his shoulder, as aware as she was that they could still be seen from the sidewalk in front. "In there."

It was a bathroom, with a single, small window high on the wall.

"No." He changed his mind, herding them out into the hall again, the two women in the lead. She cast a desperate glance toward the front, but no one appeared in the small glass pane, the only other porthole to the outside. A second later, he shoved her ahead of him into the next room. This was an office designed to meet with the public, furnished with a desk meant to impress and several upholstered chairs facing it. On a computer monitor, Rebecca saw an elegant and no doubt staged living room.

"Sit!" Tim all but threw her into one of the chairs, so that for the first time she could see him. "You, too."

Trembling, the other woman dropped into a chair as if her knees had given out. Rebecca touched her arm, trying to convey silent reassurance.

Then she met Tim's eyes, her own eyebrows raised. "What were you thinking?" she asked, as if genuinely curious. "I thought better of you."

"No, it's perfect." His face darkened. "It *would* have been perfect if *you* hadn't warned those other people. I wanted more people."

"Why?"

"To kill, of course," he said as if surprised. "Why do you think?"

Okay, we are in deep shit. Held hostage by a nutcase in a room with no windows, the building locked and so long and narrow that

Tim would have plenty of time to shoot her and this other poor woman long before an assault team could penetrate this far. That was the moment when she had the shuddering, bowel-loosening understanding of what it *really* felt like to be held hostage. It was almost funny.

Because, in astonishing naivety, she'd always believed she knew.

*****

Will had claimed a corner table at the back in the small café and was mid-order when the front door flew open, the small bell smacking the glass. The man who stumbled in had the look of someone fleeing a natural disaster – or a murderous rampage.

"There's someone with a gun," he got out. "Next door. He...he had his gun to a woman's head."

Rebecca. Tim Spiva had gotten his hands on Rebecca.

He might as well have plunged a serrated knife under Will's ribcage. The air left his lungs in a hard rush. But he was a cop. Never more than now, he needed to think with a clear head.

Will allowed himself barely a moment of terror for the woman he loved. Then he yanked hard on the reins. He would *not* let that piece of shit have Rebecca.

Unconscious of having moved, he was right in the guy's face. He showed his badge and said, "Tell me *exactly* what you saw."

A buzz of agitated conversation burst out, but he turned and leveled a flat stare on the other diners, silencing them.

The man babbled, which was normal, but Will learned another woman had been present, too. Blinds were pulled, but either the glass pane on the door didn't have one, or they hadn't gotten to it yet.

"I think I heard a gunshot," he added. "Just now."

Not Rebecca. Please, God, not Rebecca.

A scream pierced the air outside, followed by raised voices. "Stay inside!" he called as he headed out the door. He immediately spotted the trio staggering around the corner of the of the café, which sat at the end of the block, and ran toward them.

"Please." One of the men turned his head. "Someone. Call 911."

Others probably already had, but Will dialed dispatch and explained the situation in a few terse words. Reaching the trio, he said into the phone, "Likely a GSW. We need medics *now*."

Flanking the injured, older man, the couple looked to be late twenties or early thirties. The petite woman was crumpling beneath the weight of the gunshot victim, but to her credit, she kept to her feet, bore her share of his weight. Face wet with tears, she lifted her head in surprise when Will nudged her aside. "I have him."

Already able to hear sirens, he got the three to the sidewalk right in front of the café. Before he could give an order, the café door opened again and a young woman dressed in chef's white rushed out, holding a pile of folded…towels? He accepted the pile from her. Cloth napkins. Smart.

"Thanks." He was already ripping open the dress shirt to reveal what had to be the exit wound. Pressing folded napkins to the wound, he raised his head. "What happened?"

The young guy dropped to his knees beside him. "We're wanting to buy a house. We were in the office with the Realtor—" he nodded down at the prone man whose mouth gaped in a rictus of pain "—him. We were looking on the computer at houses, when a woman out front yelled, something about being taken hostage and to run out the back door."

Rebecca again, risking Tim's rage to limit the number of hostages he was able to take. Using her head. Will felt a flicker of pride through the rage of his other emotions.

"I'm thinking, oh, sure, only…I don't know. She didn't sound like it was a joke. So all three of us crowded out into the hall, and I caught a glimpse of this guy with his arm around a woman's neck. And, shit, he had a gun in his other hand. So we ran." He swallowed, looking down at the injured man. "He… I can't even remember his name." It was hoarsely said. He lifted a shaking hand to rub it over his face. "He pushed us ahead of him. Kari got the door open, and there was this sort of roar and he fell forward, so we dragged him out and got the door shut. It's metal," he finished simply.

"We have a report that there may be two women in there."

"Uh…" Shock slowed his thinking. "There might have been— Yeah, I know there was a woman in the other office. So it has to be her. Unless she was the one he grabbed."

"Okay."

Aware that an ambulance had come to a screaming stop at the curb, Will rose to his feet to allow an EMT in a dark blue uniform to crouch in his place. A second one went to his knees on the other side of the wounded guy. He glanced up and nodded. Carson Crandall, utterly focused.

"He was shot in the back," Will told them. "Bullet went through."

Another nod, and they started working over the Realtor.

Will squeezed the younger guy's shoulder and said, "Running was the right thing to do. Don't start thinking you should have been a hero."

A startled look on his face, he said, "How'd you know—?"

"Human nature," Will said. "Please go sit down inside the café and stay put. An officer will need to ask you questions and get your contact info."

The guy staggered to his feet, as if he'd aged fifty years in the last ten minutes, put an arm around the woman and led her inside.

Lights flashing, the first CTPD car blocked the street at the corner and the officer leaped out. Not one of the kids, Will realized – this was Abbot Grissom, a career patrol officer in his fifties. He wasn't a big guy, but he projected calm and had seemed competent to Will in their limited interactions.

Will snapped out, "We need someone in back in case he tries to take his hostages out that way." He made himself say, "One of the hostages is a police officer." God, there'd already been time for Spiva to get them out and into a vehicle. Except…how could he drive and maintain control of two hostages? Would he even try?

Grissom was on his radio instantly. Another police car with lights flashing raced by on the cross street. From the sound of the siren, it had turned down the alley that ran behind the buildings on this block. At least response times were quick in a town this size. Voices crackled through the radio.

"Officer Diaz doesn't see anyone," he told Will. "He's parked directly in back, hunkering down behind his vehicle to watch the door."

"Good." He summed up what he knew quickly. "Is Colburn on his way?"

"Should be here in five."

Will nodded. "I want to take a look inside."

"Let me clear the street in front first."

For all the impatience tearing at him, Will knew Grissom was right.

It took a few minutes, but Grissom managed to persuade the growing crowd to move a distance away. He asked drivers and passengers in the cars now blocked in to exit their vehicles and walk out of range of possible gunfire. And when a third officer appeared, Grissom sent him to evacuate the businesses right across the street, all vulnerable with large, plate glass windows.

When, after an eternity, he signaled a go, Will pulled his gun and edged up to the door into the real estate agency. It was all he could do to block horrific visions of what he might see. No, he told himself; there hadn't been any more gunshots. But then Mandy hadn't been shot; she'd been carved up.

He took one slow breath, and stole a look.

Nobody was visible.

They'd either made it out the back door, or were holed up in one of the rooms down that hall. Windowless rooms, he realized.

He'd call this a classic hostage situation, except for a couple, crucial elements. One of those hostages was a police officer. She also happened to be the county's only experienced negotiator. The hostage taker? He'd already killed, and must know the only way he'd come out alive was with his hands up – and he'd spend the rest of his miserable life in prison.

Not something Tim Spiva would ever consider.

Will felt himself teetering on the edge of a terrifying, bottomless abyss. He'd failed Rebecca, just like he'd failed his sister. He felt more helpless than he ever had in his life.

Seeing that his hands were shaking, he shoved the left in his pocket to hide it even as he called Lieutenant Donald Nobach's mobile number.

"I need SWAT," he said.

*****

Face suffused with dark color and his lips drawn back from his teeth, Tim leaned toward Rebecca.

"Jordan is a fucking bitch, and she doesn't *deserve* to live."

Closer, she thought. *Another couple of steps. Let me get my hands on you.*

She'd been calculating ever since she sat down. If she could slam the hand holding the gun upwards, she could grab his balls and twist. God, she wanted to do that. Kick his legs out from under him. Smash his head into the floor.

Her fear seemed to have burned out, leaving fury in its place. She'd always been able to feel compassion even for people whose lives had disintegrated to the point where they wanted to hurt others. But she'd seen what was left of Mandy. Jordan. There was no softness in her for Tim.

But she replied, "Jordan wasn't very nice to you, I'll give you that."

"*You'll* take her place," he snarled.

She frowned, as if puzzled. "You do know you won't be able to take my bra and necklace with you, where you're going. That's sort of an eye of the needle thing."

"What?" As if jolted with a cattle prod, he straightened. "You went through my stuff?"

"Of course we did. Oh, you do know we found Mandy's body, don't you?"

He hadn't known, she saw with interest. He knew about Jordan, but must have decided he didn't dare stay close enough to continue watching the police work.

"Your parents were awfully upset when I talked to them. They really believed in you, Tim."

Rebecca felt the Realtor's terrified stare. Her fury swelled, black and crackling with lightning. She would have given anything to go back, to have shot this excuse for a human being while she had the chance.

To feel Will's arms around her again, hear the rare tenderness in his rumbling voice.

But she'd keep it together. Do her job.

If not negotiate…use words as a weapon.

*****

Lieutenant Nobach had joined Will on the sidewalk in front of the art gallery on the other side of the real estate office. The lieutenant had been around back, had a man on the roof already, had somebody else bringing a ladder so they could position a team member beside the single, small window in the brick back wall.

"The guy might have to take a piss," he'd said.

Sure. Spiva would leave the two women and wander into the bathroom – exposing himself in the hall on the way – unzip, take the usual stance, and piss into the toilet – right in front of the window. Or, hey! Spiva might escort one of the women to the bathroom and be in view long enough for the officer to take a shot.

But Will also couldn't argue. People did dumb things. In law enforcement, you saw it all the time.

"We've got to verify it *is* Spiva in there," Nobach had also pointed out. "To give the snipers the go-ahead, I'd like to be sure the HT isn't some idiot that grabbed the first couple women he found to make sure the world knows he's upset."

Will didn't share the lieutenant's doubts, but he only said shortly, "We'll make contact."

Now, he waited during the SWAT leader's lengthy, frowning cogitation.

It ended with a suggestion that even Lieutenant Let's-Go-In obviously wasn't excited about. "We could go with a diversion. Use flash bangs to shake him up, maybe give Detective Walker a chance to make a move."

Will stared at him incredulously. "You call that a *plan*?"

Nobach flinched at whatever he saw on Will's face. Maybe he wasn't hiding his agony as well as he'd thought.

Daniel Colburn, the Cape Trouble police chief, walked up holding a phone. "Unless you have another idea, I think it's time to try to talk to this guy."

Will reached for the phone in automatic assumption.

Daniel didn't hand it over. "You know you're not the right person to attempt to negotiate." He made sure Will saw that he sympathized, but also that he meant what he said. "We need a semi-neutral party here. Unless you think this Spiva admires you or at least likes you—"

Wanting to lie, Will clenched his jaw. "No," he said roughly. "I think he hates my guts."

"Came down hard on him?"

"No, during interviews I stayed in the back seat, let Rebecca—Detective Walker take lead. It wasn't hard – he was riveted by her from the beginning." How honest did he have to be? It shouldn't even be a question, he realized. It *wasn't* a question. He trusted these two men. "I...let him see that I considered her to be mine. He was enraged."

Will was vaguely conscious of Nobach's surprise. Oddly enough, Daniel looked less so. He might have caught some vibes that Sunday, during the search for Mandy Shaw. Either way, he lowered his voice enough to be sure no one else could possibly hear. "*Is* she yours?"

Past the lump in his throat, he got out, "It's new, but...yeah. We were hoping to get through this investigation before we made decisions about jobs and where we'd live. I haven't talked to Alex yet, but I will."

Daniel nodded. He was even better friends with the sheriff than Will was. "Then you are the absolute last person who should make contact with him."

He swallowed; nodded.

"I gather your back-up negotiator isn't immediately available?"

"No." Will ground his teeth. "He has next-to-no experience, anyway."

"Then that leaves me." He held Will's gaze, his sharp blue eyes steady. "I haven't handled a lot of these situations myself, but there've been a few times."

Nobach said unexpectedly, "You talked that punk out of the bank a couple years ago."

"Yeah." The corner of Daniel's mouth lifted, just a little. "Rebecca arrived just in time to see him walk out."

"Do it." Will didn't care if he sounded harsh. Or desperate.

Apparently having entered the business number in his phone, Daniel tapped the screen and waited. Will was close enough to hear the rings. One. Two. Three.

Why would Spiva answer?

Four.

What if he didn't?

CHAPTER SEVENTEEN

Every muscle in Will's body was knotted tight as he stood on the sidewalk a few feet to one side of the real estate office, straining to hear every sound from Daniel Colburn's phone.

Five rings.

What if they tried Rebecca's phone instead of the real estate agency's general number? Would she be able to answer?

Instead of another ring, Will heard a muffled man's voice.

Colburn's eyes met Will's. "No," he said. "This isn't about buying a house. My name is Daniel. Is this Tim?"

A second later, he gave them a brief, confirming nod.

Will might have known who was in there, but he still went cold, suppressing his rage. He jerked his head, and Nobach walked a couple of steps with him.

"Somebody gets an opportunity, he shoots to kill," Will said. "No hesitation." And to hell with who should be making this decision.

"Got it," the SWAT leader agreed, and took another few steps, pulling out his radio.

Will walked back to Daniel, who, at the very least, was delaying Tim Spiva from whatever he intended to do next.

Like rape or kill Rebecca.

*****

"Now, which of the two women do you want me to let go?" Leaning against the desk, his hand braced on his thigh with the gun held almost indolently, Tim was smiling. "Lemme guess. It would be the hot cop."

A tiny squeak from beside Rebecca had her reaching out again instinctively, grasping the other woman's hand. Squeezing. *Courage.*

"Yeah, no," Tim said suddenly. "Not interested." He smacked the cordless phone down on the desk. "He thought he could talk me into doing what *he* wants. Do I *look* stupid?"

No, he looked crazy. Homicidal. *Oh, and holding a gun on us.*

"They have to try, you know," Rebecca said.

"Usually, it's *you* who has to try. That's why I did it this way, you know." He sounded earnest, almost boyish. "I thought it was cool, you talking nutcases into letting their poor, scared hostages go." His eyes narrowed. "How does it feel being on the inside, Rebecca?"

Keep him talking.

"Strange," she admitted.

"Like it better the other way around, huh?"

"Yes." Why deny it?

"Getting to be time to tie you two up. Especially you. I bet *she'd* do anything I told her." He lunged forward and snapped his teeth at the Realtor, who gasped and jerked back.

Unfortunately, he hadn't gotten close enough for Rebecca to get her hands on him.

"What set you off like this, Tim?" she asked, as if they had all the time in the world. "I don't understand. You loved Mandy for a lot of years."

"She was *mine*. I let her blow me off once, 'cuz okay, she really wanted to go to college. But then she fucks some asshole and comes home with his kid?" His face tightened, his voice rising and betraying more agitation. "Do you know how that felt? And then she says she isn't interested, sorry? Like *sorry* is good enough?"

Normally, Rebecca tried to soothe people in crisis. Calm them so that they could think clearly. Her instinct told her to keep him unsettled. A danger was that he'd act impulsively, start shooting, say, without forecasting his intention. On the other hand, rattled people screwed up. The cool, calculating part of Rebecca suspected that he didn't have a lot of experience using a handgun. He'd hit one of the men when he shot down the hall, but that could have been luck.

She knew one thing: no way in hell was she letting him tie her up. Her mother had been tied up for two days while that monster raped and tortured her. The memory of Jordan spread-eagled and tied was excruciatingly vivid.

If she resisted, he might just kill her. But that wasn't what he wanted, craved. He needed her submission, to see her break under pain and his sexual domination.

Just keeping him talking would be good. She had no doubt the SWAT team was outside, figuring out how they could get in. Will was there, too. If there was any way at all for them to take Tim down, Will would make sure it was done.

"The one man I've really cared about cheated on me," she heard herself say, before making a mental amendment. The only man before Will. "He said he was sorry, too." He'd found himself a woman who didn't carry a gun on the job.

Tim zeroed in on her, his intensity bizarre. "Did you forgive him? Give him a second chance?"

"No. It wasn't a one-time thing. He'd been sleeping with this other woman for weeks. And you're right. Sorry wasn't good enough."

His eyes lit. "You see?"

"I still don't, Tim." She managed to sound almost regretful. "I didn't want to hurt that guy. I just never wanted to see him again."

"But he wasn't in your face all the time. Everyone you knew wasn't on *his* side, were they?"

She thought about pointing out that friends in their group probably *had* sympathized with Tim. She hid her wince. More likely, they felt sorry for him. Pitied him. Best not to say.

"I guess not," she said, feeling her way. "But I knew I wasn't ever going to let him see how much he had hurt me. For me, it was pride. I guess you didn't feel the same way. I mean, even though you hurt her, she at least had the satisfaction of knowing how much *she'd* hurt you."

A nerve under his eye twitched. The hand holding the gun bounced up and down on his outstretched leg in a form of nervous reaction. "Bullshit!" he burst out.

Attention ostensibly on him, she was able to keep looking for opportunities, thinking. He hadn't so much as glanced at the other woman in a while, as if he'd forgotten she was there. Tim had wanted other hostages solely so that he could use them to control *her*. More than ever, she felt certain that trying to convince him to release the woman would be a monumental mistake. Asking put power into his hands – and Rebecca didn't believe for a second that he'd actually let either of them go. Once he'd decided the other woman didn't serve a purpose, he'd gun her down without a second thought.

The phone rang.

Teeth bared, he snatched it up. "No, I don't fucking want to talk!" Then he thrust the phone at her. "Hey, here's your chance to say bye-bye to your boyfriend."

She couldn't help being wracked by primal fear. But if there was one thing she'd learned this past year, it was to hide what she really felt.

She accepted the phone. "Hello?"

"Rebecca?" The voice was Daniel's, not Will's, which she should have expected. The very sound of Will's voice would have shoved Tim closer to the edge. Besides, the CTPD had jurisdiction.

"Yes, it's me."

Daniel asked about the other woman. Not looking that way, Rebecca said, "No problem." Tim's attention stayed strictly on her. She had to keep it that way.

Be invisible.

"We could get in, but he'd have too much time before we could reach you," Daniel said bluntly. "We can see in only through the bathroom window and the door pane in front. See what you can do."

His message was equally blunt. They were waiting – but she had to give them the advantage. And Will at least must know as well as she did that Tim wouldn't surrender. He wouldn't even end this the way poor Mr. Brodsky had. Tim had already proved he enjoyed killing. If he had to die, he'd want to be sure he took her with him.

"You're done." He tried to wrench the phone from her hand.

"Wait!" Rebecca struggled to hold onto it. "Tell Will—"

"He knows," Daniel said.

The reminder restored her composure. Yes, of course Will knew.

She let go of the phone. Tim's arm came back and he threw it at the wall as hard as he could using his left hand. It passed by Rebecca's head so close, she felt the bite of wind.

His smug grin faded. He didn't like it that she hadn't flinched. *Tough shit.*

"And poor Jordan," she remarked, as if their conversation hadn't been interrupted. "She's a spoiled brat, but you can't tell me you really cared about her."

Now he wasn't bouncing the gun, *he* was in motion as if he couldn't stay still. His legs twitched, his shoulders rolled, he twisted his upper body slightly from side to side. A nerve even jumped beneath his eye. And he never looked away from her. "I didn't give a shit about her. But, you know, I kind of had fun with Mandy, so why not?" Sudden rage twisted his face. "It was *you* I wanted. If Crandall hadn't come along—"

"I had my gun out. If you'd put one hand on me, I'd have shot you." She paused, shook her head. "Really, it's too bad Carson did come along."

He shot to his feet. *"He's going to die!"*

"Not happening. Come on, you blew that opportunity when you penned yourself in here. Really, why would you do this?" She went for perplexity. "There's no way out. And you were evading us so well."

His face flushed with anger. "What would running have gotten me? I *live* here. You stole my home!"

Knowing what she risked, Rebecca still let her eyebrows rise and said, "You mean, your parents' home. Can't do without them, Tim?"

The handgun came up, until she saw into the black hole that was the barrel of a lethal weapon. For a second, she couldn't look away. When she did, when she lifted her gaze to his eyes, she was sorry. They'd dilated so that the irises had disappeared, along with any humanity.

Oh, God. She'd pushed too hard. Poor impulse control, remember?

Too late.

*****

Mouth tight, Will paced in anguish, never going more than twenty feet from the sniper set up with a tripod, his rifle pointed through the glass pane in the door.

Down the sidewalk. Back.

Dennis Irvin was their best sniper at the range, but he wouldn't have been in the running in L.A. Had he ever actually had to shoot anything but a paper target? What if he froze? Missed when he had only a split second opportunity?

Will swore.

Alex Mackay, who now walked with him, said, "No problem? What did she mean, 'no problem'?"

Will had had too much time to think about it. "She didn't want to comment on her directly." Joan Tillman. Before going into surgery, the other Realtor had told them the hostage's name. "Rebecca is trying to keep his attention on her."

"Hard to imagine him forgetting someone in plain sight."

If Alex's question was meant to be a distraction, it had worked to some extent. Will slowed his pace in consideration for his boss. Whatever cataclysmic injury Alex Mackay had suffered before he took the job of sheriff here in Burris County, he had been left with visible scars and a stiff, painful gait. Will had seen how reluctant he was to swallow any of the powerful pain relievers he carried, but knew he sometimes had no choice if he was to function at all.

"Spiva did that when I was with her." He told Alex about those strange interviews, and about how Tim had reacted with a jerk when reminded that someone else was present.

"He's obsessed."

"Yes." Will had reached the seam in the concrete where he turned back.

"How do you read him?" Alex asked, turning as well. "Will shooting her satisfy him?"

Her. He meant Rebecca. Will ground his teeth. This wasn't something he could discuss academically. Seeing Alex's brown eyes read his expression, he said baldly, "I love her."

A twitch of the eyebrows, but no comment.

"I'll put out feelers for another job." *That's it, think positive. As if there'd be a future.*

"We'll talk about that later," his boss said mildly.

"And no, shooting her isn't what he wants. He *wanted* to tie her up on that same blood-soaked bed where he'd tortured Mandy Shaw. He wanted to rape her, cut her up." Jesus, his molars should be cracking by now, he thought in some distant corner of his mind.

"How much of that he imagines he can accomplish in there, I don't know. He's too crazy to have thought this out."

"The second hostage seems to complicate it for him," Alex agreed, sounding thoughtful.

"And don't forget he tried for five hostages." He shook his head. "He almost had to be intending to replicate something like the standoff with Brodsky a couple weeks ago. TV cameras, armor-clad SWAT guys in a circle around the building, negotiator trying to talk him into letting the hostages go. Fame."

He'd achieved all that, although he would never know it. Reporters and cameras were being kept behind the barricades at each end of the street, along with a crowd that included evacuated merchants and their customers as well as the usual curiosity seekers. SWAT, yeah, they were out in force, despite their limited use here. And Daniel had satisfied Spiva's need to slap down a 'negotiator'.

Alex shoved his hands in his pockets. "He wanted to show her that he was better, smarter, than those fools who'd succumbed to her silver tongue."

"Something like that." Will's response was so guttural, it was closer to a growl than actual speech.

"She's damn good at what she does. No reason to think she can't talk herself out of this," Alex said kindly.

The words were meant to be comforting. Unfortunately, Will had a suspicion that was something else Tim Spiva wanted to prove: that he could do anything he wanted to her, while she'd be unable to influence his behavior. His most desperate need would be to see her terror once she realized he was more powerful than she could ever hope to be.

For all Will's faith in her, he understood that this was nothing like any negotiation she had ever handled. Spiva might not know it, but he was demanding she die the same way her mother had.

And *that* gave Will his only hope.

*****

"You have a short fuse." Rebecca assumed a lazy pose, as if she wasn't staring down a gun barrel. She didn't cross her legs or anything that would hamper her ability to spring forward at any opportunity, however.

Still flushed dark red with fury, Tim's face altered by gradual degrees to give away bewilderment. She wasn't behaving the way she was supposed to.

"You bitch. Don't tell me you're not scared shitless."

She wasn't a good liar, so she didn't deny his accusation. Instead, she shrugged, refusing to think about anything as crippling as fear.

He was still doing a lot of twitching, shoulders moving, foot tapping. She'd kept him from feeling in control, which had him frustrated. Unfortunately, so far he hadn't given her any opening to charge him. He hadn't once relaxed enough to lower the gun.

Her phone rang.

"Give it to me," he snapped.

She handed it over, seeing that Daniel was calling.

"Him again." Tim sneered. "Boyfriend hasn't called. Think he's written you off?"

She ignored him, her mind racing. What other options did she have?

Tim answered the call. "What do you want now?"

The call had temporarily drawn Tim's focus. *So use it. Think.*

She created a mental balance sheet, what she had that might be in her favor versus everything else.

She kept fit and had some martial arts training. Maybe useful, maybe not. On the job, she did her best to avoid physical scuffles with men who were almost always larger than her. And while Tim was only two or three inches taller than her, he outweighed and out-muscled her. He was armed; she wasn't. She bet he'd brought a knife as well, but dismissed that – it couldn't be anywhere he could access it quickly.

Huge minus: the presence of a terrified woman who likely had no training in protecting herself. Plus: said woman had been smart enough to stay utterly still and quiet, as if she'd read Rebecca's mind.

Conclusion: talking their way out wouldn't work, and that was bad, given that connecting with people and helping them see the right thing to do was her greatest strength. Taking Tim down alone...that looked increasingly unlikely, too.

Negotiators sometimes had to persuade a hostage taker to make an incautious move into the sights of a sniper's rifle. Grateful never to have been put in that position, she knew now she wouldn't hesitate to talk this man to his death. But she also knew words alone wouldn't get him to step out into the hall. If she gave him a chance to think, he wouldn't expose himself.

She had to trust a sniper was there, prepared. That he wouldn't hesitate. She trusted Will. But someone else?

No choice.

She'd tuned out Tim's rant into the phone, but he signaled he was done by throwing her smartphone, which bounced off the wall, hit the floor and skidded out of sight under the desk.

He's volatile. Don't forget that. Nitroglycerin. She just had to be sure it blew up in *his* face, not hers. Not the other woman's.

What would trigger him into acting without any thought?

The answer was obvious. *Me.*

He was obsessed with her. He had to dominate her. Couldn't let her escape, couldn't let her win.

The damn gun was pointing right at her. Any minute now, he'd move on with his plan – taking the second hostage out of the equation, and somehow reducing Rebecca to the same, helpless state Jordan had been in. Mandy, too. *And Mom.*

Thinking about what her mother had suffered shored up her resolve. Now was the time to act, not once he'd succeeded in tying up or cuffing the other woman. Or – God – killing her.

A diversion would be good right now.

Wait for one from outside?

No.

I don't even know her name, and I'm going to use her. With a silent apology to the woman beside her, Rebecca glanced her way, trying to look surreptitious. Tim's gaze followed hers, and he grinned.

"You." Using the gun, he gestured at the woman. "Down on your hands and knees, facing the chair. That's it. Butt to me." As the woman stiffly rose, her shoulders hunched, he reached into the kangaroo pocket of his sweatshirt and pulled out handcuffs.

Now.

Rebecca leaped out of the chair and sprinted the short distance to the door.

"Stop!" he roared, and the gun barked.

Pain seared her arm, but she used the door frame as a fulcrum to spin into the hall. Wrong direction, but it got her out of his sight quicker.

Only he was fast, right behind her. His hand brushed her back as he snatched at her shirt, but he didn't get a hold. Knowing she'd have only this one chance, Rebecca dove forward, hitting the floor, skidding, crashing into a wall head-first. Dazed, she still heard the deadly cracks of gunfire. A howl, and then it felt as if the building had collapsed onto her. Another thump on her head. As her consciousness slipped away, she thought in puzzlement, *It's raining.*

*****

Alex had abandoned Will in favor of conversation with Daniel. The two stood in front of the café, on the other side of where the sniper was set up.

He'd learned patience during his years working the streets, vice, homicide. Like most cops, he hated stakeouts, but he could endure them. Right now, though, he was physically incapable of staying still. It killed him not to be in charge of this operation. He wasn't made to be a bystander. At the same time, he knew he wouldn't have made any different choices than Colburn and Nobach had. Any attempt to go in would force Spiva to gun the two women down before they could reach him.

And, yeah, he knew Daniel would listen if he'd had a brilliant idea.

Will would have given anything for that idea. He would do anything to save Rebecca. Trusting the woman he loved to save herself was the hardest thing he'd ever done in his life.

He reached the crack in the sidewalk and turned.

A gun fired, the sound muffled by the walls of the building. Will broke into a run as he saw the sniper's subtle shift as his muscles tightened. Watched his finger squeeze. Glass shattered. *Crack, crack, crack.*

Colburn and he reached the door simultaneously. The pile of bodies visible down the hall had terror ricocheting inside Will's chest, threatening to punch through the beating organ that was his heart.

Colburn knocked out shards of glass with his elbow, reached in and unlocked the door, and let Will go in first. Weapon in his hand, he moved faster than was safe. What if Spiva had shoved the hostages into the hall and stayed behind? He could be ready to leap from the office and start firing.

But Will knew. Dark sweatshirt, jeans, so goddamn much blood. And those were Rebecca's legs, her boots, he could just see under the man sprawling atop her.

She wasn't moving, wasn't trying to wriggle her way out from beneath.

Will had seen bloodier messes in his life, but not many. Bullets had entered Spiva's back, and one had done ugly things to his head. Will only wrenched him off Rebecca, to find her limp and covered in blood, her face turned away.

Swearing, he dropped to his knees. He didn't dare move her. Instead, he felt for her pulse. If the sniper had killed her by accident...

No, there was a flutter under his fingertips. "She's alive," he said hoarsely. "Get the medics in here." Thank God they were just outside. After transporting the gunshot victim to the hospital, they'd returned.

Colburn yelled, and other people poured into the building.

Behind him, Will heard the police chief say, "Ma'am? Are you all right? Ma'am?"

A woman taking sobbing breaths gasped out, "She saved my life. She saved my life. She's not dead, is she? He *shot* her. I saw him."

Without apology, Carson Crandall shouldered Will aside. He, too, quickly found her pulse as his partner cut her shirt from tail to collar, easing it off. Then one of them blocked Will's view and all he heard were terse, cryptic exchanges.

They put a protective collar on Rebecca before sliding a stretcher beneath her.

"I'm going with her," Will said. What if she quit breathing because he took his eyes off her?

"Follow us to the hospital," Carson tossed over his shoulder, and they kept moving, their speed intensifying Will's terror.

*****

When Rebecca opened her eyes and felt almost clearheaded, Will was the first person she saw. He sat at her bedside, watching her. Despite the nutcracker crushing her head, she managed to roll it on the pillow enough to be able to really look at him. "Wha'..." She licked dry lips, except that didn't help, not with her tongue feeling like sandpaper.

"Hey," he murmured, standing and bending over her. He stroked her forehead with a mere whisper of a touch. "Let me get you some ice chips."

They tasted better than a cinnamon bun, better than the finest wine. Will gave her more, until she sighed.

"What did I miss?"

"Spiva's dead." His usual directness was reassuring. "Joan Tillman is fine, just shaken up. She's singing your praises."

Her forehead crinkled. "Joan?"

"The other woman he took hostage."

"Oh." She pondered. "He shot me."

"He did. Then the SWAT sniper shot him. Unfortunately, when he came down on top of you, his head bounced off yours. You have two lumps – one where you bumped the wallboard, and a lot bigger one here." His fingers sifted through her hair until he found the spot that made her flinch.

Funny, she'd dreamed a screwdriver was drilling into her skull right there.

She worked through the implications. "No trial."

"No trial," he agreed.

"How long—?"

"Yesterday. You've been in la-la land for nearly twenty-four hours."

Not unconscious; she had scattered, confused memories. People talking to her – nurses and doctors. Will? Yes, Will had appeared a couple of times. She'd felt his desperation. The concussion and pain meds must have caused the confusion.

"How do you feel?" Will reached back and pulled the chair closer, taking one of her hands.

"Headache. And..." She moved one shoulder experimentally. "Hurts."

"Bullet went straight through your upper arm. Grazed the bone, which makes it more painful."

She scrunched up her nose. "And here I am again."

Will understood. She'd have expected him to smile, but the strain and worry she could see on his face didn't relent enough to allow humor. "He either wasn't trying to kill you, or he was a bad shot."

Rebecca thought about it. "Bad shot. He just…reacted when I ran."

"Just like he reacted by chasing you into the hall."

"I was counting on it. If he'd been colder, more calculating, he wouldn't have sat around talking as long as he did in the first place, and he wouldn't have taken the risk of going after me. He had another hostage. He could have held off SWAT for a long time, if he'd wanted."

Will said what she was thinking. "If he'd been cold and calculating, he wouldn't have decided to end it so spectacularly. He'd have waited to try to snatch you when nobody would see."

"Yes." What more was there to say? It was all over. Thank God, it was over.

Will's thumb circled on her palm. "I outed us."

Startled, she lifted her gaze from their linked hands to his dark eyes. "Outed?"

"I told Mackay how I feel about you. Said I intend to start job hunting."

Until this moment, Rebecca hadn't known she had really and truly made the decision. "No. I will."

He frowned. "You think I'd ask that of you?"

She tightened her grip on his hand. "It's not that." She barely hesitated. "You were right."

He went very still. "About?"

"I can find something more satisfying to do with my life. Becoming a cop, it was all about my mother. And I'm not sorry I did. I've been good at what I did, and I've learned a lot. But you saw through me, made me face stuff I'd been refusing to admit I felt."

"You're not saying this because you know it'll be harder for me to find a comparable job locally than it would be for you?"

"I'm not." A trembling smile formed on her lips, then faded. "I couldn't let myself quit because I was afraid. I'm too stubborn." That was why she had refused to acknowledge the other reasons it was time for her to move on. "I'd have worked through it, the way you said you did."

He nodded, his eyes never leaving her face.

"But today...I quit being scared. I mean, I was, because I didn't want to die. But I was able to put the fear aside and figure out what I needed to do. I bested it. You know?"

"Yeah." Now his mouth did curve, his smile tender enough to stop her heart. Pride warmed his face.

"I even know what job I want, although I might have to go back to school, or...or move away." She took a deep breath. "If you'd go with me."

"You know I would." He lifted her hand to his mouth and kissed the back of it. So gentle. "What do you have in mind?"

"I want to be a victim's advocate. I could stand up for victims of rape or assault, make sure they're treated the way they deserve, that they understand every step of the legal process." She hadn't expected a lump to form in her throat, but every word sounded so right. "I can be there in court to nod encouragement when they testify. Find counseling resources, help make decisions."

Will cleared his throat and blinked hard a couple times. "Perfect. And I doubt you'll need more education, given the experience you do have. I think it's safe to say that you could keep a part-time gig as a crisis negotiator, if you're willing. Nobody wants to lose you."

"Hmm." She smiled, even if stretching her mouth did increase the pain exponentially. "I could create a website, have business cards. Negotiator for Hire."

"And, if you stay around here, you'd start with three clients."

"I could do that." She'd felt like a failure after Mr. Brodsky killed himself. Today had been different. Instead of negotiating, she'd pushed Tim into anger, knowing he wouldn't think reasonably once his temper fired. And she *had* saved her life, and the life of the other woman – the best possible outcome. "I'll let Joan list my house," she decided.

Will laughed, letting her again see the man who lowered his guard for her, and only her. "Three and a half percent reward. I like it."

"It might be seven percent, if she can sell the place, too."

He tipped his head to acknowledge that, even as his eyes narrowed in a way she recognized as purposeful. "You will move in with me?"

She opened her mouth to ask if that was really a good idea. To say something sensible about how they ought to get to know each other better before they took a step like that. But, right or wrong, she didn't *feel* sensible.

Still, a woman had to take a stand somewhere.

"I can't live with a man whose name I don't know."

There was a long, long pause. "This non-negotiable?"

"Yep."

He groaned. "Bazyli Jaromir."

"Bazyli Jaromir Wilcynski. Has a ring."

"So, do I get an answer?"

Any amusement vanished. "If... Are you *sure*?"

"I don't waffle. Rebecca, I love you. That's not going to change. I have every intention of marrying you, but I'll give you a little time first."

There was the Will she knew and loved. Patient, deferential to her wishes. But she smiled, because she wouldn't want to change him. "Thank you."

Her mock-meekness had his eyes narrowing again, but he gave it up and laughed. When he spoke, however, he sounded entirely serious. "Just don't take too long. At least...not if you want children."

"I do." The huskiness in her voice came as a surprise. "Wouldn't want you to be too ancient when they hit those teenager years. Although maybe I shouldn't worry, given how *patient* you are."

"That's just snotty. It's lucky you don't work for me anymore."

"Very lucky," she murmured, a fraction of a second before he kissed her.

About The Author

Janice Kay Johnson is the author of more than ninety books for children and adults, including the Cape Trouble novels of romantic suspense. Her first four published romance novels were coauthored with her mother Norma Tadlock Johnson, also a writer who has since published mysteries and children's books on her own. These were "sweet" romance novels, the author hastens to add; she isn't sure they'd have felt comfortable coauthoring passionate love scenes!

Janice graduated from Whitman College with a B.A. in history and then received a master's degree in library science from the University of Washington. She was a branch librarian for a public library system until she began selling her own writing.

She has written six novels for young adults and one picture book for the read-aloud crowd. ROSAMUND was the outgrowth of all those hours spent reading to her own daughters, and of her passion for growing old roses. Two more of her favorite books were the historical novels: WINTER OF THE RAVEN and THE ISLAND SNATCHERS, written for Tor/Forge and now available in e-book format for the first time. The research was pure indulgence for someone who set out intending to be a historian.

Janice raised her two daughters in a small, rural town north of Seattle, Washington. She spent many years as an active volunteer and board member for Purrfect Pals, a no-kill cat shelter, and foster kittens often enlivened a household that typically includes a few more cats than she wants to admit to.

Janice loves writing books about both love and family — about the way generations connect and the power our earliest experiences have on us throughout life. Her Superromance novels are frequent finalists for Romance Writers of America RITA awards, and she won the 2008 RITA for Best Contemporary Series Romance for SNOWBOUND.

Visit her website at www.JaniceKayJohnson.com.

A Note from the Author:

Thank you so much for purchasing my book. This is my first independently published series, so if you enjoyed the book, I hope you will take a moment to help me get the word out to others by posting a review on Amazon or Goodreads - or "like" my Author Page on Facebook to see future updates.

I also love to hear from readers, so please feel free to contact me on Facebook or via my website at www.JaniceKayJohnson.com.

Also Available from Janice Kay Johnson

Cape Trouble, a tiny Oregon Coast town, was named for the dangerous off-shore reefs. But some of its citizens seek refuge from their own troubles…which have a way of following them.

SHROUD OF FOG (Cape Trouble, Book 1)

The secrets of the past haunt the present…

Sophie Thomsen's life had a Before and an After – marked by the terrifying morning when she found her mother dead in the foggy sand dunes, an apparent suicide. Now, twenty years later, Sophie returns to Cape Trouble, only to find her aunt brutally murdered. Although she swore never to set foot again on Misty Beach, Sophie takes over her aunt's crusade to save the falling-down Misty Beach Resort and its wild sand dunes and beach from development. But Sophie's memories threaten a killer…who doesn't dare let her remember too much.

Having come to Cape Trouble to heal his own wounds, Police Chief Daniel Colburn investigates the present day murder, but begins to suspect Sophie's mother was another murder victim, not a suicide. Everything he learns increases his fear for the woman he is coming to love.

Sophie's fate may be to die in a shroud of fog, just like her mother before her, unless she can trust Daniel to help her uncover her past in time.

SEE HOW SHE RUNS (Cape Trouble, Book 2)

When it's never safe to stop running…

One night, in her upscale California restaurant, Naomi Kendrick overheard powerful men plotting a political assassination. To save her life, she made a bargain with the devil...and then ran.

Inevitably, she is found. More than one enemy descends on Cape Trouble to learn her secrets...and silence Naomi once and for all.

Detective Adam Rostov suspects she stabbed his partner to death in her restaurant kitchen. Pursuing her to Cape Trouble, he arrives just in time to rescue her from an assault. He conceals his real purpose in Cape Trouble to stay close to her. Because if he can't keep her alive, he'll never find out if she's innocent or guilty.

Naomi's instincts scream, Run, but too late, because Adam isn't about to let her go. Not when he has begun to believe she is a victim and not a killer. Not when she is irresistible bait to draw a contract killer, a corrupt U.S. Congressman, and a crooked federal agent. And not when, despite all common sense, he's falling in love with the mysterious chef.

Once Naomi discovers Adam too has been hunting her, she must decide. Run and keep running, or trust him to keep her safe? Of course, once he knows her darkest secret, he may no longer want to protect her...

TWISTED THREADS (Cape Trouble, Book 3)

The faintest creak of the floorboards her only warning...

Emily Drake has clung to her solitude for four long years after the tragic death of her husband and child, filling empty days stitching quilts that will be heirlooms for other families, never her own. It takes a terror-filled escape from a midnight intruder to open her eyes. She desperately wants to embrace life again...if death's next approach isn't utterly silent.

Detective Sean Holbeck is powerfully drawn to his new neighbor, a woman threatened by an unknown enemy. He's already investigating a murder that he fears is just the beginning. Until he knows why the victim was chosen, he can't stop a killer…or protect Emily, who may hold the key to understanding an enraged man set on vengeance.

Dark threads of past and present, guilt and grief and pain, have twisted together until only love and trust might untangle them before a killer strikes again…

__WHISPER OF REVENGE__ (Cape Trouble, Book 4)

Loving the wrong man can be a death sentence…

Gifts from a secret admirer unsettle bookstore owner and single parent Hannah Moss. She finds herself searching every face, wondering what lies behind that smile, that stare. When renowned artist Elias Burton lends her his support, the gifts become threats. By turning to the wrong man, she's infuriated her secret admirer…and put herself and her young son in danger. But not until her child is kidnapped does she understand the terrifying price she must pay for loving a man so wounded.

A local celebrity and recluse, Elias Burton has lost every woman who has ever mattered. Because of his past, he fears to reach out to Hannah Moss…but he has never been so tempted. In protecting her, he enrages a sick, angry man who will do anything to make Elias pay over and over again for long-ago wrongs. And what better way to wound Elias than to kill the woman and child he's dared to love?

The whisper of revenge is all he has to lead him to his enemy…if it's not already too late.

What people are saying about the romantic suspense novels of Janice Kay Johnson:

•"If you are in the mood for a wonderful romantic suspense story that will have you so engrossed in it that you lose track of the time, than look no further."
-Night Owl Reviews (on Shroud of Fog)

•"SHROUD OF FOG will immerse the reader in a world of suspense and intrigue. Elements of romance throughout this captivating read will capture your heart. Johnson has penned a deeply satisfying story that is appealing to mystery lovers as well as romance aficionados. If you are looking for a tale that has plenty of plot twists and amazing characters that will remain with you, then you should rush out and get a copy of SHROUD OF FOG!"
-Romance Junkies

•"[G]uaranteed to have you looking over your shoulder more than once in this explosive, fast-paced thriller."
-Linda Silverstein, ROMANTIC TIMES (on Dangerous Waters)

•"Studded with tension and skillfully riveting, [it] will capture you from the first page and won't let go until the end."
-Kay Gragg, AFFAIRE DE COEUR (on Dangerous Waters)

•"I've never read Ms. Johnson's work before and all I can say is I will be finding everything else she's ever written. This story is so masterful it takes you inside this small town and really makes you think you are there."
-Sara HJ, HARLEQUIN JUNKIES (on Everywhere She Goes)

Turn the page for a sneak peek at the first chapter of SHROUD OF FOG - and find the entire series available online now.

SHROUD OF FOG (Cape Trouble, Book 1) - CHAPTER ONE

Why on earth wasn't Aunt Doreen answering her phone?

Disgruntled, Sophie Thomsen sipped her coffee from the travel mug as she waited at the red light. The tinge of worry, she could probably blame on the eerie effects of coastal fog. For most of her life, Sophie had hated fog. This morning it was thick enough that she felt peculiarly alone even though she was driving down the main street of Cape Trouble. The tourists passing on the crosswalk in front of her appeared and disappeared, ghost-like and colorless in their anoraks and heavy sweaters.

The morning fog might or might not burn off. You never knew on the Oregon Coast, and especially at Cape Trouble, infamous for hidden, dangerous rocks offshore and the peculiar mist that rose from the river that flowed into the Pacific Ocean and formed the southern edge of town. Sophie had spent enough time here on the coast to guess that yes, the sun would be out in another hour or two, the sweaters would be shed, the kites and beach towels would emerge, and some brave souls who didn't mind standing in waders by the hour in icy water would be spotted casting their lines in Mist River – named, of course, for its mysterious propensity for cloaking itself in drifting tendrils of gray.

She and her aunt had made vague plans to meet this morning at the storage facility, but hadn't set a time. There wasn't any real reason to feel anxiety. One thing you could say for the friendly town of Cape Trouble – sarcasm fully intended – was that if there'd been a car accident or an aide car had been summoned anywhere within a ten mile radius, everyone including Sophie would already have heard every gory detail.

Probably Doreen had simply gone ahead and was happily working inside the storage unit, sure Sophie would show up eventually. Aunt Doreen was very capable of being scatterbrained. Lucky she'd already given Sophie the code to get in and even a key to the lock.

The light changed, the green less visible than the red through the fog. Sophie looked carefully to be sure the last pedestrian had stepped onto the sidewalk. She drove more slowly than usual along Schooner Street, lined with small seafood restaurants, coffee houses, boutiques and gift shops, their lighted windows made indistinct through the gray shroud of fog.

Although it had been twenty years since she'd spent more than a few days at a time here, she knew the town well. Like other picturesque Oregon coast towns, Cape Trouble had been commercialized, but the changes were mostly cosmetic. The Victorian era homes were nowhere near as grand as those in Astoria far to the north, but charming enough to be a draw along with the lighthouse, the broad sandy beach, the never-ending waves, the much-photographed sea stacks and the whale watching tours that departed from a pier that thrust out into the river.

Sophie's family had spent summers here when she was a child. Before. That's how she thought of it. Before and After. Before the great divide that had riven her life and left her a different person on the other side of it. Sophie would gladly never have visited Cape Trouble again, or even the Oregon Coast, but unfortunately the one person in the world she truly loved lived here, so she'd resigned herself to those occasional visits.

What she didn't understand, Sophie thought with the unsettled sensation she'd had ever since arriving last night, was why she'd let herself be talked into spending the entire month of June here to help with the auction intended to raise money for a cause she didn't personally support.

Not that she could tell Doreen so. It would mean talking about things she didn't talk about. Not with anyone.

Two stoplights and one turn later, she broke out of town, heading away from the ocean, the fog thinning as she drove. She passed first the Safeway and hardware stores, the laundromat and a pharmacy as well as neighborhoods of more ordinary houses where the locals actually lived before reaching the least attractive part of town, never seen by most visitors. Two garages, an auto body shop, some kind of metal fabricating business, plumbing supply, lumberyard, two seedy bars, a wooded stretch and – finally, two turns later – the sprawling storage facility made up of long buildings encased in metal siding, covered with metal roofs, and enclosed in a high chain-link fence.

The metal siding and roof presumably explained Aunt Doreen's failure to answer her cell phone.

With a sigh, Sophie rolled down her window, punched in the eight digit code preceded by a * and ending with the # key, then waited while the huge gate rolled jerkily to one side.

Sophie glanced again at the notebook page on which she'd jotted the information. The auction committee had unit...4079. The buildings weren't clearly labeled, so she turned down the first aisle and discovered herself passing 1001 on one side and 2045 on the other. Which didn't altogether make sense. Well, the first row on her right – the 1000s - proceeded in numeric order, but the ones on her right were given to odd fits and starts.

She wasn't the first here this morning. A moving truck was being loaded at one space, a plump woman, a boy of perhaps twelve or thirteen and a man with a pot belly currently wrestling a sofa up the ramp. The man was shouting at the woman and boy, who weren't lifting their end up as high as he'd like. The woman began screaming back just as Sophie carefully maneuvered through the narrow lane between truck and the storage spaces on the other side. She flinched at the language.

Around the corner, another woman seemed to be poking rather desultorily inside a space that was packed, literally, concrete floor to ceiling and bare-stud wall to wall with...well, household possessions, Sophie guessed, glimpsing the white side of some appliance as well the plush back of a chair, the top of an end table plus lots of cardboard boxes and some bright plastic tubs. If the poor woman was hoping to put her hands on one thing, Sophie didn't envy her.

That was unit 3006. On the other side of the next aisle was...3093. The 4000s had to be here somewhere, didn't they? And surely she'd spot Aunt Doreen's aging white Corolla.

Sophie passed other tenants either putting more possessions into their rented spaces or taking them out. The place really was huge. There were occasional doors that likely opened to short hallways where tenants could access small spaces – maybe five by ten feet or ten by ten – but most units seemed be at least fifteen by twenty or more. And there were parking spaces for RVs, boats on trailers, cars covered by canvas, a horse trailer and... She stared. Good Lord, was that a carnival carousel? She'd swear it was.

A last jog, and she found herself facing a shorter row of buildings that formed an L to the rest of the facility. And yes, she was finally among the 4000s.

It wasn't until she reached the end and turned again that she discovered a couple of units were caps to the rows, and 4079 was one of those. Aunt Doreen's car was not parked in front. And she couldn't miss the lock clipped over the hasp of the closed metal door designed to roll up.

Well, damn.

Sophie parked and tried her aunt's number again. Four rings and she was back at voice mail. She had already left several messages. Wonderful. Well, she had the key and she was here, so why not open up and see for herself the stuff the auction committee had procured? Not to mention how well organized the amateur enthusiasts were.

But when she got out and tried fitting the key her aunt had given her last night into the lock, it didn't fit. Not even close. Sophie frowned. The brand name on the key didn't match the one on the lock, but she hadn't expected it would. She knew her aunt had had copies made of the original keys so practically every member of the auction committee had one – something Sophie thought hadn't been smart. So she supposed it was possible the keysmith hadn't done a good job. But...so bad the key wouldn't even go in the hole?

Had someone replaced the lock in the past few days? Without telling Doreen, who was the auction chair? That didn't make sense unless the committee had decided to expel Doreen but hadn't gotten around to telling her. And that seemed unlikely, given that Sophie's aunt was the moving force behind the whole enormous effort.

Sophie drove back to the office she'd passed at the entrance and went in. A middle-aged woman behind the counter said, "You looking to rent a storage space?"

"No, I was expecting to meet my aunt – Doreen Stedmann – here at the space she rented..."

"Oh, you're Doreen's niece Sophie." The woman beamed. "I'm Marge Hedgecoth. Why, Doreen talks about you all the time! Says you're some kind of fancy event planner."

"Well..."

"She was so excited that you were coming." She frowned. "I haven't seen her yet this morning, although I don't open until ten, you know."

Yes, Sophie had noticed the sign on the door. Tenants had access to their units from six a.m. until midnight with special arrangements required for other times, but office hours were more limited.

"She's probably just late," Sophie said, then explained that the key she'd been given didn't fit into the lock. "I'm wondering if I might have written down the wrong number for the space."

Marge verified that, indeed, the auction committee for the Save the Misty Beach campaign had rented number 4079, beginning in March when the first of the donations had begun pouring in.

"Well, Doreen gave me a key, which is unusual, but she wanted to be sure anyone who needed to drop something off could get in. So let me get my cart and I'll follow you out there."

She flipped the sign on the door to a picture of a clock that indicated she would be back in ten minutes and climbed into a golf cart parked by the back door. Sophie was able this time to drive directly – more or less – to her aunt's unit, which faced the chain link fence at the back of the property and the woods beyond. As Sophie parked again and got out, it occurred to her that it was really rather lonely back here, blocked by the bulk of the building from being seen by any other units except the one other that faced the same direction.

The golf cart arrived. A small, wiry woman with short, graying hair and skin that was beginning to look leathery, Marge got out and confidently poked her key at the lock.

"What in tarnation...?" she muttered.

Sophie saw immediately that she wasn't having any better luck.

After a minute her hand dropped. The two women looked at each other in something approaching consternation. "Hmph," she said. "I suppose they're entitled to change the lock."

"But Aunt Doreen gave me this key only last night. Could she have forgotten...?"

"Did you call her?"

"She's not answering." Sophie couldn't put her finger on why she was so uneasy, but she was. "I went by her house first, and she wasn't home. Her car wasn't there, either."

"I've a mind to cut that lock right off," Marge declared.

Sophie stared at the metal door. "I'll happily pay for a replacement lock."

"Well, then, you just hold on and I'll be back in two shakes."

The morning was chilly enough Sophie began to pace. Wisps of fog lingered. If she went one way, she could see down the aisle at the far side of the property, which was currently empty. The other way, she could see the same people working in their units that she'd earlier passed. A few covered vehicles were parked back here, too. She ended up at the chain-link fence, staring into a forest that looked surprisingly primeval, considering how long this area had been settled and that it had likely been clear-cut at one time.

There wasn't much forestry on this side of the coastal range anymore, though; winter storms and ocean winds kept trees small compared to farther inland and therefore unprofitable. These were hemlock, spruce and cedar, she thought, although she couldn't have told a hemlock from a spruce from a fir, if the truth be told. The evergreens were underlaid with shrubbery, some native, some not. Oregon grape, she thought, the ubiquitous salmonberry, huckleberries, the ferns that loved the damp climate, and other bits of foliage and even a few late spring flowers she didn't recognize.

Movement, caught by the corner of her eye, made her jump until she saw that a squirrel was scampering up the trunk of a tree. It paused on a branch to gaze at her with suspicion before darting out of sight.

She was smiling when Marge returned with a pair of lethal-looking bolt cutters.

Sophie hit re-dial on her phone and, at the sound of her aunt's voice saying, "I'm too busy to take this call," shook her head at Marge, who marched over to the door and applied the bolt cutters.

Marge appeared entirely too scrawny to cut through a quarter-inch or more of steel, but with a snap, the lock fell open. "There you go," she said with satisfaction.

Sophie took the lock off, set it on the concrete to one side, turned the hasp and heaved the door up. With a squeal and clatter, it rolled on its tracks.

Beside her, Marge gasped.

The interior was shadowy and astonishingly full, but Sophie was instantly riveted by the mess. Boxes were open, items spilling out.

Smashed ceramic and shattered glass sprinkled the concrete floor. A framed picture lay face down, glittering glass around it and a hole stomped through the back. Somebody had broken in, was all she could think. Rifled the contents without caring what was destroyed. What a disaster.

Dear God, Sophie thought in shock, had Aunt Doreen seen this? Might she have gone to the police?

The committee or her aunt had obviously bought multiple shelving units, the kind that could be easily assembled and then taken apart to be moved, because a number of them lined the walls. Most were still packed with boxes of assorted shapes. Peering in, Sophie saw framed pictures carelessly stacked to one side. Tall or awkward things filled the middle. Was that a cat climber? A huge basket that had been covered with cellophane spilled gourmet foodstuffs across the floor.

Along with her dismay at the implications of the mess, it was the clutter and the dim lighting that explained why her eyes didn't immediately focus on the figure crumpled at the back. Even when she saw…what she saw…she rather stupidly gaped at the drying pool of a dark substance that had crept far enough from the – body? – to soak the corner of a cardboard box and possibly damage the contents.

It was only then, reluctantly, that her eyes focused on that ruined head, and she saw the face.

"Oh, dear God," she whispered, at the same moment as Marge whirled, raced to the fence and lost her breakfast through it.

*****

The gate to the storage facility stood open when Daniel Colburn drove up in his squad car. Marge Hedgecoth stood just inside, waiting beside her golf cart. She didn't look so good.

Rolling down his window, he asked, "You okay, Marge?"

She summoned a smile that didn't help much. "I've been better."

Daniel nodded. "Around back, you said?"

"Far corner." She waved. "4079."

"Once I see what's what, I'll need to talk to you."

"Yes, Chief. I'll be in the office."

"Good," he said. "In the meantime, I want you to shut down the gate. No calls, either," he told her sternly. "Don't let anyone in, or anyone out. Ask folks to wait until I can talk to them."

She agreed. He figured he could trust her. He'd gotten to know Marge since he took on the job as police chief of Cape Trouble ten months ago. During his tenure, the fence around the facility had been cut a couple of times, a car stolen once, a lock cut off a unit and the contents ransacked another time. There'd been some vandalism. Marge was a tough lady.

He eyed the people he could see industriously doing whatever you did in a storage space, but drove directly to the far corner where Marge had told him the victim's niece waited.

He noted the isolation of this particular unit and automatically scanned eaves and fence line for a camera. He knew there were several sprinkled throughout the facility and that Marge kept an eye on monitors during the day in her office. He'd arrested the idiot who drove away in the very collectible, shiny red, 1962 MG roadster by watching video footage that showed the guy clear as day. But – didn't it figure? – Daniel didn't see one back here.

The car parked to one side of the gaping door was a sleek, four-door blue Prius. A woman sat behind the wheel. She got out when he parked and walked to meet him.

His immediate reaction shook him a little. Crap. He liked to look at a sexy woman as well as the next guy, but this was piss poor timing. He couldn't let himself forget that this woman was involved in some way with a death and therefore a potential investigation. And the feeling of a fist in the gut meant he was doing more than looking.

She wasn't even beautiful, not exactly. Medium height but leggy, maybe a little short-waisted which might be making her breasts look bigger than they actually were. Wavy dark-blonde hair – yeah, he did like blondes – bundled carelessly up on the back of her head with tendrils already escaping. A pretty oval face without noticeable cheekbones but somehow…delicate. As they got closer, he saw how fine-textured her skin was.

Uh huh, and how waxy pale. His nose had already caught the scent of puke. Not surprising. Rookie cops invariably puked at their first murder scenes or after seeing the gruesome result of a major vehicular accident.

"Chief Daniel Colburn," he said, holding out his hand. "I'm afraid Marge didn't mention your name."

Her eyes were green. Hazel probably, but mostly green.

"Sophie Thomsen," she told him. "That's, um, my aunt in there." She nodded sideways without looking into the storage unit. "Well, sort of my aunt."

"Sort of?"

"She's my stepmother's sister. Doreen Stedmann."

Oh, hell. "I know Doreen."

Ms. Thomsen nodded unhappily. "Everyone in town does."

"Please stay here while I take a look."

She didn't appear to be sorry to stay behind.

Daniel knew all about the auction, which was being held as part of the effort to raise the funds to buy a sizeable piece of land the other side of Mist River from town. Forty or fifty acres, he understood, of prime river- and ocean-front land that included forest, dunes, an old lodge and a string of cabins, now all but falling down. The long-time owner had passed away and his heir wanted to unload the property, which had resort chains salivating. Locals were determined to keep their pretty town pristine and save it from the evil giant condo developments that were sure to take over if that land was chopped into pieces and made available. The heir was apparently giving them a little time to raise the money. Daniel didn't see much hope, but you never know.

Doreen Stedmann was a local character, an eccentric woman known as an activist but lacking real solid follow-through, gossips said. She started a lot of projects but finished few. From the bulging contents of the storage space, she'd been doing surprisingly well on this one.

Until somebody had gone berserk in here, that is. And until she'd died or decided to kill herself amongst the auction items, if that was what had happened. He hadn't had the impression from Marge's frantic call that there'd been an accident. She hadn't asked for an aide car. She hadn't even asked for police in a generic sense. She'd wanted him, Chief Colburn.

He stepped carefully around the clutter and the broken bits, trying not to touch anything, ready to begin revival efforts if there was any chance at all. But he could tell from twenty feet away that it was too late, and had been for a couple hours, at least. What's more,

Doreen hadn't killed herself. Somebody had taken care of that for her. She was definitely dead, and the sight wasn't pretty. No wonder the sort-of niece appeared about ready to keel over.

He stood for a long time, doing nothing but studying the scene. Taking in her position, the sizable dent in her head, the cord tied around her neck as a finishing touch. The hefty, cut crystal vase that had been tossed to one side and the blood and tissue that marred its sharp cut edges.

No obvious sign of a struggle. The auction stuff closest to her was still neatly piled. The cat climber might have been rocked; it sat unevenly now, one corner of the base on top of something he couldn't see.

Why that cord around the neck? Symbolic, or had the killer been unsure the blow to the head did the job?

"Damn it," he muttered, and carefully retraced his steps. Once in the open air, he made some calls, then turned to the niece who stood with her back to him, staring into the trees on the other side of the fence. He followed her gaze, scanning for an opening cut in the chain link, but didn't see one. The ferns and salal and salmonberries appeared untrampled. Moisture from the mist glistened on leaves. From here, he couldn't see the back gate required as an emergency entrance. He'd be wanting to verify that it was still locked as soon as he had a minute.

"Why don't we sit in my vehicle," he suggested. "I've got the medical examiner coming and some crime scene folks I'm borrowing from the county."

She shivered and turned. "Yes. All right."

"Marge didn't mention cutting the lock off," he said thoughtfully. "When she called, she said only that you and she had found a dead woman. I was half-expecting a heart attack victim or suicide."

Ms. Thomsen explained about the keys not fitting this lock, and how she'd felt uneasy when she couldn't reach her aunt by phone after they'd made arrangements to get together this morning.

"I intended to change the lock anyway," she admitted. "I gather that any number of people have keys right now, and that's asking for trouble."

That was one way of putting it, Daniel would concede. Murder probably wasn't quite what she'd had in mind, though. Unless, of course, after murdering her aunt she'd just happened to have a new lock in hand because she'd intended to replace the old one anyway.

A patient interview later, he thought he knew everything she'd done from the time she drove into town last night, but her reserve was so deep, he had to wonder what she wasn't telling him. Either Sophie Thomsen was holding back on him, or she was one complicated woman. He was leaning toward the second explanation, because the one thing that rang clear was her affection for her shirt-tail aunt.

When he temporarily ran out of questions, she asked, "Was...was she strangled?"

"The cause of death will likely have to wait for the autopsy," he said gently. "That head wound looks to me like it would have been fatal."

A shudder wracked her, the most profound sign of distress she'd yet displayed. "I wonder if she saw it coming."

"Likely not. It was on the back of her head."

"I hope not," Ms. Thomsen burst out. "I hope she had no idea."

He hoped for the same. That way, Doreen's death, while brutal, was also a good one. One minute, she was involved in life, productive, maybe happy, the next, wham, one blinding moment of pain and she was gone. No lingering, knowing her fate, no misery. There were certainly worse ways to go.

Which did not mean he felt any more merciful toward the man or woman who'd killed this decent woman for no justifiable reason.

"It had to be quick," he said. "You don't have to worry about her suffering."

Some of the tension left Ms. Thomsen's shoulders. "Thank you for telling me that."

He nodded.

She breathed audibly for a minute. He was about to make his excuses when she said, "Does the gate record when people come and go? Or does everyone have the same code?"

Interesting that she was thinking so analytically. Almost like a cop.

"No, each tenant has a unique code." He already knew that much, from previous investigations. "So the answer is yes, we'll be able to pinpoint arrivals and departures based on what code they used." Maybe. The gate moved with ponderous slowness. He'd observed before that two or even three cars could pass through once it opened. If the guy was patient, he could have ridden someone else's tail coming and going and left no record of his presence at all. "You're wondering where your aunt's car is."

"Well...yes."

He'd been mulling that over himself, and now said, "I had a thought about that." He jumped out of his squad car and walked over to the row of vehicles that were being parked here presumably because of the security. He ignored the RV on the end and the camper next to it, as well as the aging but well-cared-for Cadillac that inexplicably lacked a cover. Nope, it was the vehicle on the end that was hidden under a canvas tarpaulin. He lifted one side only enough to confirm his suspicion, then let it drop.

Ms. Thomsen had gotten out, too, he saw, and stood watching him.

"White Corolla, rusting bumper?"

Looking numb, she nodded.

"The question is, how did he get out of here?"

"Or her."

He looked at the niece.

"From what I can gather, most of the people working on the auction are women. Doreen has mentioned only a couple of men."

She blanched at speaking her aunt's name, but hadn't let herself cry yet. He'd begun to suspect she wasn't the one who'd puked. Marge had looked considerably more rattled than this woman when he arrived.

Ignoring the approaching sirens, he asked, "Why do you assume the killer is an auction volunteer?"

She frowned. "Are you suggesting it was someone who just happened to wander by?"

"I didn't say that."

Her eyes widened in alarm. "There were a whole bunch of people already inside the gates when I got here. What if they leave?"

"Marge won't let 'em." He turned when a white van rolled around the corner and stopped behind his city car. "The troops are here, Ms. Thomsen. You said you're staying at the Harrison cottage? Why don't you go back there, and I'll be by to update you later. Say, mid-afternoon."

She gave a half nod, then changed her mind. "Will you ask everyone to be really careful when they're working in there? I'd hate to see anything else get broken."

He stared at her, struck by her coldness. "Why would you care at this point?"

She transferred her stare to him, startling him with the pure ferocity in her eyes. "Because Aunt Doreen cared. She cared a whole lot. And I'm thinking the only thing I can do for her now is finish something that mattered to her. Make it my memorial to her. That, Chief Colburn, is why I care."

After a minute, he said, "Got it."

She nodded and walked to her Prius. For maybe thirty seconds his brainwaves altered, letting him see only her. The confidence of her stride, the delicacy of her bone structure, the sway of her hips in snug jeans, the way she carried herself with shoulders squared and head high. Then he blinked and called, "Wait!"

He lifted a hand at the two men and one woman who'd gotten out of the van, but jogged to Ms. Thomsen.

"Is there any chance you – or someone – have a list of what should be in there?"

"Yes, in theory."

He raised his eyebrows at that.

She grimaced. "That's one of the reasons I'm here. It became apparent to me, talking to Doreen, that while the group was doing a heck of a job begging donations, they weren't doing nearly so well organizing the stuff once they had it. Apparently somebody had volunteered to enter donations as they came in and work on a catalog, but she's been full of excuses and not really doing it."

"And who would that be?"

"Rhonda...Rhoda...something." She lifted her hands. "I have a list of volunteers with contact info back at the cottage. I haven't met any of them yet, except for a few I already knew from visits to Doreen."

"All right," he said. "See what kind of inventory you do have, too." He stared at the daunting contents of the storage locker. "Do me a favor, though. Please don't call any of the other volunteers or accept any calls. In fact, don't talk to anyone, okay? I'll want to give each of them the news myself."

Still remarkably composed, she nodded. "I wonder what happened to the lock."

"I think the fact that the lock was replaced suggests the killing of your aunt was thoroughly premeditated. He – or she – came prepared. The replaced lock was likely intended to slow down the discovery of the body. Any volunteers who came out here would be puzzled and possibly annoyed because their keys didn't work, but most of them wouldn't have demanded Marge cut the lock off." Which, the more he thought about it, made Ms. Thomsen an unlikely killer. Why would she put the damn lock on, then immediately insist Marge cut it off?

"No. No, I suppose not." She hugged herself. "No." She stole a look toward the cluster of people now waiting for him outside the space and the grim sight past them, then hurried the rest of the way to her Prius.

A moment later, she drove around the corner of the building without looking back.